The December Market

RaeAnne Thayne

CANARY STREET PRESS

CANARY
STREET
PRESS™

Recycling programs
for this product may
not exist in your area.

ISBN-13: 978-1-335-92935-8

The December Market

Canary Street Press
22 Adelaide St. West, 41st Floor
Toronto, Ontario M5H 4E3, Canada
CanaryStPress.com

Printed in U.S.A.

To the brilliant Gail Chasan and the entire team
at Harlequin/Canary Street Press. Thank you for your unwavering support
and dedication in helping me bring seventy-five stories to life.
Your guidance and hard work have been invaluable.

Thank you also to my family for enduring my deadline brain time and again
for nearly thirty years. This journey would not be possible without you,
and I love you all deeply.

DISASTER STRUCK ON A SNOWY EVENING THE DAY BE-
fore Thanksgiving.

Amanda Taylor, arms overflowing with bulging grocery bags, managed to maneuver her elbow just enough to hit the button that opened the automatic door to the Shelter Inn retirement community.

She was always in a hurry or she would have tried to make two trips inside. Her day had been hectic and frenzied, and a last-minute trip to the grocery store for her grandmother hadn't helped.

One of these days, she might be able to convince Birdie to use a delivery service, but her grandmother always said she couldn't trust a stranger to pick the best fruit and vegetables and she complained they didn't always check expiration dates.

Amanda didn't really mind helping out. She loved her grandmother dearly and considered shopping for—or *with*—her one small thing she could do to make Birdie's life a little easier.

Her grandmother was planning a regular Thanksgiving dinner, though it was only to be the two of them and a friend for the holidays. She had tried to tell Birdie she didn't need to bother, but of course she wouldn't listen.

So here Amanda was, juggling five paper bags filled with last-minute items.

She balanced everything carefully as she went through the door, congratulating herself for not spilling everything.

As luck would have it, pride always seemed to be her fatal flaw. She should have known better. One moment, she was hurrying past the building's recreation room, the next her foot landed on something tiny and treacherous and slippery. Her foot slid out from under her and she toppled backward onto her butt with a small shriek as potatoes and onions and bananas flew out of the bags in a produce cascade.

Somehow, she wasn't quite sure how, she managed not to writhe around in pain. She wanted to, though.

"Uh-oh." A small, nervous-sounding voice came from the doorway of the large gathering space. "I think that was my fault. I'm really sorry."

She squinted from her graceless spot on the floor to find a small boy of about six with curly dark hair giving her a worried look through round dark-framed glasses.

She knew him, somehow, but she couldn't immediately place how. She had a vague memory of seeing him ride a bike with training wheels past her house recently but she couldn't pinpoint when that might have happened.

"Isaac. What did you do?"

The older male voice, deep and stern, coming from the doorway of the recreation room from behind her sent a shiver down her spine, for reasons she couldn't immediately explain.

"I was just playing with my race car while you were talking to *Abuelo* in there. I was driving it around out here because it goes better when it's not on the carpet. Then the lady stepped on it and she fell down."

A toy. That's what had tripped her. She looked around until she saw a small blue race car, obviously operated by the small controller in the boy's hand.

"Are you okay?" the boy asked her, his brown eyes nervous.

"Oh no. I'm so sorry. He just got this toy and he hasn't quite figured out how the remote control works yet. Can I help you?"

The owner of that deep voice moved into her line of vision. From her ignominious spot on the floor, Amanda saw worn leather boots first, then jeans covering muscled thighs, a short black jacket and up and up a hundred miles to a man with dark hair, eyes the same as his son's and lean, chiseled features.

She caught her breath.

Rafe Arredondo, the assistant fire chief of Shelter Springs, held his hand out to her. He did an almost comical double take when he must have recognized her at the same time, sprawled out at his feet.

"Amanda. Oh. Hi."

She managed a half wave, her rear end still smarting.

"Are you okay? Let me help you."

"I'm fine," she lied.

If she thought she could figure out a graceful way to stand on her own, she wouldn't have taken his hand. He grasped her fingers in his and tugged her up from the ground to her feet.

"Please tell me nothing is broken."

Her pride? Her dignity? Her vanity?

"I don't think so. I'm fine. I should have been watching where I was going. And I shouldn't have been trying to carry in five bags of groceries at once."

"We can help you clean this up. Looks like one of your bags ripped."

The bottom had completely fallen out of one of the grocery bags, spilling the ten-pound bag of flour. It was mostly intact, thank heavens.

"Go ask *Abuelo* if he can find another one," Rafe told his son.

Isaac nodded and ran full tilt back into the recreation room behind them.

"I forgot your grandfather moved in here."

"Right. A few months ago."

All of Rafe's family lived in Shelter Springs. His father, Al, had once owned a drywall business until he sold it a few years back and retired. His retirement hadn't lasted long and now he operated a handyman business.

His mother, Louise, owned one of the more popular beauty salons in town.

Amanda didn't go to Louise's shop, though she had heard that the woman and the other salon stylists all did good work.

"Seriously, are you okay? Do we need to take you to the urgent care clinic?"

"I don't think so." She mentally checked all her bits and pieces. The pain and shock were beginning to ease, though she suspected she might have bruised her behind. Also, oddly, her ankle throbbed. She must have twisted it somehow when she fell.

Isaac, meanwhile, had returned from the recreation room carrying a grocery bag. He was now picking up the produce scattered across the entry hall and packing it in the bag.

"We really are sorry, aren't we, Isaac?"

The boy looked guilty, dark eyes huge behind his glasses. "Yeah, I shouldn't have left my car in the hall." He paused. "But maybe you should have been watching where you were going, too."

She had to hide her smile at his undiplomatic response, even as she saw Rafe wince.

"True enough. No harm done. I'm fine. I have to say, that looks like a pretty cool car. I hope I didn't break it."

"I don't think you did. It *is* a cool car. It can even do wheelies. Do you want to try it?"

She shook her head, though touched by his generous offer.

"Another time, maybe. I have to take these groceries to my

grandmother's apartment. We're fixing Thanksgiving dinner here tomorrow, and she won't be able to brine her turkey if I don't get the supplies to her in time."

"I can help you carry them and then you can try my car if you want. It goes really well down the hallways."

"We'll both help you," Rafe said.

She almost refused, as she only had a few more steps to go to Birdie's apartment, but the boy looked so earnest and helpful, she couldn't find the words.

"I would appreciate your help. That would be awesome. Thank you so much."

Rafe picked up the remainder of the bags, except the one she was still somehow clutching, and the three of them moved together down the hall.

"Hey," Isaac exclaimed as she rang her grandmother's doorbell, his eyes widening behind his glasses. "This is where my friend Birdie lives."

She smiled. "Your friend Birdie is my grandmother."

She didn't tell this boy that Birdie was just about the most important person in the world to Amanda. During the chaos of her childhood, Birdie had been a constant source of strength and comfort.

Into adulthood, Amanda had even lived with her grandmother in the little house on Huckleberry Street. Rose Cottage had always felt like more of a home to Amanda than her nuclear family's grand lakefront mansion or even the condo she had purchased out of college.

After her grandmother's macular degeneration diagnosis, when her vision had begun to worsen dramatically, Amanda had sold her condo and moved back in with Birdie.

She had not considered it any kind of sacrifice. Her grandmother needed help adjusting to her new challenges. Birdie had been a constant source of support for Amanda throughout her life. Helping her in return now had been a gift for both of them.

Her grandmother opened the door, her short, spiky white hair streaked with purple highlights today. She wore dangly earrings, her favorite rainbow-knitted slippers and a sweatshirt with a silly turkey and the words *Gobble Till You Wobble* on it.

Amanda never quite knew what to expect with Birdie's fashion choices. She loved them all.

Birdie's dog sat patiently at her side. Dash was not an officially trained service animal, but he did a good job of filling that role, anyway. He helped her avoid obstacles, he retrieved items that she dropped and he alerted her to dangers like traffic and unexpected curbs when they were out and about.

"Hi, Grandma. Hi, Dash. It's Amanda. I'm here with your groceries."

"Thank you so much for bringing those," Birdie said, then frowned. "You're not by yourself. I believe you have a couple of helpers."

"Hi, Mrs. Birdie." Isaac Arredondo grinned, shoving up his glasses. "It's me. Isaac. Your friend."

"Why, so it is! How nice of you to help my granddaughter."

Isaac gave Amanda a guilty look. "I didn't really help her. More like trip her. I was playing with my remote control car in the hallway and she stepped on it and fell on her behind. It was kind of funny, but I didn't laugh because that would be mean."

Amanda supposed she should be grateful for small favors. She sent a sidelong look to Rafe and saw he looked both amused and rueful at his son's honesty.

"I imagine it was pretty funny to see me go sprawling. Like I had slipped on a banana peel or something," she was forced to admit. "I probably would have had a hard time not laughing, too. I appreciate that you didn't, even though you wanted to."

"We're going to be more careful with our toys, aren't we?" Rafe gave his son a stern look.

"Yeah. I don't want anybody else to step on it. They might break it."

"Oh dear. That would be a shame, wouldn't it?" Birdie wasn't quite able to hide her smile.

"Yeah. Because I just got it from *Abuelo* and I've hardly had time to play with it yet."

"You'll have plenty of time," his father said.

"Hello, Rafe, my dear," Birdie said with a bright smile. "How are you?"

He leaned in and kissed her proffered cheek. "I'm good, Birdie. You're looking as lovely as ever."

Amanda had no idea the two of them were anything other than casual acquaintances. Apparently they were. They seemed friendly enough and Birdie glowed at his words.

What woman wouldn't glow, being the focal point of all that gorgeousness?

"Would you like a cookie, my dears?" she asked the Arredondos. "I just pulled them out of the oven. It's the least I can do to repay you for helping carry the groceries."

Huh. Where was *her* cookie? Amanda had been the one who shopped for all the groceries, carried them in and suffered a humiliating tumble because of Isaac's toy car.

"Yes, please." The boy beamed. "I *love* cookies."

"I suppose I should have asked your father first if you can have one."

"It's fine. One cookie. I'm sure it won't spoil his dinner. I doubt anything will spoil this kid's appetite for pizza."

"Oh good."

As always, Amanda admired the way her grandmother faced her challenges. She had never let her low vision rule her life or set limits, she merely figured out a way around any challenges. Now she bustled over to the countertop, found the square container holding cookies, grabbed a paper towel to pick out two of them for her guests, then returned with them held out.

"One for you and one for your dad," she said to Isaac with a conspiratorial grin.

Amanda suspected Rafe might be one of those people who only ate healthy food, never allowing processed sugar or carbs past his sacred lips. Not so. He took the proffered cookie with a warm smile.

"Thanks, Birdie," he said. He then immediately took one bite, then another one, chewing with appreciation.

"Yum. Peanut butter kisses. My favorite. My *abuela* used to make those."

"Hers were always much better than mine," she said. "Rosita had the magic touch with everything she made. Oh, I miss her tamales."

"So do I," he said. "And her mole sauce. And her birria. Okay, everything she used to make."

Birdie gave his arm a sympathetic squeeze. His grandmother had died of pneumonia earlier that year, Amanda remembered. That likely contributed to his grandfather's decision to move into the retirement community.

"What are your plans for Thanksgiving?" Birdie asked Rafe.

"Working, I'm afraid."

Rafe, Amanda knew, was the assistant fire chief for the mostly volunteer Shelter Springs Fire Department and also one of the town's few full-time paramedic/firefighters. From everything she had heard about him, Rafe was a good man to have around in a crisis.

"I always have to work either Christmas or Thanksgiving," he went on. "We trade off. This year, I'm lucky enough to be able to take off Christmas so I can spend it with Isaac. Last year, if you'll recall, I was working during the big storm, when we had a little excitement right here at the Shelter Inn on Christmas Eve."

Amanda had been down with a bad strain of Covid the previous winter and had stayed away during the holidays so she didn't pass anything along to Birdie. The storm the previous Christmas had been legendary, though, coming in hard and fierce. The roads in and out of town had been closed, travelers trapped in their cars.

During all the chaos, her dear friend McKenna Dodd, who ran the retirement apartment complex along with her aunt Liz and lived on-site, had gone into labor several weeks early.

Fortunately, Griffin had been there to help safely deliver the baby. Amanda's brother was another good man to have around in an emergency. McKenna and her husband, Travis, had been deeply grateful to have a trained family physician there to help during the unexpected delivery.

"Well, here's hoping everyone working at the fire department over Thanksgiving has a quiet day. It's supposed to keep snowing until tomorrow night. We're set for about five or six inches, but nothing like that legendary Christmas Eve storm of last year," Birdie said.

"Right. I imagine we'll have the usual calls. Maybe a sledding mishap or two here and there and a few people who overindulged in apple pie."

"What about you?" Birdie asked Isaac. "What are you doing for Thanksgiving while your dad is working to protect the good people of Shelter Springs?"

The boy beamed, busy petting Dash, who was clearly trying to lick any trace of peanut butter cookie crumbs off Isaac's cheek.

"I'm going to my cousins' house. I'm staying over. We're going to go cut down a Christmas tree for them and for us, for *Abuelo* and maybe *Abi* and *Ito*."

"My parents," Rafe explained. "They're shortened nicknames for *Abuela* and *Abuelo*, which means grandparents."

"I hope I get to use the chain saw," Isaac said cheerfully, a pronouncement that earned a trio of winces from all the adults.

"I think that will be your uncle Joe's job," Rafe answered him.

"Maybe I can help, though. I bet I'm really good at it."

"I'm sure you are, but chain saws are for grown-ups."

When Isaac looked as if he wanted to argue, Rafe quickly went on, "We should probably get back to your great-grandfather's. He's waiting for us to take him out for pizza."

"Thank you again for helping Amanda with the groceries," Birdie said.

"You're welcome. Thank you for the cookies," Isaac said politely.

"Give Paolo my best," Birdie said, with a particular twinkling smile Amanda didn't quite recognize.

"I'll do that. Bye, Birdie. Bye, Amanda." Rafe gave them both a quick smile before ushering his son out the door.

Their departure left an odd sort of void in the room.

"He's such a nice man, isn't he?"

"Who? Rafe or Paolo?"

Birdie chuckled. "Both. Those Arredondo men sure hit the jackpot in the looks department. Don't you agree?"

"Um. Sure," Amanda said, feeling distinctly uncomfortable.

"But anyway, what do you think about Rafe? He's your neighbor now. I heard he bought Betty Scarborough's old house. You must be happy to have such a nice, strong, handsome man down the street."

Amanda frowned inwardly, though she was careful not to let a hint of her sudden unease show to her grandmother.

She really did not like that particular sly tone of voice. Birdie was a dedicated matchmaker. If Amanda showed the slightest hint of interest in any man—even merely mentioning his name—her grandmother would be quick to swoop in and try to encourage a romantic connection.

"Yes," she said carefully. "I believe he and Isaac moved in about a month ago."

The reminder left her feeling distinctly guilty. For virtually every other new neighbor on Huckleberry Street, Amanda was always quick to drop off a treat or a casserole or something to welcome them to the neighborhood.

She was fully aware that since Rafe and his son moved in down the street, she had come up with excuse after excuse not to stop by.

"It must be good to see some life in that old place. Even I could tell Betty had really let it go downhill the past few years, especially after Elmer died. And I can't see past the end of my nose. I can't say I blame her, poor woman. Her health problems made it hard for her to keep up with the yard and such. It will be good to see what Rafe does to the place. I should stop by and check it out."

"He's only been in the house a month. I don't think he's had time to do much to it."

She had noticed a big dumpster planted on the driveway for the first few weeks after he took ownership and had seen his father Al's handyman panel van parked there frequently during the month.

She could admit to some curiosity herself as to what changes he might be making, though she told herself it was only natural to wonder, as owner of one of the other historic homes along Huckleberry Street.

So why hadn't she taken the opportunity to stop by on a neighborly visit and check things out?

She knew the answer.

Because Rafe Arredondo made her as nervous as a baby bird in a thunderstorm, for a whole host of reasons.

"He's had it rough, hasn't he? Rafe, I mean. Poor boy."

Amanda nodded, though she certainly had a hard time thinking of a big, powerful guy like Rafe in such neutral terms.

"I'm sure their lives haven't been easy since…well, since everything happened with Caitlin."

"Isaac couldn't have been older than three when his mother took off, could he?"

Amanda began putting away the groceries she had brought along, as familiar with her grandmother's small, efficient kitchen here as she was of her own at Rose Cottage.

"I think so," she answered.

What a tragedy that whole thing had been. Rafe's late wife, hauntingly beautiful, had been her friend. She had been a frequent customer at The Lucky Goat, Amanda's store, and had been considering taking one of their regular classes so she could learn how to make soap herself.

Amanda had sensed a loneliness in the woman, a deep core of sadness. One day, Amanda realized she hadn't seen her around for a few months and she started hearing rumors that Caitlin had gone to rehab for a prescription drug addiction.

A few months later, she had been shocked to learn Caitlin had left the rehab program, had moved to Portland with friends and then had died of a drug overdose.

After the woman left town, Amanda had wondered if she could have done more to help her. She wasn't arrogant enough to think she could save the world. If she ever made the mistake of thinking she could, life would have quickly squashed that belief out of her. But she had sensed Caitlin was struggling with depression and couldn't help feeling guilty that she hadn't done more to reach out to her.

That was yet one more reason why she always felt...unsettled around Rafe.

As if she needed another reason beyond the fact that her father had been Dr. Dennis Taylor, whose name was still a byword in certain circles of Shelter Springs. Rafe's family in particular had strong reason to despise her father—and by connection, her.

"Too bad he has to work tomorrow instead of spending Thanksgiving with his family," Birdie said. "I hope he gets to enjoy a nice dinner of some sort at the fire station. I should take them one of my pies."

Her grandmother made a delicious caramel apple crumble pie, using fruit picked from one of the trees at Rose Cottage.

"A pie is a great idea, if you think you'll have extra."

"I've already made three pies," Birdie admitted. "I couldn't help myself. And since Griffin won't be here this year, it's only you and me and my friend Mabel Mulcahy. I think I'll have plenty."

It would be an odd sort of holiday. Amanda, her grandmother and a woman for whom there was not enough apple crumble pie in the world to sweeten her temperament.

She would definitely miss spending Thanksgiving with Griffin and his girlfriend, Natalie, another of Amanda's dearest friends. The two of them had traveled to Guatemala on another medical mission to provide health care to rural communities in need, their second since they started dating a year earlier.

She would have loved to spend the holiday with them, but how could she begrudge their time away together, especially when they were engaged in a good cause?

"Maybe you could come over a little early tomorrow and give me a ride over to the fire station so I can deliver the pie," Birdie suggested. "Given the snow we're supposed to get between now and then, I'm not so sure I should be walking the three blocks to the fire station. Especially carrying a pie. Even with Dash's help, I expect I would fall and break my hip again."

She wasn't ready to encounter Rafe Arredondo again so soon. But she also wasn't about to let her grandmother make an errand like that on her own.

"Sure. If you feel strongly about it, I'll take you, though I expect they'll have plenty of food at the fire station."

"You can never have enough pie," Birdie said.

"True enough. Maybe you should put that on a T-shirt for next Thanksgiving."

Birdie chuckled. "I think I'll do that."

Amanda wouldn't be at all surprised.

2

"I LIKE BIRDIE. SHE'S NICE."

Rafe smiled down at his son. "She is, isn't she?"

He had always liked Birdie Lovell. She was one of those rare people who treated everyone around her with kindness and compassion.

Once when he had been a kid, he and his cousin Alex had been playing street hockey on Huckleberry Street, where one of their other friends lived at the time, when Rafe had a shot go wild, the puck flying hard into her front window.

He could still remember the icy fear that had slithered down his back. Their buddy Paul had urged them all to run away and hide out in his basement recreation room, but Rafe knew they had to make it right.

He had been shaking when he went to her door to confess, Alex at his side. Birdie had only hugged them both, assured them that she understood accidents happened then had agreed to let the boys mow her lawn all that summer to pay for the repair of the window.

Remembering Alex brought the familiar pang of loss. They

had been as close as brothers, raised side by side, really. Maria, Alex's mother and Rafe's paternal aunt, had died when Alex was only nine and Alex's sister, Izzy, was six. Their father had no longer been in the picture. As a result, Alex and Izzy had come back to the area after their mother's death to live with Paolo and Rosita in Shelter Springs, just around the corner from Rafe's house.

They had always been a close family, but losing his aunt Maria had brought all the Arredondos closer together. They all rallied around Alex and Izzy.

Alex had been the best of them all. Smart, athletic, funny. He had earned a basketball scholarship shortly before his death and had been poised for amazing things.

All that promise, all that potential to make a difference in the world, had been snuffed out one December day.

He hated thinking about the sheer, senseless tragedy of it all.

"Why are you frowning, Dad?" Isaac asked him, worry creasing his own forehead. "Don't you like Birdie?"

"Sure I do. What's not to like? She's great. I was just... remembering something sad."

"Is it Mom? I get sad too when I think about her."

He hugged his son, determined all over again to make this a much better Christmas than the past few.

"I was thinking about my cousin Alex. Remember how we sometimes take flowers to his grave when we're going to visit Mom's?"

"I remember. He liked basketball and fishing and playing chess with *Abuelo*."

"He certainly did." With effort, Rafe pushed away his sadness. This was a time for gratitude. A time to focus on family and blessings and all the things they *had* instead of all the things they had lost.

"Let's go see if *Abuelo* is ready to go yet so we can take him to *Abi* and *Ito*'s house."

As his grandfather wasn't in the recreation room where they

had left him, Rafe led the way down the hall to Paolo's apartment, in the opposite wing from Birdie's. When they reached it, Isaac rang the doorbell with enthusiasm.

His grandfather opened the door right away with an apologetic smile.

"Sorry if I kept you waiting. I got a call from my accountant and decided I could hear him better in my apartment than out there. It seems an odd time to talk about my investments, but he wants to make some changes to my portfolio before the end of the year. We ended up talking longer than I expected. Get Todd started and sometimes it's tough to wind him back down."

Rafe suspected that particular conversation had not been one-way. His grandfather loved to talk to people. He had friends all over the county, former customers of the restaurant or other business owners he had met over the years.

Taking him anywhere in town was usually an exercise in patience while Paolo stopped to chat with old friends and new ones.

"No problem. The pizza is only ready now for me to pick up."

Because Rafe was working the next night on Thanksgiving and would miss the festivities, he had offered to take pizza to his mom's house that night.

Of course, Paolo did not want to miss out on all the family fun.

"I just have a quick errand. Go ahead out to your truck, if you want. I can meet you there. I only need to drop this one thing off at my friend Birdie's apartment before we go," Paolo said.

"We were just at Birdie's apartment. We helped carry her groceries," Isaac announced.

Paolo gave the boy a surprised look. "Did you?"

"Yeah. She gave us a peanut butter cookie. It was so good."

"We had a little incident with the radio control car," Rafe confessed. "I'm afraid we weren't watching it as closely as we should have been and Birdie's granddaughter Amanda ended up tripping over it."

"Oh dear. I hope she's all right."

"She said she was." Isaac frowned. "But I think she might have been limping a little when we went to Birdie's apartment."

That was news to Rafe. Why hadn't he noticed? He had certainly noticed how Amanda Taylor always smelled delicious.

"In that case, we should perhaps take an extra box of chocolates for her as well."

"I can come with you," Isaac said. "Maybe Birdie will give me another cookie."

As much as Rafe thought he should probably do something to dissuade his son from becoming a cookie beggar to all the senior citizens who lived in the building, he had to admit it was hard not to love Birdie's cookies.

He hung back when Paolo rang the doorbell, not really eager for another encounter with Amanda Taylor, no matter how scrumptious she smelled. When Amanda answered the door, he saw she had taken off her coat. She was wearing a cable-knit sweater the color of acorns that set off her auburn hair and made her eyes look an even more brilliant green.

"Oh. Hello, Mr. Arredondo. Hi again, Isaac. Rafe."

"Hi," Isaac said, marching right inside the apartment with his usual cheer. "I put the car away at my *abuelo*'s house so I can play with it again when we come to visit him. That way my cousins can play with it, too."

She blinked a little at this unsolicited information. "That sounds like a lovely idea."

"I have two cousins. One girl named Jade and one boy named Samuel. They're my friends."

"How lovely for you. I always wanted cousins but I'm afraid I didn't have any."

She had a brother, though. He knew Griffin Taylor well. They had been friends when they were younger, and Rafe often had interactions with him now when he transported patients to the local emergency room, as Dr. Taylor sometimes filled in for other doctors there.

"I understand you had a little mishap earlier," his grandfather said, his tone courteous and gentlemanly.

"Yes. But I'm fine."

"I cannot help but feel responsible since I'm the one who gave my grandson the car and urged him to try it out here in the recreation room and the hallway. I brought you a little something as a gesture of apology. I hope you can forgive us both."

She looked even more startled by the box of chocolates he held out, though Rafe could see Paolo's usual charm was working.

She sent Rafe a confused look, which he returned with a slight shrug. He wanted to tell her Paolo had a mind of his own. In his experience, it was usually best to simply let the man have his way.

"Truly. There is nothing to forgive. It was an accident. I should have been watching where I was going."

"Take the gift, anyway. I buy them from a wonderful shop over in Haven Point."

She looked at the label. "I love Cravings. They make some amazing chocolates."

"There you go. Haven't you heard that when you allow someone to give you a gift, you are giving their soul a gift in return? My soul needs all the gifts it can find."

Rafe could tell that she didn't have the heart to refuse his *abuelo*. Few people ever could.

"Thank you, then," she said with a warmer smile than she had ever given *Rafe*. "I will enjoy these very much."

"You are welcome. I actually have another box for your grandmother as well. Is she home?"

"I'm here. Hello, Paolo." She moved to the doorway to stand beside her granddaughter.

At the sight of her, Rafe's grandfather seemed to light up

from the inside. He took her hand and brought it to his mouth, which made Isaac *and* Birdie giggle a little.

"Hello, darling Birdie. I've brought you some chocolate from Cravings, as well as that game you asked to borrow."

"Oh yes. Thank you."

"I'll set them here on your entry table."

"Perfect," she said. Rafe wasn't sure if the color on her wrinkled cheeks was from the heat of the kitchen or from his grandfather's charm. He suspected the latter. Interesting. Birdie Lovell had never struck him as a woman prone to blushes.

"Amanda, this is the game I was telling you about," Birdie said. "We had such a lovely time the other night playing it. Neither of us could stop laughing. I haven't laughed that much in forever."

Rafe saw Amanda frown and give his grandfather a slightly suspicious look.

"Great," she said after a moment. "We can eat our chocolates and play the game tomorrow with Mabel after Thanksgiving Dinner."

"You're having dinner with Mabel Mulcahy?" Rafe had to ask.

"Yes. Poor dear," Birdie answered. "She didn't have anywhere else to go this year since her daughter is going to her in-laws'. I couldn't bear the idea of her eating alone in her apartment."

"You're a kind woman, Birdie," Paolo said with another of those twinkling smiles that only made Amanda's suspicious expression tighten.

"We should go, *Abuelo*," Rafe said after a moment. "Everyone will be waiting for their pizza."

"Of course. Of course. Have a lovely evening, you two. I'm sure I'll see you tomorrow morning before I head to my son's house for dinner," he said to Birdie.

"Yes. Definitely," she answered.

Paolo and Isaac both patted Birdie's dog one last time, then headed back out to the hallway.

When they walked outside to his pickup truck, they found

the wind had picked up over the past hour and now it blew snowflakes around with gleeful abandon, like a toddler throwing sand at the playground.

"That Amanda Taylor is a lovely woman," Paolo said as they made their way to Rafe's pickup truck. "She's always so kind to everyone. She comes to see her grandmother at least three or four times a week. They're very close."

Was that a dig against Rafe because he only managed to visit once or twice a week? He didn't bother to point out that was probably more often than they typically had seen each other before Paolo moved to the apartment building.

"Yes. She's very kind."

"This town would fall apart without her efforts, especially when it comes to the Christmas market. She practically runs that thing single-handed. Spends all year getting ready for it."

Yes. He knew that about Amanda. The woman loved to have a finger in every single pie, from the town's annual Giving Market to the library board to the hospital foundation to the concerts in the park.

"It's not a one-woman show," Rafe pointed out. "Many people have a hand in the market. The fire department even handles the first aid booth there as a public service."

Fortunately, Rafe was usually able to leave that to the EMTs.

"Yes, of course. You're right. But I doubt the market would have grown as it has without Amanda's efforts over the past five years or so that she has been running things. She's quite unstoppable when she puts her mind to something. I believe she gets that from her grandmother."

"No doubt," Rafe said as he helped his grandfather up and into the passenger seat of his truck, then moved to the back seat of his king cab to help Isaac into his booster seat.

His thoughts kept returning to Amanda even after he had picked up the pizzas and garlic bread from their favorite local pizzeria and drove to his parents' home.

He had known her forever, though she was a few years

younger than Rafe, and their acquaintance had always seemed on the periphery of his world. Their paths didn't intersect all that often, though he expected that might change somewhat now that he had bought a house down the street from her, and his grandfather lived in the same senior apartment building as her grandmother.

Despite her energy and enthusiasm for different civic causes, Amanda Taylor had always struck him as…sad, somehow. It wasn't anything she said, just shadows in her eyes that even the brightest smile couldn't hide.

She certainly had reason for her pain. Growing up the daughter of Dennis Taylor could not have been easy for her. Her father had left a legacy of pain in Shelter Springs that would be hard for anyone to escape.

Amanda had also lost her childhood sweetheart in a tragic avalanche. Rafe had been on the ski patrol twelve years earlier, before he had become a paramedic. He had been one of the first responders who had scrambled through snow and ice trying to dig out Jake Shepherd, and Rafe had been there when the man had been pulled to the surface, his features blue and lifeless.

He had rushed to help Griffin Taylor, who had been snowboarding with Jake, perform CPR, to no avail.

As far as he knew, Amanda had not dated much since her fiancé died. When it came to town events like the Founders Day parade or the fire department's annual breakfast, she always came alone or with her grandmother or friends.

Was she still grieving for Jake, more than a decade later? He had no idea. The only thing he knew for certain was that Rafe needed to do his best to stay away from her.

He had made the grave mistake of marrying one woman with baggage, demons from her past she had been unable to outrun. He and his son were still trying to recover from the jagged hole Caitlin had ripped through their world.

He had learned his lesson well.

3

HER GRANDMOTHER HAD A BEAU.

Amanda wasn't quite sure what to think about it.

The day after Thanksgiving, she stood behind the checkout counter of her store, The Lucky Goat, watching Birdie and Paolo Arredondo walk arm in arm through the crowded aisles.

They seemed to be having the time of their lives, sniffing products and comparing prices as they filled a basket that Paolo carried.

At least she thought they were enjoying themselves immensely. She didn't really have time for more than fleeting glances their way. This was Black Friday and for that day and the next, Small Business Saturday, she expected to be running full tilt.

She had come into the store before dawn to make sure everything was ready and open early for bargain shoppers and likely wouldn't leave until long after the store closed.

She didn't mind the long hours and hard work. She loved running her store.

Once, her grandmother had operated an art gallery on this same property. After Birdie decided to close the gallery and retire, when her vision first started to go, Amanda wanted to use it for something herself. She had petitioned her grandmother to let her buy the small building from her.

Amanda knew she wanted to open a store that would help others in the community, especially women looking to augment their family's income. Through a series of fortunate circumstances, she had decided to focus on locally produced skin care products and handicrafts.

She would never get rich from the store, but she really didn't need to. Upon her father's death, she and Griffin had both inherited a sizable chunk.

Griffin had used his to go to medical school and open his family medicine practice.

Through careful investments and moderate spending, Amanda still had much of hers left, even after she purchased the store, as well as Rose Cottage, from her grandmother.

She loved being able to help entrepreneurs. Her suppliers were usually mothers or grandmothers eager to earn a little extra money with a side hustle, making soaps and lotions and lip balms. Amanda also featured a small line of eco-friendly shampoos and conditioners.

On the craft side, she sold handworked fine jewelry, pottery and whimsical items like wind chimes and wood carvings.

Her store was popular with both locals and visitors to Shelter Springs, which was exactly what she had hoped when she decided to open it.

She loved being able to provide quality products to her customers while also helping local craftspeople and entrepreneurs.

"Is that Birdie over there with the hunky older gentleman?"

Her assistant manager and dear friend, Cat Lewis, angled her head toward the older couple.

Amanda peeked at them, trying not to be too obvious. She

didn't need to bother. They weren't paying attention to anyone but each other. Paolo and Birdie had their heads together now, bent over some cinnamon-scented gingerbread ornaments in the shape of hearts and stars and Christmas trees.

"Apparently. He recently moved into the Shelter Inn and I guess they have become close friends."

Cat looked delighted. "They are adorable together! Are you sure they're only friends?"

She wasn't sure of anything—only that something about Birdie's burgeoning friendship with Paolo left her distinctly uncomfortable.

"Yes," she said firmly, trying to convince herself as much as Cat. "They're only friends."

"Fun fact. I heard the steepest increased rate of venereal diseases is among those who are over sixty-five years old. Can you believe that?"

She frowned. "I don't need to even think about that right now, thank you."

"I'm just saying. I guess it's because they know they can no longer get pregnant so they prefer to, shall we say, ride bareback."

"That's so gross." Twenty-year-old Scarlet Bennett screwed up her face like Cat had just sprayed her with some new skunk-scented air freshener.

"Let's change the subject, why don't we?" Amanda said. She was relieved when one of her regular customers set an armload of products on the checkout counter.

"Did you find everything you needed?" Amanda asked.

"And then some," Kimmy Hill said with a laugh as she watched her ring up the totals. "Actually, not quite everything. Are you planning to have a kiosk again at the Christmas market this year?"

"Are you kidding?" Cat answered. "Amanda is the chairperson of the market committee. She's been working on plans for it since the last one closed. It would be a shame to put in all that effort and then not have a stall at the market."

"Yes. We will definitely have our regular stall there. We've been stockpiling inventory for months. If you went last year, we will be in the very same spot. Different products, though."

Shelter Springs' annual Giving Market was both a highlight of Amanda's year and a huge amount of work.

"I think I went to the market three times last year and purchased items from your stall every single time," Kimmy said with a laugh. "I wish I could have waited to buy these gifts for my book club."

"They will love these," Amanda said, gesturing to the dozen Booklover candles, with a scent that always reminded her of old pages, rainy nights and warm fires.

"Well, I would have liked to see a portion of the proceeds go to the charity you're supporting this year but I have to get these now. We're having our December meeting next week, before the market opens."

"Perhaps you missed the sign on the door that announces we're still donating twenty percent of our Black Friday sales to the food bank."

Kimmy's eyes lit up. "I did miss the sign! That's wonderful. In that case, I think I'll add that bath bomb gift basket you had back there. I can never figure what to get my sister-in-law but I know she adores taking a good bath. Can you give me a minute to go grab it?"

She ran off before Amanda could point out the two other customers already waiting behind her.

Fortunately, Scarlet quickly moved to the backup cash register. "I can help the next customer," she said.

Kimmy returned only a moment or two later with one of their bath bomb gift baskets in hand. Amanda had packaged it with a bath scrub and small containers of lemon-scented soap and lotion, as well as an inflatable pillow.

Amanda quickly rang up the woman and had just finished gift wrapping the basket in cellophane tied with a wide buffalo print ribbon when another customer opened the door to enter the store, letting in the strident sound of sirens.

Amanda wasn't the only one who turned to look out the wide front windows in time to see a fire truck stop in the middle of the road, right in front of her store.

"What's going on?" Scarlet asked, looking panicked. "Is there a fire?"

Amanda gave the young woman's shoulder a reassuring squeeze. Scarlet still suffered from post-traumatic stress disorder after her family's home in the countryside outside town was consumed by a fast-moving wildfire a few years earlier. She and her parents and siblings had barely escaped alive and were still in the process of rebuilding.

"I'm not sure. Cat, can you take over this cash register? I'll go check it out."

She quickly grabbed her coat from the hook inside the supply room and hurried outside. The street was buzzing with people and firefighters, all focused on something happening on the roof of the yarn shop across the street, Cozy Creations.

She watched as a second fire truck approached, this one fitted with a bucket.

"What's going on?" she asked a bystander.

"Somebody is stuck on the roof, apparently. They went up to hang a few Christmas lights and panicked. That's what I heard, anyway."

On the roof? Who on earth was it?

Amanda had a sudden suspicion. The twin sisters who ran the shop, Opal and Pearl Barnes, were both as stubborn as they were frugal. The women tried to do everything themselves, whether that was shoveling snow, repainting their storefront or building new display cases inside.

They hadn't put up Christmas lights in years past, as far as she could remember. They usually only decorated their front windows with lights around a huge stuffed knit penguin they had made together.

Why hadn't they asked Amanda for help or hired one of several professional companies that would hang lights for residences or businesses alike?

How had they even gotten up there? She saw a large extension ladder going up the side of the building, which gave her the answer.

The women were in their early seventies. They had no business up on the roof!

She watched the flurry of action as a firefighter she couldn't recognize from here climbed into the bucket of the truck and it extended up two stories to reach the roof. Amanda caught her breath as the rescuer climbed out, then sidestepped toward the figure she could now see huddled near the edge of the roof.

The crowd on the ground cheered as the firefighter wrapped a blanket around the figure, helped them to their feet and carefully guided them along the roofline.

The sky began to spit snow as a cold wind blew off the lake. Amanda shivered. Her store was packed and she knew she should return to help her customers but she couldn't drag herself away from the drama happening out here in downtown Shelter Springs.

She had to make sure Opal or Pearl, whichever twin was up there, made it to safety.

"Paolo tells me this is where you went," a voice suddenly said beside her. "What's going on? Is there a fire or is someone hurt?" Birdie asked.

Because of her advanced macular degeneration, her grandmother could only see things that were close to her face. Of course she wouldn't be able to have any idea what was happening all the way across the street. If not for Paolo, hovering closely at her side, Birdie wouldn't have been able to find

Amanda on the crowded street. He must have pointed her out and led Birdie here.

"I don't know for sure. There seems to be someone stuck on the roof. I don't know if it's Opal or Pearl."

"Oh no! Those poor dears!"

Her grandmother bought yarn and other knitting supplies from Cozy Creations and was friendly with both women.

"What happened?" Paolo asked. "How did they get up there?"

Amanda watched as the firefighter helped the woman back into the bucket. He seemed to be attaching a safety harness to her.

"I'm not sure. I heard from someone they were trying to hang Christmas lights and panicked. I'm not sure if that's what happened, though."

"Neither of those nice ladies should be up on a slippery roof," Paolo said, frowning with concern.

"Agreed. But they are, apparently."

She moved slightly to the right, where she had a different perspective. Now she could see a woman in a blue coat, knit scarf and hat, standing in front of the store with both hands pressed to her mouth.

"There's Opal, across the street." Though her grandmother certainly couldn't see that far, Amanda pointed to the woman. "So that means the person on the roof must be Pearl."

"And her with those bad knees! She has no business climbing onto a roof." Paolo's face twisted with concern, and Amanda had to wonder if he knew all the women of a certain age in the entire town.

"The rescuer is trying to help her into the bucket, it looks like," she explained to her grandmother. "They're going to lower her down that way."

The town had only recently purchased the bucket truck, she had read in the weekly community newspaper, after their previous ancient one that had been in service for more than thirty years had broken down beyond repair.

"Hey! That's my grandson up there!" Paolo said. She looked at the firefighter on the roof.

She should have realized. How could she have missed that powerful frame, those broad shoulders inside the firefighter uniform?

Her heart gave a little kick in her chest that severely annoyed her.

She had no business even noticing the man, let alone finding him attractive. In the slightest.

Amanda was fully aware that Rafe Arredondo was likely the last man in town who would ever be interested in her.

Now that she knew it was him, she couldn't help watching the scene unfolding now through a new perspective, as if she had once more moved to a different viewpoint along the street.

Pearl seemed reluctant to climb into the bucket, clinging tightly to Rafe. He shook his head at something Amanda certainly couldn't hear, with the increasing wind. Amanda held her breath as he finally managed to help the older woman inside. After a moment, the bucket began to lower, slowly and smoothly at first, then with a sudden lurch that made the crowd gasp.

"What is happening?" Birdie frowned, her face lifted and snowflakes coating her dark glasses.

"The bucket was going down with Pearl in it but it seemed to wobble a little. I'm sure she's okay."

"I wonder why Rafe is not riding down with her to make sure she stays safe," Paolo said, his brow furrowed.

One of the firefighters standing around the scene must have heard the slight condemnation in his voice. He took a step closer to them. "Can't. It's against procedure to let a victim go by themselves but in this case it's probably the safer option. You know how we bought the truck used from a fire department in Texas?"

Paolo nodded. "Yes. My grandson flew down there to drive it back a few months ago."

"Apparently, there's a good reason why we got such a good deal on it, despite all the testing we did beforehand and the safety inspections. It's glitchy. An aerial bucket should be able to hold about six hundred pounds but ours gets shaky if there's more than about half that inside it. Otherwise we would have sent two guys up there. I imagine Rafe didn't want to risk it. You shouldn't worry about Pearl, though. He harnessed her in. She should be fine."

Amanda watched as the bucket was finally lowered all the way to the ground. A trio of other firefighters swarmed to help her out, and she saw Opal rush over and grab her sister in a tight embrace, to a resounding cheer from the crowd.

Phew. Crisis averted.

Amanda let out a relieved sigh. She ought to return to her store and all the Black Friday customers, but for some reason she couldn't seem to tear herself away. Rafe was still on the roof and Paolo and Birdie seemed transfixed by the scene. The man was giving Amanda's grandmother a play-by-play of the action.

Amanda couldn't quite see what was happening. Rafe seemed to be crouching down on the edge of the roof, then would side-step along and bend down again every few feet.

"What is he doing?" Birdie asked.

"I'm not quite sure," Paolo answered.

Amanda narrowed her gaze, then realized he had something in his hands.

"I think he's finishing the job of hanging the Christmas lights for Opal and Pearl."

Oh. What a kind thing to do. Despite the pelting snow and the wind knuckling under her coat, Amanda felt warmth seep through her.

He finished in less than ten minutes, a job that likely would have taken *her*—and most people—an entire afternoon.

When he plugged in the lights and they came on, the crowd below gave another round of applause. Under his helmet, she saw a flash of a smile, and Rafe gave a slight bow in the increasing snow.

This was more excitement than their little downtown business area had seen in a long time. For the sake of the local merchants, she had to hope all the onlookers would return to their shopping when it was over.

"Will they send the bucket back up for him?" Paolo asked the firefighter who had told them about the cut-rate truck.

"I don't think they want to risk it, especially with the wind getting worse. That's why they're putting up the ladder."

Sure enough, two firefighters had placed another ladder near the shaky one Pearl must have used to climb onto the roof.

Rafe turned and began to climb down. He made it only a few feet when the ladder tilted slightly. One boot slipped out from under him in an alarming way that made the crowd gasp. Firefighters below rushed to support it but it was too late. The shift had thrown Rafe off-balance and his boots scrambled for purchase on the ladder. The next instant, he was falling, falling, at least a dozen feet, then landing with a sickening thud on the sidewalk.

For one horrified moment, Amanda could only stare, then she was racing across the street. She had no idea what she hoped to do, especially with other firefighters and paramedics on-site. She had rushed over only on instinct, wanting to help if she could.

Fearing what she would find, she was relieved to see Rafe sitting up, swearing a blue streak and holding his arm.

"What happened? Are you all right?" Paolo asked, fear and urgency in his voice.

Rafe looked up, brow furrowed. "*Abuelo*? What are you doing here?"

"We were shopping across the street when the fire truck

pulled up. We stayed to watch you in action and had more of a show than we expected."

Rafe's gaze met Amanda's and he looked even more confused. She couldn't blame him. It made sense for his grandfather to rush over after he fell, concerned for his safety. She, on the other hand, had no legitimate reason to be here. She hardly knew the man.

"I think you broke your arm, dude," one of the firefighters said, giving him a cursory examination.

"And you should feel damn lucky that's the only thing," the town fire chief, Mike Bennett, growled. "It could have been your neck."

"It wasn't. I'm mostly fine," Rafe replied. While he said the words casually, she could tell he was in pain.

"You should have come down the minute Miss Barnes was safe, before the wind ratcheted up and snow made the ladder slick as snot," Mike said.

Rafe shrugged. "I didn't want Opal or Pearl to feel like they had to go back up on the roof to finish the job."

The two older women had also joined the growing crowd around Rafe. "Oh, thank you," Pearl exclaimed. "We wanted to have our great-nephew help us. I'm so glad we didn't. He would have been killed."

What about Rafe, who nearly had been?

Amanda swallowed down the words. It wasn't the women's fault. They had only been trying to make their shop a little more festive.

"Good thing we've got the ambulance here. You've earned yourself a ride to the emergency room," Mike said gruffly.

"I don't need an ambulance ride. Somebody can just drop me off."

"It's here and at the ready. You're taking it." The chief spoke in a tone that brooked no argument.

"Will he be okay?" she heard Birdie ask Jordan Foster, one of the volunteer firefighters, whose mother worked with Amanda on the market committee.

"Chief A is tough," Jordan answered. "It takes more than a little fall off a ladder to stop him."

She didn't find his words necessarily reassuring. Poor man, when he had only been trying to help a couple of elderly sisters who eked out a small living at their yarn shop.

How could she help him? she wondered as she headed back to The Lucky Goat and the holiday shoppers. The man lived down the street from her. She had to do something. She couldn't continue to ignore her new neighbors. He was a single dad, doing his best for his son and for the community.

She would have to see if she could take a meal or something to him and Isaac.

If he could be kind enough to risk his own personal safety, she could certainly step outside her own comfort zone for a moment, at least long enough to help a man who was down.

4

"DAD! I THINK SOMEBODY'S HERE."

Rafe shifted on the sofa, moving pillows to accommodate the ridiculously large fiberglass cast. At the slight movement, pain iced up his left arm, from his fingertips to his shoulders.

Everything ached. He had fallen ten feet onto concrete and had bruises on top of bruises. But the only thing broken, according to the extensive X-rays he had undergone at the emergency room, had been his arm, broken in two places, likely from where he had banged it on the blasted ladder on his way down.

He knew things could have been worse. He hadn't required surgery, for one thing. The orthopedist had assured him they were clean breaks that should mend on their own in six to eight weeks, as long as he took things easy and kept his arm as immobilized as possible.

He still didn't want to deal with any of it and wished he could have gone back in time ten seconds so he could made sure the ladder was completely stable before he started to climb down it.

Bad enough that he was injured. Worse, he had taken a fall in front of the whole damn town. The guys were never going to let him hear the end of it.

The doorbell rang. "I was right!" Isaac said. "Can I answer the door?"

"Sure. Go ahead. It's probably your grandma or your aunt Julia. They both said they wanted to stop by and check on me."

His family tended to hover whenever one of their number needed help. Usually he wasn't the *hoveree*, he was on the other side of the equation. That was a role he found much more comfortable.

"I don't think it's *Abi* or *Tia* Julia. It's a lady."

"*Abi* and *Tia* Julia are both ladies."

Isaac frowned. "I know. But this isn't either of them. It's that pretty lady who fell on my car at *Abuelo*'s new house. Amanda!"

Before he could process that, Isaac thrust open the door.

"Hi there, Isaac." The woman's voice was soft, warm and very familiar.

"Hi! You're the lady from the Shelter Inn. My friend Birdie is your grandma."

Rafe shifted on the sofa, remembering her pale, frightened face, one of the first he had seen after that tumble off the ladder.

She had been there to witness the whole disaster, much to his chagrin. He found it bad enough that she already had seen him at one of his lowest moments earlier that day. This wasn't much better. Here he was with his arm in a stupid cast, in desperate need of a shave.

Why was she here?

"That's right. I'm Amanda."

"I remember," Isaac said cheerfully.

"Is your dad home?"

"Yeah. He broke his arm. Did you know that? In two whole places. He has a cast and everything. I've never broken any bone in my body. Have you?"

She seemed a little caught off guard by the question. "Yes, actually. When I was very small, I broke my collarbone after I fell off a wall in our back garden that I shouldn't have been climbing on. Oh, and I broke a toe when I was a little older than you are. I fell while riding my bike. That's about it, though."

"Does it hurt a lot when you break your bones? My dad says it doesn't hurt much but I don't believe him."

"I can't really remember, to tell you the truth."

"I never said it didn't hurt." Rafe finally spoke up. She lifted her attention from his son, and he saw her eyes widen at the sight of his cast.

"Oh. Hi."

"I never said it didn't hurt," he repeated. "I only said that I felt okay. They gave me medicine at the hospital to help me feel better."

"Did it?" she asked.

He shrugged. "I'm sure I'll be fine in a couple of days. Is there something I can help you with?"

He again had the impression she wasn't quite sure why she was there. After a few seconds, she appeared to remember the two large insulated grocery bags she carried.

"Yes. Right. Sorry. I feel terrible about you breaking your arm, especially while you were trying to help Opal and Pearl."

"It's part of the job. I haven't fallen off a ladder since I was a rookie. It shouldn't have happened."

He knew Mike was furious that the ladder hadn't been completely secured before he started down, and procedure hadn't been followed to make sure it remained stable.

"The stupid part is, we just spent way too much for a bucket truck that doesn't work the way it's supposed to. If that had been functioning correctly, I could have taken the bucket down with Pearl and wouldn't have needed to climb down a slippery ladder."

"I can see why that must be frustrating. Why it happened—

however it happened—I realize you're probably going to have a tough time in the kitchen for a little while and could maybe use a couple of easy meals for you and Isaac."

He blinked. "That's...very kind of you."

Why was she being so nice to him? They hardly knew each other.

It was hard to avoid Amanda completely when she seemed to be involved with every civic and Chamber of Commerce committee, but their paths rarely crossed.

After he and Isaac moved into the house on Huckleberry Street, he had been startled to realize she lived only down the street, in her grandmother's charming old cottage. As further proof that their worlds seldom collided, until he moved in, he had no idea she still lived there after Birdie moved to the retirement community.

"I wasn't sure what kind of food the two of you preferred so I picked up three different meals from restaurants around town."

"You didn't have to do that."

"You're right. I didn't have to. I wanted to. Don't worry. I had gift cards saved up from all the times The Lucky Goat has done joint promotions with these places."

"You still must have gone to a lot of work, ordering everything, then driving around to pick it up."

A hint of pink seemed to dance across her cheekbones. "It was nothing. Really. I tried to pick menu items that can be stored in the refrigerator for a few days and reheated. You can always freeze everything too, for another day when you need a quick meal."

"Thank you. I really appreciate that."

He had no idea what else to say. He wanted to blame the painkiller medication the emergency room doc had made him take, though he suspected it was more likely the unexpected kindness of the gesture that left him feeling all warm and gooey.

"I can put it away in your refrigerator, if you would like."

"Thank you. I would appreciate that."

He really hated accepting help, but figured she could do the task in half the time since he was temporarily one-handed.

Fortunately, he had just cleaned out the refrigerator a few days earlier, purging it of any scary leftovers.

"Guess what?" Isaac asked.

He didn't wait for her to answer before he went on. "My dad can't go to work. They won't let him drive the ambulance or a fire truck because his arm is broken. He can't fight any fires either or help people who are hurt. So that means I get to stay here every night and I don't have to go sleep overnight at my grandma's house or with my cousins. I don't mind sleeping at their houses, but I like being with my dad better."

"Wow. That will be a change for you."

He nodded, then gave her a mischievous look. "*Abi* told *Ito* that my dad is going to be tearing out his hair by tomorrow. She said he likes to stay busy, but the doctors said he has to take it easy for at least a couple of weeks."

Rafe frowned. His parents really needed to stop talking about him when his son was within earshot. Especially when they knew Isaac had absolutely no filter and shared everything he saw, heard or felt with the entire world.

She sent Rafe an amused look that somehow left him feeling a little lightheaded.

The painkillers again, he told himself.

"Oh dear. I guess it's lucky he can only tear out half of his hair, since he only has one working arm right now."

Isaac giggled. "So he'll only be half-bald. That would look so funny!"

"Wouldn't it?" she agreed.

"I'll do my best to find something to keep me busy," Rafe said, trying not to sound whiny. "At least we have food to eat now, and I don't have to try to slap together peanut butter and jelly sandwiches for every meal with a cast on my arm."

They moved to his kitchen and she easily found room in the refrigerator for the take-out boxes.

"Dad, can I show Amanda the picture I painted at Aunt Crista's house today?" Isaac asked, then turned to her. "My aunt Crista is an artist. She paints really pretty pictures."

"I know. I have one of her watercolors in my house. I love her work. I would love to see what you created."

"Okay. I'll go get it."

He ran out of the room before Rafe could tell him another time might be better.

When they were alone in the kitchen, he was struck again by how pretty Amanda Taylor was, with green eyes and hair the rich auburn of maple leaves in October. The years had only made her more striking.

"Thank you for the food," he said, feeling suddenly awkward and uncomfortable for reasons he couldn't quite explain.

She flashed a quick smile, there and gone again, like a lazuli bunting flitting around his mother's backyard bird feeder.

"You're welcome. I hope it helps a little. I also hope I picked meals Isaac will enjoy."

"I'm sure it will be great. He's a pretty indiscriminate eater. The only thing he doesn't like are artichokes."

"Not an artichoke in the whole lot," she assured him.

"Whew," he answered.

"How long do you expect to be out of commission?"

He tried not to growl his frustration. "Because the injury happened on the job, the chief is forcing me to take time off. He wanted me to take a month but I'm doing my best to whittle that down."

She gave him a sympathetic look. "That can't be easy for you. I'm sorry."

"I keep trying to remind myself it could have been worse."

"Much worse," she agreed. "When I saw you fall, I thought surely you must have broken several bones, not only your arm."

"I mean, I guess it could have been worse. But yeah. It could also have been better, if I hadn't fallen at all."

"What will you do to fill the time?"

"Hang out with Isaac, when he's not in school, I guess. He and I can work on a couple of projects we're making as gifts for Christmas." He shrugged. "Maybe we can fit in some snowboarding."

She gave him a long look. "You have a broken arm. Granted, I'm not a doctor but I'm not sure snowboarding should be on the agenda."

"I broke the other arm in high school and played right through the rest of the basketball season with it, plus competed in a couple of snowboard races."

"You're not a teenager anymore," she pointed out.

Before he could answer, Isaac rushed in and thrust out his picture. "Here it is. Can you tell what it is?"

She took the paper and examined it carefully. He had to hope she was better at interpreting a six-year-old kid's art project than he was.

"Sure I can." She crouched down to Isaac's level and pointed to the drawing. "It's a Christmas tree, right? With a bunch of presents. What's that big one in the candy cane wrapping paper?"

"Something I really want Santa Claus to bring me this year," he said happily. "I can't tell you what it is, though. It's a surprise."

Rafe huffed out a breath. He had been working hard for weeks to figure out what Isaac was hoping to find under the tree. Even a small clue would be nice.

"Got it. That's a lovely picture. I especially like the purple ornaments."

"My friend Maverick said purple isn't a Christmas color, though."

"Well, I love it. You tell Maverick that any color works for a Christmas ornament. I should know. I have a store that sells Christmas ornaments in every possible color."

"I'll tell him," he said, clearly delighted by her answer. "I can draw you a picture, if you want. I don't have paints but I can use crayons."

"That would be lovely. Thank you!"

Isaac rushed away with the single-minded focus he could sometimes exert. When he left, Rafe thought Amanda looked a little nonplussed.

"I didn't mean right now," she said.

"Don't worry. We can drop it off for you sometime. He's always happy for any excuse to take a walk, even in the snow."

She nodded. "He's very sweet. You're lucky."

"Yeah. I am."

"Actually, while he's busy for a moment, I wanted to talk to you about something else."

"Oh?"

"I don't really know how to bring it up."

"Seriously? I find it hard to believe that Amanda Taylor, the woman known for taking charge and getting things done in Shelter Springs, is ever lost for words."

She made a face. "Yes. I know. I have a bad habit of signing up for more projects than I can legitimately handle. It's a problem."

"I hope I'm not another one of your projects." He gestured to the empty bags on the countertop.

Color soaked her cheekbones. "No. Not at all. I was simply being neighborly, especially as you were hurt helping some friends of mine."

"I was doing my job. And not very well, obviously, or I wouldn't have taken a tumble off a stupid ladder."

"Hanging the decorations for Opal and Pearl was thoughtful. I'm very sorry you were hurt while doing a nice thing. I can tell you that from the perspective of the bystanders, it was terrifying to witness you fall."

She sounded genuinely upset at the possibility, which gave him an odd little burst of heat in his chest.

"Anyway," she went on, that color spreading, "you moved in a month ago. I should have brought cookies or something before now."

Why didn't you?

The question seemed to hover between them.

"I did not realize you were the welcoming committee for the neighborhood, along with all your other town responsibilities."

She gave a small, embarrassed smile. "Not officially, maybe, but I do try to reach out when new people move in on our street, to welcome them with a plant or a treat as a housewarming gift. Building a community where people watch out for each other takes a concerted effort."

"And that's important to you?"

"Yes. Very. Isn't it important to you? You've chosen to raise your child here in Shelter Springs. I would think the stakes are even higher for you to make sure Isaac has a warm, supportive, safe community to grow up in."

He did care about that. He had been offered a job in Boise after he finished his paramedic training. At the time, Caitlin had urged him to take it since the pay had been substantially higher. They had debated it for a long time before finally deciding to stay in Shelter Springs.

He was deeply grateful now that he had turned down that offer. In light of everything that happened later, he couldn't imagine trying to raise Isaac on his own in a larger town, away from the safety net of his family.

"Yes. It's important to me. I wouldn't have stayed in Shelter Springs if it wasn't. I see a lot of things in my line of work that can sometimes be grim. I also see plenty of good, too. This town is filled with decency and heart, for the most part. We're lucky, aren't we?"

She flashed him a smile, more genuine than any she had given him yet that evening. Again, that funny warmth seemed to flash through him like fireworks over Lake Haven.

He cleared his throat. "So what was it you wanted to talk to me about? Let me guess. You're throwing together a neighborhood watch or something, and you want me to sign up."

"No. Though that isn't a bad idea. I'll jot that down for next year."

"Then what?"

Her slight smile seemed to dim and she suddenly looked troubled. "I was looking for your opinion on something. But never mind. It's not important."

"Now you have me curious. What is it? You're here. You might as well ask me."

She hesitated, her expression suddenly wary. Finally she went on in a rush.

"Do you think something might be going on with our grandparents?"

Of all the possibilities that had cycled through his brain in the past few seconds, their respective grandparents hadn't come close to making the list.

"What do you mean by that? What do you think might be going on?"

"I was just wondering if they might be...dating."

He thought for a moment he was maybe imagining this entire conversation. Maybe those painkillers they had forced on him in the ER were befuddling him more than he thought.

"Birdie and *Abuelo* dating? Seriously?"

She seemed to regret bringing up the topic. "They seemed... very friendly the other day when I saw them at the Shelter Inn before Thanksgiving. Your grandfather took Birdie chocolates."

"And you, if you'll remember."

"Right. But I think I was merely an afterthought. And then they came into my store today shopping together. They were there when you had your accident, remember? They were arm in arm the whole time."

"That's just Paolo's way. He can be very protective. I expect he thinks he has to provide a little extra support to Birdie, with her vision struggles."

"That could be it." She hesitated. "I don't know. They just… they seem to be spending a lot of time together."

Rafe frowned. "Why is that a problem for you?"

"Not necessarily a problem. A concern, maybe."

"Semantics. Why would you possibly be concerned about two widowed people in their golden years who enjoy spending time together?"

Her mouth tightened. "My grandmother has been very vulnerable since she started losing her vision. I would hate to see her get hurt."

Rafe narrowed his gaze. "You think *Abuelo* would hurt Birdie in some way? Or any woman?"

"I don't know. I hardly know him. All I know about him, really, is that he and your grandmother ran Rosita's in Haven Point. One of my favorite restaurants."

He thought he picked up a barely perceptible note of suspicion in her voice. Under other circumstances, he would have found that amusing. The two small towns had a long history of friendly competitiveness.

"Yeah. He and my grandmother were in the restaurant business for nearly forty years. It's a local treasure."

"I agree. They have delicious fajitas."

Rafe had worked there summers and after school since he was old enough to bus tables. He had learned how hard and relentless the work could be and had nothing but admiration for his grandparents, who had kept it going for years.

He had to admit, he liked working for the fire department much more than the hospitality industry.

"He was sorry to sell it after my grandmother died but he couldn't run things on his own. My cousin bought it from him, and she and her husband run it now."

"Your grandmother died in January, didn't she?"

Thinking about his *abuela* still ached. Rosita had been a constant example of courage and grace throughout her life. Watching her grow increasingly ill had been one of the most helpless times of his life.

"Yes. Pneumonia. She had preexisting respiratory issues, maybe from all her years of working in kitchens and breathing cooking fumes and flour particulates. When she got sick, she couldn't fight it off."

"Winters can be hard on older people here in the mountains. My mom wants Birdie to move down to Florida with her, but my grandmother won't hear of it. Shelter Springs is her town, she says. She was born here and intends to go out here, too."

Birdie was definitely a character. He could hear her saying that. He liked and respected the woman. If his grandfather was going to start a relationship with someone again, he could do far worse than Birdie Lovell.

"My grandfather is a good man. If he and your grandmother enjoy spending time together, I can't see that it's any business of yours or mine. Unless you have something against hardworking immigrants."

She stared at him, her eyes filled with outrage at the suggestion. "Of course I don't! That has absolutely nothing to do with it. I like your grandfather very much, the little that I know about him. But I've come to realize that over the last few weeks, every time I talk to my grandmother, Paolo is either at her apartment, coming over soon or has just left. It's surprising, that's all. My grandfather died years ago and Birdie has never shown the slightest interest in anyone else, in all the years since."

"I guess my grandfather must still have it."

"She's eighty years old! Also, he lost his wife less than a year ago. Don't you think it's a little soon for him to jump into something else?"

"Trust me. Grief is a completely individual experience. There is no one-size-fits-all playbook when you lose someone you love."

Three years after his marriage broke down and then Caitlin's subsequent death, he was still figuring out his way, sorting through the jumbled mess of loss, anger and regret.

"*Abuelo* is a grown man," he said, his voice quiet. "It's not my place to be bothered if he chooses to ease his loneliness by befriending a dozen women at the Shelter Inn."

Her eyes widened. "Has he?"

"Not that I'm aware of. I meant that only as a figure of speech. My point is that Paolo doesn't have that much time left on this earth. Neither does Birdie. If they make each other happy, like I said, that's their business."

"I suppose you're right," she said after a moment, still looking unhappy.

"You don't seem very convinced."

"I'm sorry. But your grandfather seems to have become extremely involved in Birdie's life in a relatively short amount of time. I can't help but worry."

"Maybe I'm the one who should be worried. My grandfather lost the love of his life less than a year ago. He's vulnerable and alone. Maybe Birdie is the one taking advantage of the situation. He's only seventy-six, so she's an older woman."

He meant the words as a joke, though he could tell she wasn't particularly amused. Before she could respond, though, Isaac rushed back into the room, his hand outstretched.

"Here's your picture," he said. "It's another Christmas tree. See? And that's you and me standing by it."

Rafe could see two stick figures with very large heads, one

taller and with red hair and the other smaller with curly hair and glasses.

"Thank you. It's wonderful," she exclaimed. "I love it. I'll put it up on my refrigerator."

Isaac grinned happily. "If you want another one, let me know."

"I'll do that."

"I'm hungry, Dad. Can I have one of those cookies our friend Amanda brought?"

He pointed to the counter, where a box from the local bakery sat enticingly. "Just one. You have to save room for dinner. Fortunately we have a few options to choose from now, thanks to our kind neighbor."

To Rafe's surprise, Isaac went to Amanda and wrapped his arms around her waist. "Thanks for the cookies and stuff."

She hugged him back, an odd expression on her lovely features. "You're very welcome," she murmured, then quickly stepped away.

"I should go, so you can have your dinner and your father can get some rest. It was good to see you again, Isaac. Rafe, I'm sorry once more about your accident. If you need help with anything, I'm just down the street."

He was most concerned about dealing with logistics. Getting dressed and undressed, wrapping his cast in a waterproof covering so he could take a shower, putting toothpaste on his toothbrush with one hand. Somehow he didn't think Amanda Taylor would appreciate him giving her a call her to help him take off his hoodie at the end of the day.

Or anything else.

An inappropriate image of the two of them in his bedroom flashed through his mind but he quickly shut it down. She certainly wouldn't appreciate *that*.

How was he supposed to fight this unwanted attraction to

her when she smelled delicious and her mouth appeared so soft and inviting?

"Thanks again for the food," he said, his voice more gruff than he intended.

"You're welcome." That soft mouth lifted into a polite smile.

With one last wave to Isaac, she walked outside. Rafe followed her out and stood in the doorway, watching her climb into her small SUV, drive four houses down the road and pull into the driveway of the house that used to belong to her grandmother.

After she pulled into her small attached garage, he finally went inside.

Amanda Taylor was a curious woman. Rafe did not know quite what to make of her.

She was not the woman for him, even if he were open to a new relationship. While she was nice enough and seemed devoted to Shelter Springs, he could not make his way past the haunted shadows in her eyes.

Amanda Taylor had baggage and plenty of it.

Rafe knew his own weaknesses. He was drawn to wounded birds, compelled by some innate instinct to try to help. He suspected it was something genetic. The men in his family, from *Abuelo* to Rafe's own father, were always looking toward the needs of others.

He wouldn't say the Arredondo compulsion to help others was necessarily a terrible trait. Most people would find it commendable, even.

Unfortunately, sometimes that urge to ease someone else's pain led a man to choices that would only prove self-destructive in the end.

Caitlin once had the same haunted shadows in her eyes, filled with ghosts he once optimistically thought he could vanquish for her.

He had been sadly mistaken. Despite his best efforts, he

hadn't been able to save the woman he loved. Worse, Isaac was the one who had paid the price for Rafe's poor choices.

Isaac was the most important thing in his world.

With every single decision, Rafe had to ask himself if his son would be helped or harmed by his choices.

Rafe could no longer afford to let himself be involved with a woman simply because he was attracted to her.

If he ever again entered into any kind of long-term relationship, his son's well-being had to remain at the forefront of his decision-making.

Right now, Rafe couldn't imagine a world where Amanda Taylor and her baggage and her shadows and her suspicions about his grandfather would ever be a healthy choice for him or for his son.

5

THOUGH THE NEXT DAY WAS NEARLY AS CHAOTIC AND busy at the store as Black Friday had been, Amanda couldn't seem to get the awkward encounter with Rafe out of her head.

What was wrong with her? She interacted with people all day long. She had become excellent at dealing with irate customers who ultimately didn't like a product they had chosen and purchased, with parents who ignored their children as they raced through the store opening bottles and knocking things off shelves, with suppliers who missed deadlines and unexpectedly increased prices.

Why, then, had she completely botched that conversation with him? From the moment she showed up out of the blue with an abundance of meals for him and Isaac to her fumbled attempts to ask him about Birdie and Paolo, she had been unnerved and off-balance.

He probably thought she was some kind of weirdo do-gooder.

She sighed. What did it matter what Rafe thought of her?

While they were neighbors now, both living on Huckleberry Street, she expected she would have very little to do with him or his son, if their past history was any indication.

Unless, of course, their grandparents ended up embroiled in a hot and heavy relationship. Would that make them... stepgrandchildren?

She had no idea and didn't want to think about it—or Rafe—another moment. That's what she told herself, anyway, until the next time the awkward memory of their encounter popped into her head.

During one of the rare slow moments at the store, she was trying her best to focus on juggling the complicated schedule for December—given that for two weeks, half of her employees would be working The Lucky Goat stall at the holiday market—when the bells on the door jingled. She automatically looked up and was both shocked and delighted to see her dear friend Natalie Shepherd walk through.

"Nat!" Amanda exclaimed, setting aside her laptop and rushing to hug her friend. "You're back! I thought you weren't flying home until next week."

Natalie looked burnished and beautiful, alive with health and happiness.

"Yes. We were supposed to fly home on Monday but with all the Thanksgiving travel traffic, the airline called and said they either had to bump us a few days or they could get us home on a red-eye last night. As Griffin has to work in the urgent care Wednesday, we opted for the red-eye."

While Griffin had his own family medicine clinic in town, he and other physicians in the area shared shifts in order to staff the local urgent care clinic.

"I'm sorry you had to cut your trip short."

"Only by about thirty-six hours. It's fine. We had an amazing experience. You should have seen how many people in Guatemala he was able to help. And they were all so very grateful, too."

This was the second time during the year they had been together that Natalie and Griffin had gone on a trip overseas so that Amanda's brother could work with a medical charity that provided free care to people in need.

"Oh, that's wonderful. It must be so rewarding for both of you."

"I didn't do much except hand him bandages and tongue depressors occasionally. It was still wonderful. You should come with us next time. The organization we were working with asked Griff to consider a longer trip over the summer, maybe to eastern Africa. He's thinking about it."

She couldn't help but notice how Natalie glowed when she talked about Griffin. It made Amanda's heart happy, even as she was aware of a small twinge of envy.

Natalie was so good for Griffin—and vice versa. The two of them seemed to fill in all the cracks that sorrow and pain over the years had etched on their hearts.

"We got you something. Griff helped pick it out." Natalie handed over a gift bag.

"Oh. Thank you. That is so nice of you both."

"Go ahead. Open it."

When she did, she pulled out a gorgeous hand-beaded hummingbird in brilliant colors, dangling from a looped ribbon.

"Oh! It's wonderful. Thank you! I love it!"

"As soon as I saw it, I thought of you and your trees here at the store."

She had two Christmas trees at The Lucky Goat, one decorated with ornaments for sale that had been made by local craftspeople, the other, in the window, adorned with her own personal collection of handmade ornaments from around the world.

"I'll hang it right now. Thanks, Nat."

She moved to the front window and found a spot between a carved wooden crèche ornament and a hammered iron twisted candy cane.

"How was Thanksgiving?" Natalie asked after Amanda stood back to admire the tree. "Griff is hoping Birdie will forgive him for missing it this year."

"You know she will. Birdie never holds a grudge, and she certainly doesn't mind that you weren't there, especially when you were engaged in a good cause."

"He was still sorry not to be able to spend it with you both."

"We missed him, too. And you as well. Thanksgiving was quiet. Me and Birdie and Mabel Mulcahy."

Natalie winced. "Sorry about that."

"Mabel was actually quite lovely. I think she has mellowed a little over the years."

Birdie's neighbor in the apartment building had once owned a small market near the elementary school featuring a huge candy selection, offerings far sweeter than Mabel had ever been to her young customers.

"That's good to hear."

"Yes. It was a nice day." She paused, remembering the day before and Birdie and Paolo walking arm in arm through the store. Should she say something to Natalie? She debated for only a moment, then decided she owed Griffin a little advance warning.

"I should probably give you and Griffin a heads-up so you're not caught by surprise like I was. I think Birdie might have a boyfriend."

Natalie's quick laugh faded quickly when she saw Amanda didn't join her.

"You're serious."

Amanda nodded. "Totally serious. I should say that I'm not a hundred percent certain and I might be making a big deal out of something that's not there. But she has been spending a lot of time with a new resident at the Shelter Inn. A widower. Paolo Arredondo."

Natalie blinked. "I know Paolo. His daughter-in-law Louise was one of my mother's good friends. She used to come to our house and style my mom's hair, even in her last days of hospice."

"Oh, how kind."

While Louise had always been cool to *her*, Amanda could appreciate the woman's compassion toward Natalie's mother, who had died of cancer when they were teenagers. Jeanette Shepherd's death had been a pivotal event for Nat and her siblings. It had hit Jake particularly hard. He had never stopped mourning his mother and had been in a dark place for more than a year after her death.

"She was always really wonderful to Mom," Natalie said, then frowned again. "You think Birdie is dating Paolo? Really? Are you certain they're not just good friends?"

"Maybe. But I've seen them together several times now and she mentions him often when they are *not* together. Yesterday, they came into the store Black Friday shopping together and Birdie had her hand tucked in his arm the entire time as they walked around."

Even as she said the words, she realized how silly they sounded. She remembered what Rafe had said, about Paolo wanting to help.

Of course Birdie would have her hand tucked in Paolo's arm. She could not see well and sometimes needed assistance navigating the world around her, especially when she was in places that were not as familiar to her as her own apartment.

Amanda should never have said anything to Natalie—or to Rafe the day before. She cringed again, remembering the awkwardness of their conversation.

"Good for Birdie! Paolo is a great guy."

When Amanda did not answer, Natalie gave her a closer look. "You don't agree? Is there something wrong with Mr.

Arredondo, something I don't know about? Some compelling reason Birdie should not be spending time with him?"

Apparently Amanda was the only one uneasy at the idea of her eighty-year-old grandmother dating someone, when Birdie had never shown interest in anyone before.

If it didn't bother anyone else, why did Amanda find it so concerning? Was it possible she was envious that her grandmother might have someone in her life when Amanda was alone, as always?

No. She wasn't that selfish. She loved her grandmother and wanted her to be happy. She was just concerned that Birdie would end up hurt.

She had only been thirteen when her grandfather died but Amanda could still vividly remember how deeply her grandmother had grieved for him. For nearly a year afterward, Birdie had withdrawn into herself. She had stopped inviting them to dinner and had nearly lost her art gallery because she seemed to have stopped caring about anything.

None of their efforts to reach her had worked. For the only time in Amanda's memory, Birdie had been without her ready smile and warm hugs.

She couldn't bear thinking about Birdie being hurt again, after everything she had already endured.

"There's nothing wrong with Paolo, as far as I know. I wouldn't have even brought it up except I was shocked to see them together, and I wanted to give Griffin some advance warning so he wasn't caught by surprise, too."

"I'll let him know. I think he'll find it sweet, though."

Natalie brushed a strand of hair out of her eyes, and as she did, Amanda caught a glint of something sparkling there in the lights of her window display Christmas tree.

She gasped. "Natalie! What is that on your hand?"

Nat gave an innocent look that did not fool Amanda for a moment. "What? This?" She held out her hand, where Amanda could see the gleam of a beautiful diamond and emerald ring. She couldn't believe she had missed it until now.

"Griffin proposed? You're actually doing this? Oh, Nat. We're going to be sisters, just like we always talked about."

Even as she said the words and hugged her friend tightly, Amanda felt a little ache in her chest. When they had talked about it, back in their teenage years, they thought they would become sisters when Amanda married Natalie's brother, not the other way around.

"Tell me everything," she exclaimed, ignoring the ache. "When did he pop the question?"

Natalie smiled with so much joy that Amanda had to hug her again.

"Apparently, he bought the ring a few months ago and has been waiting for the right moment, carrying it around in his pocket. It's a wonder it wasn't stolen or lost somewhere along the way."

Amanda could just imagine her brother waiting for the perfect occasion to propose.

"Our last night in Guatemala, we were walking on the beach near our hotel. The moon was glimmering on the water and we were both a little sad to be leaving when there were still so many people needing help. We were talking about where we would go next and he suggested we should block off some time in our schedules for something besides travel. Then he popped out the ring, knelt right there in the sand, told me he loved me with every breath inside him and asked me to marry him."

"Oh," she breathed.

"It was the perfect proposal. Exactly right."

Of course, she had to hug her future sister-in-law all over again.

"I'm so happy for both of you," she said. "There is no one on earth I would rather see with my brother forever."

Natalie gave a soft, dreamy smile. "I was wondering if you

would consider sharing maid of honor duties with McKenna. I've asked her to be the matron of honor but with three small children, she will likely need help."

She was so very grateful to have Natalie back in her life. For many years after Jake's death, they had both let grief and guilt interfere with their friendship, until the previous Christmas had finally allowed the healing between them to begin.

"Of course! I would be honored."

"Thank you. We're thinking summer. Neither of us wants to wait long. We have to work out all the details around my few remaining travel obligations, but I'll keep you posted when we figure out the timing."

"Perfect. Summer works. I am so happy for both of you, Nat. This is the best news. Have you told Birdie yet?"

"No. We're heading over this afternoon."

"She'll be over the moon. Fair warning, though, she will probably take credit for the whole thing and claim she's the one who brought you two together last Christmas."

"I don't mind. She can take all the credit she wants. How can I complain when I'm the one who benefited from her match-making efforts?"

"Don't tell her that or you will never hear the end of it."

Natalie smiled. "You know, maybe you ought to let Birdie take a hand in your love life. She seems to have pretty good instincts about people and who might be the perfect match for them."

Amanda huffed out of breath. "What love life?"

"That's what I'm talking about." Suddenly serious, Natalie reached for her hand. "Mandy. Jake's been gone a long time. He wouldn't want you to put your whole life on hold for him."

She slipped her hand away and forced a smile, trying to hide her discomfort at the turn of topic. "I haven't done that. I've dated plenty of men since he died. I've had a few serious boyfriends and almost got engaged a few years ago, before you came back to Shelter Springs. He was a very nice engineer from Boise."

"Right. Ben. The twins told me about him."

What else had Holly and Hannah told Natalie about the man? She knew neither of their friends had particularly liked him, mainly because he had refused to consider moving to Shelter Springs. And, okay, maybe because he had not been completely over his ex-wife, even though the woman had left him for someone else, running off to Hawaii and leaving him to be a single father to their two young girls.

They had dated for six months and had talked about getting married. She had become friendly with Ben's mother and his sisters and had adored his daughters, who had been seven and five at the time.

When said ex-wife had reappeared in the picture, repentant and wanting to repair their marriage, Amanda had done the right thing and stepped aside.

She had grieved those adorable girls more than she had mourned the end of her relationship with Ben, she had to admit. With their sweet laughter and warm hugs, they had carved away a little chunk of her heart. She still thought of them often and hoped they were doing well, now that their parents were back together.

After that painful experience, Amanda had also vowed that she wouldn't date anyone else with children. It was too messy, difficult for all parties involved. Unfortunately, that definitely narrowed the field when she was thirty-one and most men of comparable age had a past that often involved children.

"I date," she said again. "But between the store and my grandmother and all the work I do with the market and my other projects, my time is limited. To be honest, I haven't found anybody lately who is tempting enough to distract me from all I have to do."

For some ridiculous reason, she thought of Rafe Arredondo,

with his dark hair tousled and that sexy mouth tight with a pain he didn't want to show. He had looked wounded and grumpy and completely adorable.

He had a child, she reminded herself. A precious six-year-old boy whom she suspected would carve much more than a chunk out of her heart if she let herself fall for him or for his father.

"I'm sorry I said anything," Natalie said. "I'll stop bugging you. It used to drive me crazy when McKenna and all my other well-meaning friends who were in healthy relationships tried to give me dating advice."

"Did you listen to any of them?"

"Absolutely not!"

They both laughed and Amanda was grateful any awkwardness had passed. "We need to have an engagement party! We should at least get our friends together to celebrate during the holidays, now that you're home. My schedule will be packed once the market starts but I could maybe swing an evening this week to go out to dinner."

"What a great idea! I would love that."

"Let me know after you've had a chance to tell everyone about the engagement and I'll set up a text chain to try to arrange something."

"Actually, don't tell them anything about the engagement. Just say you want to get together for the holidays. I would love to surprise everyone at dinner."

She smiled, imagining the delight of their friends. "Sounds great. Again, I'm thrilled for you, Nat. You and Griffin are perfect together. You've always been dear to me, but even if you had been my mortal enemy, I would have loved you anyway for making my brother so happy."

Over the past year, her brother had glowed with joy, more at peace than she had ever seen him. It made her own heart happy, especially after everything Natalie and Griffin had endured before finding their way to each other.

"I should run. I just wanted to drop off the ornament and share our news with you. I probably should have waited until your brother could come with me but I was too excited."

"You never could keep a secret."

"True enough. Bye, Mandy."

They hugged again, then Natalie left with a wave to the other workers in the shop, all of whom she knew.

Cat came over as soon as the door closed behind her, features avid with curiosity.

"I wasn't eavesdropping, I promise. But I could not help overhearing the happy news. I gather Natalie and Griffin came back from Guatemala engaged. Yay!"

Amanda again felt that funny little pang of mingled joy for her brother and his new fiancée and sorrow for the hope-filled girl she had once been, wholly believing she and Jake would have their happy-ever-after.

"Yes. It's so exciting."

"They are an adorable couple. I know it's a cliché but they each completely light up when the other one is in the room. I love it. Reminds me of when Sean and I were first dating. I still have that little tingle when I haven't seen him for a few hours."

Amanda found that adorable, especially since Cat and her husband had been married for more than two decades and had four children.

"Don't say anything to anyone, okay? She wants to wait a bit to tell everyone."

Cat mimicked twisting a key in a lock against her mouth, then both returned to their customers.

6

"YOU'RE NOT SUPPOSED TO BE HERE. I THOUGHT WE agreed you would be off work until after the new year."

Rafe fought down a shudder. He had spent three days watching daytime television and slowly going a little stir-crazy from the enforced inactivity.

He tried not to glower at his fire chief—and friend—Mike Bennett.

"I'm fine. Really. I can go back to work anytime. It's just a dumb cast. No problem at all."

"Maybe not for you, but the department has a strict policy that any job-related injuries have to be completely cleared by a doctor before you can return to active duty. Your doc said at least three weeks."

Rafe knew himself well enough to be completely certain that wouldn't work for him. He had adult ADHD, unmedicated, and needed to stay busy. He knew he couldn't endure sitting around for even a few more days.

"There has to be something I can do. I can work the phones,

teach a couple of classes, do some first aid training. Whatever you need."

Mike shrugged. "We finished our final first aid class of the year last week and we don't have another one scheduled until January. Remember, last year we figured out nobody wants to sign up for CPR or first aid training while they're busy with the holidays."

"Come on. There has to be something I could do. I don't care what. I can deep clean the station kitchen or organize files or something. I can't stand doing nothing."

His friend looked at him with compassion. "I get it. I'm the same way. But rules are rules. The mayor would chew my butt from here to Haven Point if I put you back on the schedule. And you know how fond my wife is of that particular part of my anatomy."

Rafe managed to hide his wince at this. Mike was fifty years old and while he was built like an ox and perfectly capable, always passing his annual physical, his wife's delicious cooking had added on a few love handles over the years.

"I know how shorthanded things get around here in December. People take year-end vacation time, there are more bugs going around. You can't afford to lose me for three weeks or more. I want to work and I'm totally capable of it."

"I know that and you know that. Unfortunately, we don't make all the decisions. The city has to protect itself."

Mike glanced down at his desk and his expression suddenly lit up in a way that filled Rafe with foreboding.

"There is one thing I'm willing to consider letting you do, but I know it's a job you typically try to avoid."

"What's that?" he asked warily.

Mike held up a festive red and green brochure for the Shelter Springs Holiday Giving Market. "Usually, your cousin Izzy, Jordan Foster or Tyler Jenkins sign up to handle the first aid station at the market. But this year Jordan and Tyler are taking those classes in Boise for their paramedic certification so they're out. Izzy can't do it by herself, as much as she likes the overtime. I was just about to send out an email asking if anybody else wanted to volunteer. We need at least one EMT or paramedic on hand at all times."

Oh man. He would almost rather deep clean the station bathrooms than have to sit all day, every day at the popular town market that drew visitors from across the region.

The market was a big deal around town and in his family. Not only did Izzy always work the first aid station but his sister-in-law Crista typically had a booth there, selling her lovely watercolors. His mom helped her out as often as she could get away from her salon.

He looked at the brochure as if it were a rattlesnake. "The market. Seriously? Don't you have anything else?"

"Not that I'm willing to let you do with a cast on your arm. Even that is pushing it. If we weren't so shorthanded, I wouldn't consider letting you do even that much."

Though Rafe couldn't believe he was even considering it, he really hated the idea of sitting at home throughout most of December. He would even rather stay occupied by working at the community Christmas market, where at least he would be doing something more than bingeing Netflix shows he really didn't care about.

"Fine," he said, before he could talk himself out of it. "I can help out at the market."

Yeah, the job would still involve a lot of sitting around, but people-watching was generally more entertaining than staring at a screen, and at least he might have the occasional twisted ankle or paper cut to deal with.

"Oh good." Mike look delighted. "Izzy will be happy to hear that. She's in charge of coordinating schedules. Let her know I'm adding you to the rotation. The market is open for over two weeks this year, from this coming Friday to the Saturday before Christmas. It opens at noon and ends at nine each night, Monday through Saturday, closed on Sunday."

"That should work. I can get Isaac off to school in the mornings and maybe he can hang out with my dad or one of his friends in the afternoon and evening."

Mike frowned with sudden misgivings. "Are you sure you're up to this? What if someone has a heart attack or something? It's not easy to do CPR with one hand."

"You can, though. One hand is better than nothing if someone needs emergency help. Also, I've taught CPR classes long enough to know that you *should* only use one hand on a child. Plus I assume I'll have a defibrillator available, which is better, anyway."

Mike gave him a long look, then finally sighed.

"You're a stubborn cuss, Rafe Arredondo. Has anybody ever told you that?"

Rafe thought of all the teachers who had been ready to pull out their hair with his energy level and his poor sainted mother, who had basically sat with him night after night throughout elementary school to make sure he finished his homework.

He smiled. "I'm well aware. Thanks, Mike. I owe you."

"I'm not sure if I'm really doing you a favor."

"It's better than the alternative," he said, sincerely hoping that was true.

7

"THIS WAS A GREAT IDEA. THANKS FOR ARRANGING it, Amanda!"

Amanda smiled at Nat and the rest of their friends, gathered around the table at their favorite restaurant, the Spur & Saddle.

"We don't get together often enough. I miss talking to you all," she said.

"I think the last time we were all gathered like this was that barbecue we had over the summer at Griffin's place," Natalie said.

McKenna, Natalie's younger sister, made a face. "I had to miss that one. Remember, Hazel had just had her tonsils out and I was busy handing her ice cream and snow cones."

"But you did get to enjoy a few weeks of relative silence." Natalie's tone was teasing but Amanda knew she adored her two nieces, Hazel and Nora, as well as their baby brother Austin.

"True enough. It was almost worth going through the tonsillectomy for that," McKenna said. "I feel lucky I was able to come tonight and we were able to coordinate everyone else's schedules. Thanks again for making it work, Amanda."

Amanda didn't really have time for a social event with her girlfriends right now, considering her store was so hectic and the town market opened in only a few days. But she knew if they didn't do it now, the days would fly by and it would be January before they could all arrange their schedules. That wouldn't do, as Natalie was leaving on an extended trip for six weeks after the New Year.

She had made it work, regardless of her schedule. Hadn't she resolved to create more time during this holiday season to slow down whenever possible so she could savor the connection with those she cared about?

She only had one brother and he was marrying a dear friend. She had to celebrate their engagement, even if it meant somehow squeezing out time she did not have.

She loved these women. Every one of them had been a powerful role model to her, showing her by example how to handle life's curveballs with grace.

"It was a wonderful idea," Vivi Morales said with a grin, though she looked exhausted after a long day of teaching at the elementary school.

"The best." McKenna gave an emphatic nod. "Austin is teething and the girls are bouncing off the walls with Christmas on the horizon, now that it's actually December. I am so glad for any excuse to escape our place."

"I'm always happy for the chance to see you all. But I must admit, I had an ulterior motive for arranging dinner. Natalie has news."

"What news?" Vivi asked.

In answer, Natalie picked up her wineglass with her left hand, where her lovely ring glinted in the candlelight.

The others at the table immediately picked up on the unmistakable hint. The twins shrieked and Vivi clapped her hands together.

"You're engaged?" Vivi exclaimed. "When did this happen?"

"While we were in Guatemala. I've been dying to tell everyone but thought it would be more fun to spill the beans in person."

"Why am I always the last to know all the exciting stuff?" Holly demanded.

"I didn't know either, for once." Hannah looked disgruntled.

"I mean, it can't be that big of a surprise to everyone, can it?" McKenna said with a wry smile. "They've been inseparable for the past year. Whenever Nat is in town, I have to beg her to tear herself away from Griffin's side so she can come visit her nieces and nephew."

"Ha. That's totally untrue and you know it. I love seeing them. In fact, I'm pretty sure they all get sick of me."

Since the previous Christmas, when Natalie had returned during the holidays for the first time in years, she had developed a deep bond with her sister's children. She had become even more of a doting aunt than she used to be long-distance, when she had carved out a life as a digital nomad, house-sitting and working as a freelance writer and editor.

The children were as happy as their mother that Natalie had decided she loved being home in Shelter Springs with them, with McKenna and especially with Griffin.

"When is the big day?" Vivi asked.

"Neither of us wants to wait long," Natalie said, with that same soft joy on her expression. "We're thinking sometime in the summer, anyway. Maybe June. My last job is scheduled for April and that would still give me a little time to work out the final details."

"We can help you even when you're off seeing the world," Amanda said. "We'll take care of all the small details so you only have to show up and look gorgeous."

After ordering their food, the conversation returned to the upcoming wedding plans.

"I can't wait for another wedding. What was the last one we planned?" McKenna asked.

The table fell silent when Holly raised her hand with a rueful expression. Hannah reached out and squeezed her sister's other hand, and Amanda would have hugged her as well, if she hadn't been seated across the table.

Holly's slimy husband had walked out on her the previous Christmas season, leaving her alone to raise their four-year-old daughter, Lydia, who happened to have Down syndrome.

"Are you going to stop traveling?" Holly asked, and Amanda could tell she was determined not to be the center of attention.

"No. I still want to do some travel writing but I'm going to stick closer to home now and focus on destinations in the Rocky Mountain states. We have plenty to see nearby, enough unique and beautiful travel spots to keep me busy for a long time."

"Exactly," McKenna said. "I've been telling you that for years."

"I haven't heard much about your trip to Guatemala. You were working at a medical clinic, right?" Hannah asked.

"Oh, it was wonderful. We're going again, as soon as we can arrange it. You should come, too. I'm certain there's need for someone trained in physical therapy, like you."

She told them about the clinic where they had worked and about all the people they had helped, talking with enthusiasm until the server brought their appetizers and salads not long after.

As the conversation shifted, Amanda turned to Holly, seated next to her.

"Where's Lydia tonight?" she asked, her voice low.

"With my parents. They love any chance to spend time with her and she adores them."

She was grateful Holly had a warm, loving family to support her through her divorce, especially as Amanda had heard through the grapevine that Holly's ex, who had taken off to

California after he walked away, was already engaged and living with his new girlfriend.

"How are you doing?"

"Hanging in there." Holly's smile seemed forced.

Amanda had never really liked Holly's husband, who had always struck her as self-centered and somewhat controlling.

Her dislike had solidified into something more harsh when she saw him struggle to adjust to having a child with an obvious developmental disability that would present a lifetime of challenges.

She couldn't understand anyone not completely embracing Lydia. The little girl was joy personified. She was loving, generous and filled with a light that drew people to her.

"Is Lydia as excited for the holidays as Hazel and Nora?"

"Oh yes. She loves to play with the little wooden Nativity set my parents got her and she can stretch out under the Christmas tree for hours, looking at the lights."

"Same," Amanda said with a smile.

"How are *you* doing?" Holly asked, her features soft with compassion. "I know how hard this time of year always is on you."

"It's my own fault. I take on far too many projects and then I don't have time to breathe until January."

Holly frowned. "That's not what I meant and you know it. I was talking about Jake. We're close to the anniversary of his death. It's been, what? Eleven years now?"

"Almost twelve."

The events of that Christmas were burned into her memories as if they had happened twelve days ago instead of twelve years.

The months leading up to that December day had been a nightmare. Jake had been spiraling out of control, getting drunk every weekend and often during the week, too. He had been grieving the death of his mother and furious at his father, for running away to live off-grid in Alaska, right when his three children needed him most.

Amanda had tried to be a compassionate, understanding fiancé. She had endured as long as she possibly could, but when she realized that she was falling into the very same enabling behavior that her mother had exhibited throughout Amanda's entire childhood, she had decided enough was enough. With her heart breaking apart, she had ended their engagement.

A week later, he was dead.

For a long time, she had feared his death had not been accidental, that he had snowboarded into that hazardous off-limits area at the ski resort on purpose—knowing the avalanche danger, but still set on his same unerring self-destructive path as the past few months.

Griffin, Jake's good friend, had been with him at the time. Only later had Amanda learned that Griffin also blamed himself for Jake's death. The two friends had fought on the way up the hill on the ski lift, with Griffin asserting that Jake was already drunk and in no state to take to the slopes. He was a danger to himself and others, Griffin had snapped out.

Jake hadn't listened to his friend any more than he had listened to Amanda when she had begged him to get some help for his drinking.

She pushed away the hard memories and forced a smile for her friend.

"I'm fine. Really. I will always miss Jake and the future we might have had, but it's been nearly twelve years. I've gone on with my life."

"Have you, though?"

The quiet question seemed a gut punch coming out of nowhere.

"Yes! You know I have. I'm busy all the time. I have a shop. I have the market. I have all of my other volunteer work."

"But you don't date. Not much, anyway."

Why on earth was everyone so obsessed with her love life right now?

"I do not need to have someone by my side in order to have a full, rewarding life."

"Agreed," Holly said. "If I've learned anything over the past year, it's the hard truth that it's far better to be alone than trapped in an unhappy, destructive relationship."

For some reason, Holly's words made Amanda think of Ben again and his daughters. He had been the first man she had truly let herself care about since Jake died.

If she were honest with herself, though, with the wisdom she had gained over the past two years since their breakup, Amanda could admit that she had loved the idea of being a mother to Lila and Jane more than the idea of being Ben's wife and life partner.

"You should get out there again. Have you tried any of the various dating apps?" Holly asked.

She shook her head, setting down her fork. Her chop salad no longer seemed appealing. "That's how I met Ben," she said.

"Oh yeah." Holly gave a sour look that clearly conveyed her opinion of the man. "Well, you can't always get it right the first time."

"Where else do you expect to meet guys?" Vivi joined the conversation from her spot across the table. "You spend your whole life either at Birdie's retirement community, where the median age is about seventy-five, or at your shop, which is frequented by mostly women."

Amanda sighed. "Why is everyone suddenly trying to set me up? Am I wearing some kind of sign that says Desperate Single Woman on it? I'm not! I'm perfectly happy with the status quo. I have my house, the shop, my cats. I don't need anything else."

Amanda gestured to Natalie. "Anyway, tonight isn't about trying to fix my nonexistent love life. We're here to celebrate Griffin and Natalie. Where do you guys think you'll live after you're married? Griffin's condo?"

Natalie gave her a careful look, seeing right through Amanda's completely transparent effort to change the topic. Apparently she decided to go along with it, much to Amanda's relief.

"We're looking at a lot above town. We're thinking about building."

"Oh yay! Nothing would make me happier," she declared.

She had worried that Griffin and Natalie might decide not to stick around in Shelter Springs. While Griffin was determined to practice medicine in the area, where he could serve the community, Natalie loved to travel. Amanda didn't think it was completely out of the realm of possibility that she might influence him to move his practice somewhere else.

If they were considering building a home in the area, the chances of Griffin pulling up stakes and starting over somewhere else seemed unlikely. That meant she would have her brother and her dear friend around for a long time.

The conversation drifted to the price of building lots then possible wedding venues, and Amanda sat back, enjoying her soup and her friends and the restaurant with its twinkling lights and holiday decorations.

They had just ordered dessert when a new party came into the restaurant. Amanda felt her shoulders tense when she recognized Rafe's mother along with his sister, Julia, and sister-in-law, Crista. The hostess led the three of them past their table, where the two groups greeted each other with warmth.

Shelter Springs was a relatively small town and most people who had lived there a long time knew each other.

Louise's smile dimmed noticeably when her gaze reached Amanda, but she gave a polite nod as the hostess led them to a table in the other dining area of the restaurant.

While they were waiting for their dessert order, Amanda excused herself to go to the restroom. She was washing her hands when the door opened and Louise walked through.

The other woman always looked elegant and put-together,

with expertly applied makeup and her honey-colored hair showing no trace of gray.

"Oh. Hello," the other woman said.

Amanda nodded. "Hello, Louise. How are you this beautiful December evening?"

"I'm doing very well, thank you. We're heading to the movies. Crista and I will be busier than usual with the market for the next few weeks, so we thought this might be our only chance for us girls to have an outing together before Christmas."

Louise was obviously close with her daughter and daughter-in-law. Amanda had seen the three of them shopping together in town or attending book events at the library or summer concerts in the town's main park.

If she were honest with herself, Amanda could acknowledge that seeing their loving relationship always left her with an uncomfortable ache.

She loved her mother, but they weren't particularly close. She hadn't been sorry when Lena remarried and settled permanently in Florida.

Still, she talked to her mother on the phone two or three times a month and they texted more regularly.

As much as she would have savored the same kind of close relationship Louise shared with Crista and Julia, Amanda didn't know how to get to that place.

She knew the fault was hers. Even as an adult, she struggled to truly forgive Lena for the long years spent enabling her father, covering for his addictions both socially and professionally. Her mother had been obsessed with appearances, pretending everything was perfect in their home, when it had been far from it.

She pushed away the memories. "That sounds lovely," she said to Louise. "I hope you have a wonderful evening together."

"Looks like you and your friends are enjoying yourselves."

"We're celebrating tonight. Natalie and my brother are getting married."

Louise looked startled. "Oh. I hadn't heard. How nice for them."

"They have only been engaged a short time. They're planning a summer wedding."

Though she knew she should let it go at that, she couldn't resist adding, "I'm thrilled to see Griffin so happy. He deserves it."

She knew Louise had been one of those residents not thrilled at the idea of another Dr. Taylor moving to town.

"Will they stay here in Shelter Springs?" Louise asked.

"I believe so. Griffin loves this town and caring for the people here."

The other woman dried her hands with a paper towel. "I understand I owe you a debt," she said after a moment.

"Me? Why?"

"My grandson told me you stopped by the other night to take dinner to Rafael and Isaac. Several dinners, actually. Isaac reports it was all delicious. It was very thoughtful of you."

Amanda sincerely hoped Louise could not see the flush of heat washing over her when she remembered that awkward encounter with Rafe.

"It was nothing. I picked up a few things around town, that's all. To be honest, I was feeling more than a little guilty that they have been living down the street for a month and I had still not welcomed them to the neighborhood with cookies or something. Things have been so hectic, getting ready for the holidays at the store and all the advance preparations for the market."

She was making excuses, and she suspected Louise knew that as well.

"Well, I'm sure they appreciated it. Rafael said you took enough meals to last them all week."

"I was happy to do it," she lied. "Poor man. It can't be easy for him, not being able to work."

Louise made a face. "Unfortunately, he will be working after all. I think he should rest but my son is stubborn. He was able to convince Mike Bennett to let him help out with the first aid station at the market. I suspect you'll be seeing a lot of him over the next few weeks."

Amanda blinked, not sure how to respond. Rafe would be working at the market. Their paths would inevitably cross frequently over the next few weeks.

So much for going out of her way to avoid the man.

She tried to tell herself the little twist in her stomach was nerves. It certainly wasn't anticipation, right?

"Oh, that will be great," she said, doing her best to hide any trace of reaction from Louise. "It shouldn't be too arduous for him. We don't have many injuries at the market, other than the occasional slip and fall. Actually, we might see more of those this year, since half of the booths will be outside in the ice and snow."

"I had heard you were opening more booths and taking advantage of the outside courtyard to the convention center."

"It only made sense. We've been maxed out in booth space for the past few years."

Louise nodded. "I don't doubt people will enjoy bundling up and shopping outside together."

"I hope so."

"Well, I should get back to the girls. Thank you again for keeping for keeping an eye on Rafe and my grandson. I do my best, but my son has never been a big fan of being coddled."

Amanda would not be surprised if the man had come out of the womb tough and independent, ready to take on the world.

"I hope you have a lovely evening, Mrs. Arredondo."

"Thank you. You as well."

They walked out together back to the restaurant with Amanda thinking that was the most cordial conversation she had ever had with Louise.

THE HOLIDAY MARKET HADN'T OPENED YET—AND
wouldn't until noon the following day—but Rafe was already
heartily sick of listening to Christmas music.

He had only been there an hour, checking out the first aid fa-
cilities and supplies in the small examination room on the edge
of the conference center hall. In that time, he had already heard
"Jingle Bells" and "Rockin' Around the Christmas Tree" twice.

He had a feeling it would be a long two weeks.

He liked Christmas music as much as the next guy. More,
maybe. His sister was very musical. Julia played the piano and
also had a beautiful voice. Every year, she sang in the church
Christmas choir. Rafe had always enjoyed listening to her practice and perform.

Listening to his sister sing was one thing. Hearing relentlessly perky canned Christmas music over the conference center audio system was another entirely.

Apparently he was in the minority, though. Everybody else

setting out their products at the various stalls seemed cheerful and eager for the market to start.

"Are you sure you're ready for this?"

Rafe frowned at his cousin Izzy.

Pretty and bright, she had worked as a volunteer firefighter since she was eighteen and now was an emergency medical technician, training to be a paramedic. He wanted to think she had followed his own example, but Izzy had always walked her own path.

"Can't wait," he said dryly.

She laughed, brushing her long dark hair from her face. "You're such a bad liar, *primo*. This will be torture for you. All this holiday cheer will make your teeth ache."

"Hey. I have holiday cheer. We even have a Christmas tree up. We decorated it last night."

"Did you? I have to come by and see it."

"Definitely. Besides that, Isaac is pushing me hard to put up some lights on the house."

"No offense, but are you sure that's the best idea? The last time you tried hanging some Christmas lights, things didn't exactly go well. And now you've got a bum arm that will make hanging lights a real adventure."

"I tried to tell Isaac that. But he's six years old and wants what he wants. If he wants twinkly colored lights on our new house, I'll figure out a way to put them up. Don't worry, though. If I decide to hang some lights, I'll see if Joe or one of the guys at the station can come over and help me."

"I can help you," she retorted. "I'm one of the guys at the station, aren't I?"

He held up a hand of apology to head off her annoyance. "Absolutely. But you won't exactly have a lot of extra time over the next few weeks."

"Point taken," she said with a wry smile. "I can come out this Sunday or next, though. The market isn't open on Sunday."

"I'll call you if I need you. I figured I would try to talk him out of it first. Maybe we'll get an inflatable or something."

She made a face. "You want to see inflatable Christmas decorations, just take him to *Abuelo*'s new apartment. They have a whole army of them on the ground there."

"I'll do that."

"Looks like we have everything we need," Izzy said, stocking the last drawer with extra bandages. "We should be good to go for tomorrow. The last thing on the list is the safety inspection."

"Oh right. Mike mentioned that."

"I'll let you handle it, since I've got to run to an appointment."

"Thanks a lot."

"You outrank me, anyway, Chief," Izzy said with a grin, before she grabbed her coat from the hook by the door.

She pointed through the open door of the small first aid room. "There's Amanda Taylor. She's the boss lady around here and is probably the one you would work with for the safety inspection."

Rafe looked in the direction she pointed, where he found Amanda Taylor, clipboard in hand, looking lovely as always.

At the sight of her, Rafe felt a little burst of heat, the same one he had felt every time he thought of her over the past few days.

Amanda appeared to be in the middle of settling a dispute between neighboring vendors about something. Power cables, by the sound of it.

"Are you sure you don't have time to finish the inspection before you have to leave?" he pressed.

Izzy shook her head. "Considering I was supposed to be there fifteen minutes ago, no. Sorry."

He sighed and picked up the fire department tablet with the checklist on it that they used for all public event safety inspections.

"Great. Thanks."

Izzy smiled and waved at him as she headed out the door. After a moment, when yet another version of "Jingle Bells" started playing over the sound system, Rafe shut the door to the first aid room and headed over to Amanda and the two vendors.

She looked festive—and, yes, he could admit it—*adorable* in a holiday sweater with a grumpy cat on it as she gave the vendors a calm smile.

"You know the rules, Ed. You get one string of lights. We all have to work together here."

The vendor frowned. "My stall is twice as big as his. I'm also paying more than he is for the space. Therefore I should get twice as many lights."

"If we had unlimited power capabilities, maybe. But we don't. You signed the same contract as everyone else that stipulated every stall gets one string of lights."

Rafe did not know the guy, though he looked familiar. His stall offered hand-carved ornaments, walking sticks and other holiday decorations. Only fitting, since the guy was built like a tree.

He looked as if he wanted to get in Amanda's face and argue the point. Before Rafe could step forward with the protectiveness he really didn't want to feel, Amanda gave a disarming smile. She placed a calming hand on the man's arm. "Keep in mind, we're going to have bright overhead lights on throughout the market. You really don't need more than one string of lights to compete with that. Besides, your wonderful items will do more than any Christmas lights could to bring in shoppers to your stall, trust me. Everyone is going to love your work, Ed. I know I do. I want to buy one of your walking sticks for my grandmother. I'm definitely stopping by first thing tomorrow when you'll have the biggest selection."

"They really are great," the other vendor said. "I know my grandchildren would love one of those whistles you have for sale, though their parents might not. How long does it take you to make one of those?"

The crisis seemed to be averted as the two men talked now about their various crafts.

Amanda had a way of calming people. He didn't know exactly how she did it, but he could tell everyone seemed to have complete confidence that she could solve their problems.

As soon as she moved away from the two men, other vendors hurried up to talk to her. Rafe waited on the sidelines until they seemed to be done, looking slightly less frenzied than they had as they approached her.

"I'm told you're the one I need to speak with about the final safety inspection."

She looked up from her clipboard, startled, and he was interested to see a smudge of color rise on her cheekbones.

"Oh. Rafe. I didn't see you. Sorry. I'm a little distracted today."

"Understandable. You seem to be in the middle of a few things."

"Only a few," she said with a small smile.

"I don't want to give you one more thing to add to your list, but I apparently need to walk through the market for the final safety inspection before the doors open tomorrow."

"Of course. We're very focused on safety here. We want the Shelter Springs Holiday Giving Market to be a positive experience for everyone."

"We have the same goal, then."

Rafe admired the team that had been working so hard behind the scenes to put on the market. Many organizations claimed they were committed to altruism and philanthropy, but the market organizers followed through. Each year, the market raised thousands of dollars for various causes around the community. This year, as their signs proudly proclaimed, a portion of all sales would be split between the local food bank and the after-school program that Rafe sometimes sent Isaac to when he had to work but couldn't make other arrangements with his family members who helped out.

Before Caitlin left, Rafe never imagined how difficult juggling childcare could be for a single parent, and he was grateful for caring teachers and well-run extracurricular programs.

"Is there a good time this afternoon we could do the safety inspection?"

She appeared to consider her schedule, looking down at the clipboard again. "Now works as well as any other time," she finally said. "I can show you around as soon as I drop off these vendor maps at the information booth."

"Great. I'll walk with you."

He suspected that if he let Amanda out of his sight, she would end up being waylaid by other people who needed things from her and it might be another hour before he could find her again.

"Oh, you don't have to do that. I'll only be a minute. I can meet you back here."

"No problem. I can use the exercise." It was only a small white lie as he had worked out in his home gym that day, focusing on leg exercises and hand weights with his good arm. He would hate to lose muscle tone while his left arm was stuck in a cast.

Rafe worked hard to stay fit. He took his job as a firefighter and paramedic seriously and didn't want any health issues to interfere with his ability to carry out his duties.

The endorphins from working out also helped with his restlessness and frustration over being sidelined from doing what he loved.

"Suit yourself," Amanda said, her tone brisk as she set off through the market.

As he had predicted, on the way to the information kiosk, she was approached by four other people asking her questions. She treated everyone with calmness and cordiality, even when two people were upset about the Wi-Fi speed inside the building for processing payments, something Amanda likely had absolutely no control over.

At the information desk, they found Liz Cisneros Shepherd and her new husband, Steve.

Their relationship had been the talk of Shelter Springs the previous Christmas. Liz was the younger sister of Steve's late wife, who had died many years ago from cancer.

Rafe had heard the gossip, with some people saying how strange it was that Steve was marrying his wife's younger sister now. As far as he was concerned, if they were happy together, it was nobody else's business.

"Hi, Amanda," Liz said with her cheery smile. "Love that sweater! I haven't seen it in your collection. Is it new?"

Amanda looked down at her sweater with a rueful smile. "Yes. Opal Barnes knitted it for me. She gave it to me when I dropped off a few meals for the sisters after their terrifying ordeal last week."

Rafe raised an eyebrow. So he and Isaac had only been two more on Amanda Taylor's charity list. He wasn't sure how to feel about that. Her concern on their behalf had been heartwarming, if more than a little unexpected. It was somewhat deflating to know she handed out kindness indiscriminately.

Amanda was someone who worked hard for the people of Shelter Springs. How much did she receive in return?

"I love it," Liz declared, angling her head for a closer look at Amanda's sweater. "I think I might even like this one more than the hamster sweater that was my favorite last year."

"I'm sure you'll see that one again. It's still in the rotation."

"I look forward to seeing them every year."

Amanda smiled at the other woman. He saw her smile include Steve Shepherd, though that one was a little less genuine, he was interested to see.

"Wearing so-called ugly sweaters throughout the month of

December helps me get in the holiday spirit. I'm not naturally this festive, you know."

For some reason, she sent a sideways look toward Steve Shepherd. It took Rafe a moment to understand, remembering that Amanda had once been engaged to marry Steve's son. An engagement that had ended in tragedy.

They had that in common, he realized for the first time. Each of them had lost someone they loved.

"This time of year sometimes seems to overflow with memories, doesn't it?" Steve said quietly. "Unfortunately, not all of them are easy."

"No. They're not."

"I try to focus on the holiday memories that bring me joy," Liz said. "I still remember sledding in the park with Jeanette, driving around to look at Christmas lights with my family, sitting by the fire while my mother read Christmas stories to us."

Amanda smiled softly. "I try to remember the good moments too, even when it's not easy. And every year, just like my ever-expanding ugly sweater collection, I try to add a few more memories."

She gestured to the information desk. "Do you have everything you need here?"

"Yes. We have maps, charts and our own little FAQ."

"And you're fully staffed with enough volunteers?"

"Oh yes. I think everyone at the Shelter Inn who's not working at our booth wants to have a turn at the information desk. Our residents love to be in the middle of the action. For the next two weeks, the place to be in Shelter Springs is here at the market. Birdie and Paolo plan to be here nearly every day."

Rafe glanced at Amanda and saw her mouth tighten slightly at the way Liz seemed to link her grandmother and his grandfather together automatically.

"That's great," Rafe said. "I'm glad *Abuelo* has something

to distract him this year from his own sad memories of my grandmother."

Amanda looked as if she wanted to say something, but whatever it was, she swallowed it down. "Thank you both for agreeing to organize the info desk volunteers."

"We're excited," Liz said with a smile. "It's shaping up to be an amazing market. Bigger and better than ever."

"I hope so."

"Thank you again." Amanda hugged the other woman. After a pause, she hugged Steve as well.

If circumstances had been different, the man would have become her father-in-law. Rafe wasn't at all sure why he suddenly found that idea so discomfiting. He *was* certain it probably wasn't a good idea to try to analyze his reaction.

When they walked away from the information desk, she turned to Rafe. "Where should we start with the inspection?"

He looked down at the tablet and the digital checklist he had to go through.

"I need to examine the exit doors and look over your evacuation plan in the event of an emergency. I heard you talking to a few of the vendors about their light displays. I need to check the electrical system to be sure it's adequate for the load. And finally, I need to check the food vendors to make sure they're following fire safety procedures with their cooktops and ovens and have fire prevention mechanisms in place."

She appeared momentarily overwhelmed at the list but seemed to square her shoulders. "Okay," she said brightly. "Lead the way. I'll come along with you to answer any questions you may have."

She already looked exhausted. He imagined she had probably been on her feet all day, working through the details of the market.

He wanted to tell her to find a chair somewhere, put her feet up and take a rest. Unfortunately, he needed her help. The job would take at least twice as long without her along to explain things.

"Since we're close to the inside food court, let's check that out first."

"What do you need from me?"

"I just need you to stick close in case I have any questions."

And because I like the way you smell, like sugar cookies and strawberry candy canes. Of course he couldn't tell her that. It shouldn't matter to him how she smelled. He was here to do a job, and the sooner he forced his attention back to the checklist, the better for both of them.

9

SHE HAD A MILLION THINGS TO DO. TWO MILLION, RE-
ally, but instead of focusing on any of them, Amanda found
herself following along behind Rafe Arredondo while he carefully went through the list of fire department safety checks.

She found it fascinating to watch him work. He was thor-
ough, she would give him that. They went through every possible precaution the festival organizers followed, checking and
double-checking everything.

She tried not to think about all the work still ahead of her to
set up her own market stall. She just had to trust that Cat and
Scarlet had helped out at the market enough times that they
knew how to set up the display without her.

Her phone beeped with an incoming text, as it had been
doing throughout the hour she had spent with Rafe. She
glanced down to find a question from one of her committee
members about parking.

She answered it quickly, then looked up to find Rafe watching her with an intensity in his dark eyes that unnerved her.

"We're almost done. I'm sorry to take you away from the countless other demands on your time."

She shook her head. "Safety is our number one priority. I appreciate your attention to detail."

"How many people are you expecting throughout the course of the market? Do you have a way to monitor visitors inside the venue to ensure the crowd doesn't exceed the capacity?"

"Last year we averaged about two thousand people a day. We have added four more days this year and don't yet know if that's going to attract more people or if our historical crowd average will be diluted by the extra days."

"Is that why you're staying open longer? To spread out the crowds a little?"

"One of the reasons. The market has really exploded in popularity around the region over the past few years. With that growth, we had so many more requests from vendors who wanted to have market stalls that we really had no choice but to expand outside, since we were already at capacity in the convention hall."

"Makes sense."

"It's good in many ways, making it feel more like a traditional European Christmas market. We expect that our expanded footprint will allow us to better handle overflow crowds and stagger admission inside when the crowds are too heavy. I will have committee members with clickers standing at the entrances to make sure we don't exceed the fire code capacity."

She was grateful again for her large committee of dedicated volunteers, who worked tirelessly to make sure the holiday market went off without a hitch.

Once more, though, she had to ask why she did this to herself. Every year she promised herself she would back off from being so involved. Wouldn't it be lovely if she could simply be another of the vendors, concerned only with setting up her own storefront instead of working behind the scenes to iron out all the details for everyone else?

Somehow, despite her best intentions, she inevitably found herself sucked back in.

For a good cause, she reminded herself as she followed Rafe around. She loved knowing a good percentage of the profits from the market went toward helping others, working together to make their community better.

She tried to focus on that as Rafe continued checking things off his list. After finishing his inspection inside, they donned coats and walked out into the starry December evening, crisp and clear and lovely.

Her breath came out in little puffs as she followed Rafe to one of several outdoor heaters.

"These are provided by a company out of Boise," she said. "They have all already undergone extensive safety testing and we have certificates for all of them."

"Sounds good. I would still like to see one of them in operation. Any idea how they work?" he asked. He fiddled around with the switch, a task made harder with a cast on one arm.

"Here. Let me help."

"It's fine. Everything just takes me a little bit longer than it would if I didn't have this dumb thing on my arm."

She stepped back and watched as he worked the switch and finally had the propane heater going.

In the moonlight, he looked big and tough and masculine, and Amanda was aware of a soft flutter of awareness rippling through her.

No. She didn't want to be attracted to him. What was the point? She was the last person in town who would ever interest Rafe Arredondo, which was exactly how she liked it.

That's what she told herself, anyway.

"How is your arm feeling?"

"Fine. It's achy once in a while but it hasn't been too bad. I'm just frustrated that I can't do everything I want."

"I can imagine that would be tough on you."

Rafe wasn't someone who liked to be on the sidelines. He was always in the middle of the action.

The previous summer, she had been attending an outdoor concert at the park when a young tourist sitting near her suffered an anaphylactic reaction to a hornet sting and didn't have her EpiPen on hand. Her face had swollen and she had started wheezing.

Amanda could still vividly remember her deep relief when the paramedics pulled up, Rafe leading the charge, and rushed to help the girl. She had followed up with the family and had heard the girl suffered no ill effects from the incident and was now careful not to go anywhere without her epinephrine kit close by.

"I'm sorry about your frustration, but I'm grateful to have an experienced paramedic on hand in case of an emergency here at the market. I don't expect you to be very busy, but there are the occasional mishaps."

"Like what?"

"Well, three years ago, one of the kids performing with a musical group fell off the stage and got a bloody nose."

"Something to look forward to, then," he said, his voice so dry she had to smile.

He gazed at her for a long moment, as if he had never seen her smile before, which she knew couldn't be true.

Something in his intense expression made her shiver.

What was *that*?

She was definitely working too hard if her imagination could even contemplate the possibility that Rafe might be as attracted to her as she was to him.

"Where's Isaac this evening?" she asked.

"He's with my brother and his kids, since Crista and my mom are here getting her booth ready. He loves hanging out with his cousins."

"How nice that you have a strong support network to help you with him."

"Yeah. I would have been lost without my family, especially after Caitlin left."

"You're lucky."

He raised an eyebrow. "Because my wife left me and then died four months later of a drug overdose? *Lucky* is not necessarily the word I would have used."

Amanda winced at her own thoughtless words. "I'm sorry. That's not what I meant. I should have said you're lucky because of your family. I envy how close you all are. I have Griffin and my grandmother but that's about it."

As soon as she said the words, she regretted bringing up her family, the reminder of her father and all the lives he had destroyed.

"Did you say your mom was in Florida these days?" Rafe asked as they continued walking around the outdoor kiosks.

"Yes. St. Pete's. She's remarried and seems to be happy enough. We're not really close, though."

Though her parents already had been divorced at the time, her mother had left town only months after Dennis Taylor's death and the fiery accident that had taken four innocent lives.

I can't bear everyone staring at me, whispering about me. I lived with it for all those years while we were married and he was still alive. I can't do it another moment. You understand, don't you, darling?

Amanda knew the memory shouldn't still burn, so many years later. She understood her mother's motives in leaving Shelter Springs as soon as she could. How could she not, when she and Griffin had endured the same kind of whispers and stares. Her mother hadn't been here for Amanda during the two darkest times of her life, after her father's alcohol-fueled accident or after Jake's tragic death in the avalanche that seemed to have buried her heart along with him.

"Lena can't understand why I've chosen to build a life here in Shelter Springs, if you want the truth. She thinks I should have taken my business degree and worked on Wall Street or for a big bank somewhere. Barring that, she would love me to move to Florida to be closer to her."

"Your mom grew up here, though, didn't she? Isn't she Birdie's daughter?"

The women were so very different, it was sometimes hard for Amanda to remember that. "Yes. But she had never wanted to stay here in Idaho. My parents used to fight about it all the time, with her urging Dad to open a clinic somewhere more lucrative than a small family medicine practice in the middle of Nowhere, Idaho."

"Why didn't he?"

Amanda shrugged. "Tradition, I guess. His father had been a town doctor here. And before that, his grandmother had been a midwife to some of the early European settlers. I guess it was easier to maintain the status quo than to reach outside his comfort zone."

She paused. "So instead, he reached for a bottle."

His expression sharpened to one of compassion and understanding, an acknowledgment of all the pain they shared and the commonalities. They had both lived with and loved addicts. They belonged to the same unfortunate club.

"Sorry," she said, wishing she had never taken the conversation in this direction. "I don't know where that came from. We have enough to do without taking a pointless wander down memory lane."

Before he could answer, a new vendor to the market, a woman from southern Idaho who was selling intricately crafted Father Christmas figures with carved faces and richly sewn robes, approached Amanda to ask a question about the vendor discount on concessions.

She shifted her attention away from Rafe to answer the question.

"Thank you," the woman said. "I'm so excited about this event as I've been coming myself to shop here for years. I am thrilled you expanded and I could find a spot."

"I hope you won't be too cold out here."

"The stalls are heated and I also packed plenty of warm clothes. I'll be fine."

"I hope you have a wonderful time. Make sure you fill out our vendor survey. We're always trying to improve."

After bidding the woman farewell, she and Rafe continued with the inspection. Amanda managed to refrain from spilling any more embarrassing personal insights while Rafe finished going through his safety checklist.

Finally, after he seemed to have examined every single exit, outlet, power cable and heating source inside and out, they returned to the convention hall, where he signed the safety certificate and handed it to her.

"There you are. You should be good to go."

"Whew. That's a relief. I would hate to have to tell all these people the market is canceled and we have to shut it down on your say-so."

He smiled down at her and Amanda again felt that little shiver of awareness.

"We can't have that. Where would all the people in Shelter Springs go to hear 'Jingle Bells' a hundred times a day?"

"Maybe not a hundred times a day. I would guess forty or fifty, at the max."

He was still laughing when Natalie Shepherd walked around a row of stalls. She seemed to stop short when she spotted them.

"Oh. Hi, Amanda. Rafe."

"Hey, Nat," he said with a friendly nod.

"I was just looking for Amanda. We have a little problem at the Shelter Inn kiosk. When you two are finished, would you mind stopping by?"

"We are done here," Rafe said. "Thanks for being patient with the safety inspection."

"Not a problem," she lied.

She couldn't tell him it was a *big* problem—and not only

because of all the demands on her time right now. Because of him. Because she was becoming entirely too drawn to him.

She was a grown woman who had no business indulging this ridiculous crush.

For one thing, she couldn't spare the time. For another, what was the point, when any relationship between them beyond this tentative friendship was completely impossible?

She would simply have to do her best to ignore her reaction. Eventually it would probably go away, right?

"So. Rafe Arredondo?" Natalie said after he walked away, angling an eyebrow.

"What about him?" Amanda asked in a voice she hoped sounded casual.

Nat studied her for a long time. "I don't know. You just look good together, somehow. Rafe is a great guy. I've always thought so. I might have had a little crush on him when we were in school."

"Did you? Is there something I need to talk to my brother about?"

Nat laughed. "Not at all. Griffin has absolutely nothing to worry about and he knows it. He's my person. End of story. I was thinking Rafe would be great for you."

"Don't let your imagination get away from you. We were only having a safety inspection. That's all. He will be helping out at the first aid station here during the market and we were going through a checklist from the fire chief to make sure we're following all the correct protocols. Nothing exciting at all."

"Too bad," Natalie said with a grin.

"Now, what is the problem at the Shelter Inn kiosk?"

"Nothing major. There are a couple of lightbulbs missing and they're wondering where they go to find more."

"That should be easy enough to fix. I'll come take a look."

She followed her friend, wishing every problem she had to face as the holiday market coordinator—or in life—was as simple to address.

AMANDA TRIED TO HIDE A YAWN AS SHE WALKED INTO
the convention center the next morning, juggling her coffee
and her messenger bag.

It was already midmorning and she had been working at her
downtown shop location since before dawn. She suspected she
was in for a very long day, working to iron out all the first-day
logistical problems of opening the market.

She had scheduled extra staff to work at her market stall all
day, mainly because she knew she would be too busy putting
out fires as chairperson of the committee to spend much time
at her own storefront.

With all she would likely have to deal with, she wished she
felt at the top of her game. She hadn't slept much the night before, her mind buzzing and her eventual dreams tangled. She
had finally awakened an hour before her alarm clock and had
decided to head into The Lucky Goat for a few hours.

While she wanted to tell herself opening-day jitters were to
blame for her insomnia, she suspected her sleeplessness might

have more to do with a certain assistant fire chief with a crooked smile and a cast on his arm.

When she walked inside the large hall hosting the market, she found the hectic chaos of the evening before had eased. A few vendors were still setting out products to display but many stalls were shuttered, locked up until closer to their official opening time, in two hours.

Amanda turned to head to her stall when she spotted a huge ladder coming toward her, carried by none other than Rafe Arredondo, as if he had stepped right out of her dreams.

She stopped in her tracks. "Excuse me. What does the first aid station need with a giant ladder?"

He looked up from his task and for an instant, she thought his features lit up, then he shrugged. "I came in early to make sure everything was ready and to add a few more first aid supplies I thought we might need. That took less time than I expected so I was looking for something to do and remembered an issue I noticed yesterday when we were doing the inspection."

"Oh? What's that?"

"The big hot cocoa mug on the sign above the food vendors looked a little loose. I would hate for it to fall on somebody. Wouldn't that be a lousy start to the market?"

She could only agree. That would be a nightmare. *So would watching Rafe fall again*, she thought as she watched him set up the ladder underneath the wooden sign. "No offense, but are you supposed to be up on a ladder?"

He glanced at her with surprise. "Sure. Why not?"

"I mean, your track record on ladders isn't all that great right now."

"A guy falls off one lousy ladder and has to hear about it for the rest of his life."

"Hardly the rest of your life. It only happened a week ago," she pointed out. "Also, you still have the cast on your arm from the last time."

"I'm fine. This will only take a minute."

She could tell by the stubborn jut of his jaw that she wouldn't be able to dissuade him, and she couldn't think of any way to keep him off the ladder. With a resigned sigh, she set down her messenger bag and her coffee on one of the small round café tables set up near the hot cocoa stand.

"I can at least stabilize the ladder for you."

"It's not necessary. I'm sure you have a million other things to do right now."

"I do," she answered tartly. "My to-do list absolutely does not include having to scrape our first aid paramedic off the ground when the ladder topples and he falls over."

His mouth worked as if he wanted to smile but he finally shrugged and began scaling the ladder. She tried not to pay attention to the ripple of muscle in his shoulder and along his back as he moved up the rungs, using only one arm. She noticed a screwdriver and hammer in one of the side pockets of his navy blue cargo pants.

The sign *was* hanging a little off-center, she noticed. She was surprised she had not seen it the day before or that he had not pointed it out to her during the inspection.

When he reached nearly the top of the ladder, he pulled out the screwdriver and, bracing his weight against the cap of the ladder, he extended both arms up to the sign, holding it in place with his cast while he worked the screwdriver with the other hand.

She held her breath, remembering again that horrible moment when she had seen him topple off the roof across the street.

"How does that look from down there?" he called.

She had a hard time focusing on anything else except him, but she did her best. "Better, I think. Thank you."

"You're welcome. I'm heading down."

He put the screwdriver back in his pocket and began lowering himself down the ladder, again using only one arm. She didn't think she took a true breath until his boots hit the ground again.

"Mission accomplished," he said looking up at the sign, now perfectly aligned.

"Good job," she said as he folded the ladder again. "I can put that away for you."

"I've got it."

She shook her head. "You are a stubborn man, Rafe."

He gave her a smile that made her feel a little lightheaded, much to her chagrin. "So I've heard. My *abuela* used to say I'm more stubborn than a mule *en un puente*. On a bridge. Don't ask me why mules are more stubborn on bridges than in, say, the middle of the road. I have no idea. Over the years, I've learned to own it."

She smiled in response, charmed to hear about his relationship with his grandmother. He must miss Rosita terribly. How would she cope when it was finally time to say goodbye to Birdie? She didn't like even thinking about it.

"Guess what? I'm stubborn, too. If you won't let me put the ladder away for you, I can at least help you do it."

He gave her a long look, then apparently recognized she wasn't about to budge. "Okay. We can do it together."

Leaving her coffee and her bag for now, she grabbed one end of the ladder. He moved forward to the other end, and together they made their way through the aisles between booths toward the utility room outside the main convention hall, where Amanda knew from previous years that miscellaneous tools were stored.

The room smelled of lemon and pine from the various cleaning products stored on shelves. It wasn't an unpleasant smell, reminding her of visiting her father's medical clinic.

"Thank you again for fixing the sign," she said after they had stored the ladder in its designated spot. "I appreciate you being so conscientious, especially when I'm sure you are not particularly thrilled about having to spend the next two weeks working at our first aid station."

"At least I'm not stuck at home, being bored senseless."

She smiled. "Don't take this wrong but I really hope you're bored senseless here. With any luck, things will be quiet the entire two weeks of the market, with nothing more exciting than a paper cut."

"I'm fine with that possibility. I brought a book for the slow moments."

She wanted to ask what he was reading but she reminded herself she didn't really have time for small talk, any more than she had time to be holding a ladder for him.

She didn't need to know his reading tastes. Unfortunately, she was far too curious about the man.

"What about you?" he asked, before she could pursue the topic. "Will you be spending the next two weeks here or do you alternate between the market and your shop in town?"

"The second one. I already spent a few hours there this morning. I basically have to stick around here during all the hours we're open, at least for the first few days. Until we manage to work out all the kinks. After that, I'll leave things to my committee and divide my time between my Lucky Goat kiosk here and my store downtown."

"It must be busy at both locations. I imagine not everyone wants to come to the market to do their shopping. You can't close down your other store."

She shook her head. "But I have good employees, who are perfectly capable of taking over when I'm not there. While the market is on, I typically go into the store first thing in the morning to take care of a lot of my administrative tasks. Payroll, scheduling, that sort of thing. I come here in the afternoons and usually stay until close."

"That makes for a long day."

She had never really minded the long hours, mostly because she didn't have all that much to go home to except her cats.

Why that thought should depress her so much right now, she put down to being tired. She was happy with her life. She loved living at Rose Cottage, spending time with her friends and her grandmother, helping the community she loved.

"I don't mind. It's only for a limited time. I couldn't keep up that frenetic pace indefinitely, but when I know it will only last for two weeks, I can handle it. Last year, I ended up with Covid and was stuck at home for nearly a week, unable to help here or at the store. My poor employees had to pick up the slack for me."

"When you work at a breakneck pace, that kind of thing is inevitable, especially if you don't take care of yourself. It will always catch up with you. Eventually your body will step in to force you into taking a break."

If he would stop interfering with her sleep patterns, she might be able to get enough rest, she thought wryly. Of course, she couldn't tell him that.

"Interesting advice coming from a man with a broken arm who refuses to take a day off even when he has a perfectly legitimate excuse."

He laughed, a low ripple of sound that made her suddenly aware they still stood in the small utility closet.

He had a delicious laugh. It eased the austere planes of his face and made him appear younger and more relaxed.

He smelled of laundry soap, sharp and clean, and some kind of masculine soap that reminded her of summer evenings in the mountains.

She couldn't seem to stop staring at his mouth, wondering what it would be like to kiss him, as she suddenly realized she must have during those restless dreams during the night.

She caught her own thoughts. Good grief. What was *wrong* with her? She was acting as if she were back in junior high, with a silly crush on a star athlete.

Annoyed with herself, she wrenched her gaze from his mouth to meet his own gaze, which suddenly seemed to flash with a heat she didn't think had been there before.

"I should…" She gestured a little vaguely toward the door and the market and all the demands on her time.

"Right. Same here. We wouldn't want to miss the opening jingle bell."

"We don't open the market with a jingle bell, though that's not a bad idea. I'll make a note for next year."

They parted ways as they walked into the convention hall. Only after she retrieved her now-cold coffee and her messenger bag and headed toward The Lucky Goat kiosk did Amanda suddenly realize that her storefront was located just across the way and down a few stalls from the small room along the exterior of the hall used as the first aid station.

Why hadn't she noticed that before now? If she hadn't been so busy troubleshooting everyone else's problems the day before, she would have been able to foresee the dilemma she had just presented to herself.

When Rafe was at the first aid station and she was at her storefront, they had a clear line of sight to each other. She would not be able to avoid him. If she had thought about it, she could have rearranged the layout as soon as she learned he would be working at the market. She easily could have traded spots with another store before everyone started to set up, coming up with some good excuse for moving her kiosk somewhere else.

Like at the far end of the market, where she wouldn't have to bump into her inconvenient crush constantly.

She could handle it, she told herself. She would simply have to remind herself a few dozen times a day of all the reasons they could never be together.

No problem at all.

"WELL, YOU SURVIVED YOUR FIRST MARKET DAY SHIFT, only handing out a few bandages and some ibuprofen. Was it as bad as you feared?"

Rafe frowned at his cousin, who had come to relieve him.

"First of all, I never thought it would be bad. And I was right. It was fine. I finished four chapters of my book, I talked to probably a hundred people asking what I did to my arm and I heard from a dozen more who were actually there when I fell and thought for sure I had broken my neck. Oh, and this morning I reinforced the hot cocoa sign so the mug didn't fall out and roll through the market, causing destruction and mayhem all along its path."

"You're a hero." Izzy grinned.

"I do my best," he said dryly.

"Did you have a chance to walk through and see what everybody is selling?"

He did not want to confess to his cousin that the only booth he was really interested in was the one across the aisle and down a little, where Amanda Taylor had been busy all day talking to store customers, committee members and other market vendors.

She must be exhausted. Even from here, he thought he could see dark smudges under her eyes that made him want to pick her up, carry her to his truck and drive her home so she could head straight to bed.

"Not really."

"Before I start my first shift, I always try to make my way through all the stalls to see everything. If you go early, nobody has sold out of anything yet. I make notes of things that interest me and then go back during my breaks or at the end of the night to buy the things I want. It's awesome. I get half my shopping out of the way in only a few hours."

"Sounds like you have a system."

"I stopped at Crista's booth, too. She was too busy for much chitchat but I knew she would never forgive me if I didn't at least make an effort to say hi."

He had stopped by once to say hello, and his sister-in-law and his mother had in turn stopped to greet him on their way back from the restroom or from grabbing a soda. Izzy was right. They had little chance for conversation, as the market had been packed with shoppers all day.

"You should take some time to walk around a little before you head right home."

"I'll be working here for two weeks. I'm sure I'll get a chance to check out everything."

"I'm still looking for something to get Bo's mom. She's picky and hated the purse I got for her birthday in September."

The mother of Izzy's current boyfriend, who had lasted longer than most, was a notorious sourpuss. Irene Clyde had been his algebra teacher in high school and Rafe could still remember all those excruciating parent-teacher conferences he had to sit through, listening to her detail all his shortcomings at length.

"Did Irene tell you she hated it?"

"Not in so many words. But I have never seen her use it."

"Maybe she's saving it for a special occasion."

"Ha. I'll pretend I believe that. You should at least check out the Shelter Inn booth. It's one row over, on the south side of the aisle. You can say hi to *Abuelo*."

"I didn't know he was here," Rafe said in surprise. "I haven't seen him today but I guess I haven't gone past that way."

She nodded. "He and Birdie Lovell are working the booth together. From what I could tell, they appear to have a system. She chats up all the customers while he rings up the sales."

"I guess if it's working, they should go with it."

"From what I saw, he seems to be having a great time. I'm glad he has the distraction. It's good to see him smile again."

He glanced across the way, to where Amanda was talking to a couple of women whom he knew served on the festival committee with her.

Amanda was not thrilled about the friendship between their grandparents. Had she visited the Shelter Inn booth to see Paolo and Birdie having a good time together, in front of the whole town?

He hoped it no longer bothered her. If Birdie could ease his grandfather's deep sense of loss a little, Rafe had no problem with their relationship.

"I have to go pick up Isaac. But yeah. I'll stop by to say *hola* to him before I go."

"Sounds good. Anything else I should know about your day?"

I couldn't stop staring at the shop across the way? Or at least the woman running the shop?

He wasn't about to tell his nosy cousin that particular information.

"Nope. Good luck. Have fun."

"Oh, I will."

As she settled into his chair next to the entrance of the first aid room, Rafe grabbed his coat. When he walked out, he considered going in the opposite direction so he could avoid The Lucky Goat storefront, then decided he was a big tough firefighter. He wasn't about to run away from one small woman, or his sudden interest in her.

He walked toward her kiosk and saw that her committee members had left. She stood talking to one of her employees. As he neared, she looked up and he thought he saw her eyes light up.

She was wearing a brightly patterned holiday sweater, covered by a black apron that had The Lucky Goat logo imprinted on it.

"You look like you're leaving for the day. That hardly seems fair. You'll miss the busiest time, when everybody gets off work and decides to come shopping."

"Izzy and I are trading shifts. I'll mostly be working during the afternoons and early evenings. It's easier with day care, then I can have the chance to spend a few hours with Isaac for dinner and bedtime."

"Makes sense. Well, have a good evening."

"You, too."

Get some rest, he wanted to add, especially when he saw the shadows under her eyes up close. He decided to hold his tongue, not sure she would appreciate the unsolicited advice.

"Before I leave for the night, I'm heading over to the Shelter Inn storefront to say hello to my grandfather. Any message you'd like me to pass along to Birdie?"

"No. Thanks, though. I'll try to pop over when I get a moment so I can say hello."

He nodded. "Sounds good. See you tomorrow. Hopefully, I won't have to climb up any more ladders."

She smiled, but before she could answer, a customer who had been browsing through the kiosk asked a question. With an apologetic look and a wave to Rafe, she turned to answer.

As he walked away from The Lucky Goat booth, Rafe had to admit hers was by far the best-smelling area of the market, filled with delicious scents that made his mouth water.

Or maybe that was only Amanda.

He pushed away the thought as he made his way two rows over, to the Shelter Inn booth that was about halfway down the row.

His grandfather, he saw as he approached, was wearing a cheerful green plaid holiday cardigan and a broad smile as he chatted with Birdie and a couple of middle-aged women Rafe didn't know.

His smile widened further when he spotted Rafe approaching.

"*Hola, mijo!*"

His grandfather opened his arms and Rafe bent down to hug the smaller man. *Abrazos* were a big deal to Paolo, one of the many things he loved and respected about his grandfather.

"How's business?"

"Been good. Brisk. Birdie is excellent at reeling in the customers. She knows everyone."

"Not quite everyone." She smiled. "Rafe, dear. Hello."

She must have recognized his voice, he realized. "Hi, Mrs. Lovell."

She frowned. "Stop that. You call me Birdie like everyone else does."

"Birdie, then. Great to see your storefront is doing well."

"So well." Her voice brimmed over with pride. "We've sold out of all the needle felt ornaments we brought and our wooden dinosaur cars are a big hit."

He looked at the cars, shaped like brontosauruses and triceratops. "I was thinking Isaac might like one of those. What do you think, *Abuelo?*"

"Definitely. That boy loves cars *and* dinosaurs."

He looked at them for a moment and finally selected a green triceratops car and handed it over to his grandfather to ring up.

"This one looks good."

"He'll love it," Paolo said.

"Which one did you pick?" Birdie asked. She took it from his grandfather and held it close to her face, turning it around in her hands. "I adore this one. Isaac will definitely love it."

"I don't need a bag. I can put it in my pocket. I'll have to hide it somewhere in my truck until he's asleep and I can put it with all his other presents."

"Oh, I remember those days with our children," his grandfather said. "So much fun."

"Did you all make these things?" Rafe asked, gesturing around the stall overflowing with crafted ornaments, toys and quilted blankets.

Birdie nodded. "The residents of the Shelter Inn spend all year working on things to sell at the market. It keeps our hands busy and we like to think we're doing something good."

"A hundred percent of what we make goes to the Giving Market Foundation," his grandfather said, his features beaming.

"A hundred percent? You don't save some for overhead?"

"Not a penny. We all donate the labor and the materials for our projects," Birdie said.

"I made those wind chimes over there," Paolo said, his voice bursting with pride.

Rafe wasn't a big wind chime fan but he thought his mother would love to have one of Paolo's creations in her garden, so he added that to his order.

After saying goodbye, Rafe walked outside to find the outdoor market as busy and bustling as the indoor had been. Maybe more so. Everyone seemed cheerful, bundled up against the cold and holding mugs of cocoa or wassail.

As he walked to the fire station, where he had parked his

truck, Rafe noticed all the lovely decorations downtown, including the lights he had strung for Pearl and Opal Barnes.

It was hard not to feel festive, surrounded by all this holiday cheer. He relished the feeling, especially as the past few Christmases had been rough for him and for Isaac.

This would be his third Christmas alone with Isaac since Caitlin lost her battle with sobriety and gave in to her demons.

For a few months, she had lived in Portland with friends from her old life, giving constant promises that she was going to turn her life around soon and return to them.

He had wanted to believe her but somehow hadn't been surprised when she died of an overdose right before Christmas.

Rafe had still been grieving the woman he had once loved the next Christmas, when Isaac was four. Then the previous year, he had been working through the holidays, busy with what turned out to be a crazy storm.

He was in for an interesting time trying to wrap Isaac's presents with only one arm, but he would figure out how to make it work.

After their few rough years, he was ready to do anything necessary to make sure his son had an unforgettable Christmas.

12

MUCH TO HER RELIEF, AMANDA DIDN'T DREAM OF RAFE that night.

She didn't *think* she did, anyway, though it was always possible. She was so exhausted when she finally dropped into bed after staying at the convention center until nearly midnight on the first day of the market. When she returned home, she fell asleep without even taking off her clothes, other than her shoes and the bra she had whipped off the moment she walked inside her house.

One moment she had been on the sofa eating a frozen dinner, the next, she woke up with her cheek pressed into the cushions and her phone telling her it was 3:00 a.m.

She had managed to make her way to her bedroom, where she quickly changed into her favorite sleep pants and an old T-shirt. She had remembered at the last moment to set her alarm, then had fallen immediately back to sleep.

She woke up a few moments before her 6:00 a.m. alarm and saw through the slats on her window blinds that the snow that had been falling lightly when she drove home from the market must have continued through the night. She could see several inches weighing down the limbs of the pine tree outside her window, which meant she had at least that much on her driveway.

She sighed, wishing she could pull the blankets back over her head and catch another hour of sleep. Shoveling was not her favorite task, but it had to be done.

She decided to wait to shower until after she finished clearing her driveway and the front walk.

At least she wouldn't have to feel guilty about not making it to the gym, since she figured the aerobic benefits from shoveling her own driveway—and sometimes her neighbors'—was enough of a good workout.

After donning silk long underwear and insulated jeans, she was grabbing her coat and her favorite matching hat and scarf that Birdie had knitted some time ago, when her phone buzzed with an incoming text message.

She saw it was from her mother, a message that was simple and to the point.

Call me when you have time. No rush.

She hesitated, then deciding she should probably get it over with, she dialed the number and placed her phone on speaker.

Lena answered on the second ring. "Hello, darling," she said, sounding breathless.

"Is this an okay time to talk?"

"I did say no rush, but this is perfect. I'm walking Pepper and Peaches. Don't worry, though. I have my earphones in, so I can talk and walk and hold their leashes at the same time."

She could clearly picture her mother's small white poodles, who were as spoiled as they were adorable.

"How are you, my dear?" Lena asked.

"I'm good. The market opened yesterday so things have been a little hectic."

"You're still working on that? Can't they find anyone else in town to do it? I think you've served your sentence, don't you?"

"It's fine. I don't mind. I like being involved with the market, especially as it always benefits good causes. This year we're helping fund the local food bank as well as an after-school program at the elementary school."

Her mother made a small huffing sort of sound. "Well, don't wear yourself out."

Amanda pictured herself sound asleep on the sofa in the early hours of the morning, still in the clothes she had worn all day. "I'll do my best," she murmured. "Did you need something, Mom?"

Her mother quickly switched gears to her purpose in calling. "I'm assuming you know your brother and Natalie Shepherd became engaged over Thanksgiving."

She tried and failed to gauge any undercurrents in her mother's voice. She had never really been able to ascertain how Lena felt about Griffin and Natalie dating. She did know her mother had not been happy about Amanda's relationship with Natalie's brother, though she suspected Lena would have had the same reaction, no matter whom she might have dated as a teenager.

Lena had married young and had argued hard against Amanda making the same decision. In retrospect, from her advanced age of thirty-one, Amanda couldn't really blame her. She was a completely different person than she had been back then. She wanted and needed different things from a partner now. Maybe Jake would have grown into the man she always believed him to be. And maybe not.

"Yes, I heard. Natalie came into the store last week to tell me."

"I wanted to check in with you to see how you're doing about the whole thing."

She frowned, trying to figure out what direction Lena was taking with the conversation. "I'm fine. Why wouldn't I be? I think it's wonderful. Nat has asked me to share maid of honor duties with McKenna."

"That seems a little insensitive of her, doesn't it?"

Her confusion deepened. "Why? We're dear friends. I'm honored."

"Doesn't it…hurt a little to see them planning a life together? I mean, you were once engaged to her brother. Marrying Jake was everything you ever wanted. His death was such a terrible tragedy."

She had loved Jake dearly and some part of her would always grieve for him. But she wasn't completely convinced that marrying so young, before she really knew her own mind, would have ended happily for them.

She couldn't see what that had to do with Natalie and Griffin, though.

"I'm thrilled for them," she said again. "They both deserve every ounce of happiness that comes their way and I can't wait to celebrate with them. What about you? I'm assuming you and Randall will come back to Shelter Springs for the wedding celebration."

Lena's sigh sounded put-upon. "I suppose I'll have to, won't I? It won't look very good if the mother of the groom stays away. When Griffin called to tell me about the engagement, I tried to convince him they should get married here in Florida. We have a lovely beach near our house. But he was having none of it."

She could only imagine how that particular conversation must have gone down. Why would Lena think Griffin would possibly want to get married at some random beach in Florida, where he had no connection whatsoever to the place?

Her brother was committed to building his future in Shelter Springs, despite the sad memories he and Natalie both had here.

"Is that the reason you called? To talk about Griffin's engagement?" Amanda asked.

"Partly. But I also wanted to invite you down to spend Christmas with us. Randall and I would both love to see you. It's been too long, my dear. His daughters are coming to stay and bringing their children, who are so adorable, though a little bit noisy, if I'm honest. It should be a houseful of fun."

"With all of that happening, you certainly don't need one more person to entertain."

"We haven't been together during the holidays in ages," Lena said, her voice disappointed. "I miss you."

Lena could win a gold medal in the Olympics if they had a guilt category. She had perfected her technique over years of being married to a husband with alcohol use disorder. It had never worked, but that didn't stop Lena from trying. The guilt trips didn't work and neither did the yelling or the crying or the appeals to his conscience.

"I can't, Mom. The holiday market takes so much time and energy and when it's over, I am always slammed with work to do, catching up at the store and doing our year-end inventory. It's just not a good time for me. I'm sorry. Besides that, I don't feel good about leaving Birdie alone for the holidays."

"Griffin and Natalie will be there, won't they? They can watch out for her. Besides, she has all her friends at that retirement community."

Yes. And you'll have Randall and his two daughters and your five stepgrandchildren, the new life you have created away from us.

"It's not a good time for me, Mom," she repeated.

Lena sniffed. "I understand. I expected that answer. Every year I get my hopes up that this year might be different, but I should know better."

Oy, the guilt.

"The holidays don't work for me. But I *was* thinking about getting some sunshine after the new year, when things slow down," she improvised. "What if I came down in January for a few days? We can Zoom with Natalie about the wedding plans, do some shopping. Maybe visit the art museum where you volunteer."

"Oh, I would love that." Lena's tone perked up. "My friends would all love to meet you, too. A few of them have sons who are very eligible bachelors. I would love to set you up."

Amanda could think of few things she would enjoy less than going on a blind date with the son of one of her mother's Florida friends.

"Maybe," she said, careful to keep her tone noncommittal.

They chatted for a few more moments, making tentative plans for a trip that hadn't even existed in her head ten minutes earlier, then Amanda caught sight of the clock in her kitchen.

"I need to go, Mom. I'm sorry. We had about three inches of snow last night, so I need to shovel the driveway and the sidewalk out front of Rose Cottage before I head into the shop."

"I don't miss the Idaho snow, I'll tell you that much. The humidity here kills me sometimes, but I would rather deal with frizzy hair than have to drive in a blizzard."

They hung up soon after, and Amanda quickly finished gearing up to go outside and grabbed a snow shovel out of her small garage.

The sun wouldn't be fully up for another half hour but in the early light of dawn, the world looked magical. Her neighbors had left their Christmas lights on all night, and they gleamed through a layer of snow, bright and festive.

She loved this place.

Not just her beloved cottage, but this street, this town, where neighbors looked out for each other.

Lena couldn't wait to leave Shelter Springs. She had wanted to go even before the accident, when Amanda's father had climbed behind the wheel with a blood alcohol count twice the legal limit and had ended up decimating so many lives.

Prior to the accident, she had stayed because Amanda had begged to finish high school in Shelter Springs. Afterward, Lena had wanted to move immediately, unable to bear the whispers and the gossip about her ex-husband.

Amanda had been eighteen when her mother took off. Lena had begged her to go with her to Florida. She had wanted Amanda to finish high school there and then attend a Florida university.

Life would have turned out much differently if she had given in and agreed to the move, but she hadn't been willing to leave Jake or her friends.

What would have happened if she had left? She wondered anew as she started clearing the driveway. It was impossible to know which of her choices might have taken her in an entirely new direction.

If she had moved to Florida, she and Jake likely wouldn't have become engaged. She wouldn't have ended up giving him back his ring in hopes that it would help him come to his senses.

If none of that had happened, would he have gone on a bender, drunk before he ever headed out to go snowboarding with Griffin and decided to ski into the avalanche prone off-limits area?

She would never know the answer to that but she was still thinking about the ripple effect of choices when she heard someone call her name.

She turned toward the street to find two figures standing where her driveway met the street, a tall, muscular man and a small boy, each holding snow shovels.

"Hi, Ms. Taylor," Isaac chirped cheerfully. "Can we help you shovel? I have my very own."

He held out a miniature shovel with a blue plastic blade.

"I see. It looks great. But you don't have to do that. I'm nearly done, anyway."

"We're helping all the neighbors," Isaac said. "I asked my dad if we could do yours next and he said yes."

Without waiting for a response, he started pushing snow in a wobbly line on the sidewalk that ran in front of her house. The boy looked so pleased with himself, chewing his bottom lip in concentration, she didn't have the heart to discourage him.

Rafe took a few steps toward her. He wasn't wearing a hat or beanie and a few random snowflakes caught in his dark hair.

"Sorry," he murmured. "He's not perfect at it, but he loves to help people."

Isaac was as hard to resist as his father. She gestured to Rafe's cast.

"I should be helping you clear your own driveway. I doubt shoveling snow is on your doctor's list of approved activities."

"Like climbing ladders?"

"Exactly."

His smile flashed in the pearly predawn light. "I'm only using this arm for leverage. The right one is doing all the work."

As she watched him dig beside her, she saw that he was holding the shovel against his cast and pushing and lifting with his right arm. She still didn't think it was a good idea, but she certainly was not his mother and had no right to tell him what to do.

Together, the three of them cleared her driveway, the sidewalk that ran along the front of her cottage and the one leading up to her porch.

They then moved next door to her neighbor's house and had that one done in no time. As far she could tell, all the other houses on the street had already been cleared.

"How long have you been out here shoveling for everyone?" she asked. Her breath came out in puffs and she could imagine her nose and cheeks were rosy with the cold.

"About an hour," Rafe answered. "We're about to take a break and go home for some breakfast."

"We're working men," Isaac chimed in. "We have to keep up our strength."

He looked so proud of himself that Amanda had to smile. "Exactly right."

She paused, an idea forming. The words spilled out before she could think them through. "If you have time, I would be happy to fix you breakfast. I make really good Mickey Mouse pancakes."

Rafe looked startled at the offer. "You don't have to do that."

"It's the least I can do to repay you for helping me shovel and for taking care of the neighbors so that I don't feel compelled to help them on my own."

"I'm sure you have a million things to do this morning. You have to get to your store, don't you?"

She was suddenly filled with misgivings, wishing she had never said anything. Amanda knew she should probably take the out he was offering her. Then she looked at his cute son, glasses fogging up and a red beanie pulled down over his forehead. Yes. Isaac Arredondo was completely irresistible.

"I have an hour before I need to head in. Pancakes sound delicious to me. I'll make them for myself, with or without guests."

"Can we, Dad?" Isaac urged. "I love pancakes."

He sighed. "If you're sure it's no trouble."

"Positive," she lied.

She led the way up the steps, stamping snow off her boots on the front mat that featured a cute little robin in a Christmas sweater.

When she opened the door, Amanda experienced a whole host of misgivings. She wasn't certain she wanted Rafe inside her private sanctuary.

Too late now. She could not renege on an invitation. She would simply have to make the best of it.

She led the way inside, wondering what he would think of her little cottage. She hadn't made any major redecorating changes since her grandmother had moved out two years before, though she had replaced the carpeting that tended to trip her grandmother, finishing the wood flooring underneath by herself.

"You can leave your coats and things here," she said, gesturing to the coatrack in the entryway at the same moment that her two cats sauntered into the foyer, tails raised and ears perked at the newcomers.

"You have cats! I love cats," Isaac said. "What are their names?"

"The black one is Oscar and the orange-striped one is named Willow."

"Can I play with them?" he asked, already shrugging out of his coat, mittens and hat.

"I think they would love that. They are very nice and they love any kind of attention."

She turned on the gas fireplace for warmth in the open-plan space before moving to the kitchen area that she and Birdie had renovated after she moved in with her grandmother, when Birdie's eyesight began to worsen.

Their efforts had made the kitchen more efficient, and Amanda loved the extra window they had added above the sink, which brought in more light and warmth.

She had already made coffee while on the phone with her mother earlier and now she poured some for Rafe. He took the mug from her and sipped.

"This is nice," he said, leaning against the counter and gesturing to her comfortable space.

"I like it," Amanda said, pulling items out of the refrigerator. "My grandmother lived here all my life. Most of hers, actually. She and my grandfather bought it only a few years after they were married."

She set several strips of bacon in the frying pan then placed her griddle on the other burner.

"How can I help? I can watch the bacon for you, if you want."

"That would be great. Thanks."

He moved to the cooktop while she started mixing together the ingredients for pancakes, wishing she were wearing something a little more attractive than jeans and a blue silk long underwear top.

There was something cozy and domestic about working together in the kitchen. He seemed perfectly at home turning the bacon with the tongs she provided, while delicious scents swirled around them.

When she stepped toward the cooktop to add pancake batter to the heated griddle, her shoulder brushed his and she was instantly hot from more than the cooking flame.

The proximity was both unnerving and strangely exhilarating.

Their gazes locked and she saw a flare of awareness in his dark eyes as sudden heat seemed to crackle between them.

What was happening? She let out a breath, forcing herself to relax.

"Isaac is such a sweetheart," she said, forcing herself to focus on something else. "You're doing a good job with him. It can't be easy as a single father."

He turned back to the bacon, and she breathed a sigh of relief and added batter to the griddle.

"Thank you, but I'm not sure I'm doing even an adequate job most of the time. It sometimes feels like I'm barely keeping our heads above water."

Compassion seeped through her, alongside the glittery awareness. "I can't imagine how tough it must be to handle everything on your own."

"I'm not really on my own. My family is a big help. He spends more time at his grandparents' house than he does at our place."

"He must miss his mother," she said, then immediately regretted bringing up the subject. At least it helped her focus on something else beyond her instinctive response to him.

"Yeah. Sometimes. But Caitlin has been gone for three years. His memories of her have faded over the years."

What about your memories?

She didn't say the words as she carefully flipped the pancakes, while beside her, he removed the bacon from the frying pan and took it off the burner.

"Time can be a gentle healer," she said softly as she scooped the first batch of pancakes off the griddle to a plate, concentrating on the task instead of the man she found entirely too fascinating. "I have found its passing helps the pain to fade a little more every day."

"Yes," he agreed. His voice sounded raspy and her gaze again flew to his. He was looking at her with an expression that made her pulse speed and her breath catch.

She couldn't seem to look away, caught by his intense study of her.

Later, she wasn't exactly sure which of them moved first. One moment, they were standing side by side at the cookstove. The next, his mouth lowered to hers and she was frozen by shock and a sharp, delicious thrill.

Was Rafe Arredondo actually kissing her here in her kitchen, or was this just another of those strange dreams haunting her?

It certainly felt real enough. She could smell the clean, masculine scent of him, more mouthwatering than the breakfast smells around him. He tasted of coffee and mint and something indefinable and addictive.

His body was warm and muscled against her, a steady sort of strength she longed to sink into.

The kiss couldn't have lasted long. A few seconds, maybe. They might have kissed longer, until the kitchen burned down around them, when something hard thumped against her shoulder, shocking her back to reality.

What was *that*? She slid her mouth away from his and took a shaky step back, blinking hard as the kitchen came back into focus.

This definitely wasn't a dream. She was standing in front of a hot stove kissing Rafe Arredondo—who had a large fiberglass cast on his arm.

13

IT TOOK RAFE'S BRAIN A FEW SECONDS TO CATCH UP
to what had happened.

One moment he was kissing Amanda Taylor—how on earth
had *that* happened?—and the next, he realized he had conked
her shoulder with his cast.

His arm throbbed but he was more dismayed than truly
hurt. He had only wanted to pull her closer. She was warm and
smelled delicious and he moved his arm out of natural instinct,
completely forgetting about the stupid fiberglass cast he wore.

"Oh man. I am so sorry. Are you okay?"

She gazed up at him for several long seconds, and he could
almost see her trying to regain her composure, inch by inch.
She looked warm and rumpled and it was all he could do not
to pull her back into his arms, cast be damned.

"Are you sorry for kissing me or for slugging me with your
cast?"

He debated his answer then finally decided on the truth.
"How about both?"

He was not the kind of guy who suddenly kissed a woman out of nowhere, especially when it wasn't as if they were in a relationship.

She blinked and turned back to the stove, picking up the container of pancake batter and carefully pouring more circles onto the still-hot griddle.

Was he wrong, or was her hand trembling slightly as she poured?

"The cast thing was an accident. The other part...well, that was probably an accident, too. Or at least a mistake, on both our parts. Is your arm okay?"

His arm burned but the rest of him, the parts that very much wanted this soft woman with the big green eyes and the slightly swollen lips, ached worse.

Somehow it seemed exactly like her to worry about his injury when she ought to be bashing him with one of her frying pans.

He released a long breath. "For the record, I don't go around kissing every woman who offers to cook me breakfast."

She sent him a sidelong look, then poured more pancake batter onto the griddle. "Good thing, or you likely would have more breakfast offers around town than you would know what to do with."

Her tart words surprised a strangled laugh out of him. Oh, he liked her.

"I'm serious. I shouldn't have kissed you like that. We're not even...dating or anything."

"Rafe. Stop. It's fine. We kissed." She shrugged, with a nonchalant sort of expression he wasn't sure how to interpret. "It was lovely, don't get me wrong. But it's done now. Let's just...move on."

Rafe suddenly wasn't so sure whether he *wanted* to move on, or if he would rather spend the next year or so kissing that soft mouth every chance he found.

He certainly couldn't say that, so he just nodded, trying to be as nonchalant as she seemed to be. "Got it."

She smiled, though he was oddly comforted to see her fingers were definitely trembling a little on the spatula she held. "I'm going to throw out the first batch of pancakes, since they must be cold now. These will be ready in only a minute, if you want to call in Isaac."

"Right. I'll do that."

He walked through her small, cozy house until he found Isaac sitting on her sofa looking perfectly happy as he petted a purring cat with each hand. His son grinned at him.

"I think they like me," he said.

"Of course they do. Who wouldn't?" Rafe answered, doing his best to ignore the little pang of guilt that they didn't have any pets.

He knew it was for the best. His schedule was so chaotic that a dog or cat—or hamster—would be left alone for large portions of the day. It was tough enough arranging care for Isaac. Rafe couldn't see himself adding in another living creature to their small family.

"Amanda has breakfast ready for us. Let's go find a bathroom so you can wash your hands. We should probably hurry and eat so we can see if any other neighbors need their sidewalks cleared."

"I'm so hungry, I could eat a brontosaurus all by myself," Isaac said as he headed into the kitchen after a short pit stop to the bathroom to wash his hands.

"I afraid I don't have any of those," Amanda said with a smile. "Will a Mickey Mouse pancake and some bacon do?"

She scooped a pancake off the griddle that was one large round shape with two smaller round shapes for ears.

"Hey. My dad makes those, too. You must have the same recipe!"

"We must." Amanda smiled at the boy with so much warmth and tenderness that Rafe couldn't seem to look away.

Over breakfast, she and Isaac filled up most of the conversation space, leaving little for Rafe to do but listen. They talked about race cars, they talked about his favorite soccer team, they talked about the trip to Disneyland he was dreaming about.

She had a wonderful way with children. Or at least a wonderful way with *his* child. She treated Isaac with respect and genuine interest in everything he wanted to talk about, and he glowed under her attention.

Sometimes, Rafe worried that his son was suffering because he didn't have a mother in his life. When those thoughts occurred, he reminded himself that Isaac had a grandmother and two adoring aunts to help fill that void.

But now he wondered again what it would be like to have someone by his side, helping him make all the tough parenting decisions. Not to mention preparing Mickey Mouse pancakes and bacon in the mornings, while she looked soft and warm and kissable.

"I can't wait to see Santa Claus," Isaac said, once he had eaten every crumb of pancake on his plate. "My dad said he will be at the market this afternoon."

"That's right."

"I know a secret," Isaac said in a conspiratorial whisper.

"Do you?"

He nodded and pushed up his glasses. "That Santa won't be the real Santa Claus. That's what my cousin told me. It will be one of his helpers. The real Santa Claus is too busy helping his elves pack all the presents for Christmas."

"Good point. I imagine that's a pretty massive undertaking."

"I'm going to ask *Ito* if we can go see him today."

"That would be fun. Make sure you come to find me at my store. I might have some stickers for you and possibly a candy cane, if your dad says it's okay."

"I love candy canes!"

"Same. They're delicious. What's your favorite flavor?"

They compared peppermint and cherry and strawberry for a few moments, and Rafe sipped at his coffee, enjoying their comfortable chat immensely.

"I don't have candy canes *or* stickers," he finally said into a pause in the conversation. "I could give you a *Star Wars* bandage but that's about it. Will you still stop by to see me, too?"

Isaac giggled. "Maybe. I like *Star Wars*."

Rafe smiled at his son, the most wonderful gift he could ever hope to receive. "That's good. I'll save one for you."

When Isaac had eaten the last of the bacon on his plate, Rafe slid back from the table. "That was a delicious breakfast. We should probably head back out so we can finish shoveling and Amanda can get on with her day. What do you say to her?"

To his surprise, Isaac slid his chair back and hurried over to throw his arms around Amanda for a hug. "Thank you for breakfast. You make really good bacon."

She smiled and hugged him back. "That's very nice, although your dad made the bacon. I only did the pancakes. Thank you for playing with Oscar and Willow. I am sure they loved the attention."

She followed them out to her front entryway, where Rafe helped Isaac back into his boots, coat and gloves and awkwardly threw on his own over the cast.

"Thanks again for breakfast. I enjoyed it. I guess I'll see you in a few hours at the market."

"You are most welcome. It was my pleasure."

She looked so warm and tousled, auburn hair falling out of a loose updo, that he had a sudden fierce urge to kiss her again, right there in front of Isaac. Somehow he managed to refrain as he ushered his son out the door.

The sun broke through the clouds as they grabbed their shovels and walked back down the street toward their house. Delores Parker, the elderly widow who lived next door to them, came out to her porch in a red plaid coat, holding a mug of something that sent curls of steam into the air.

"Were you the two angels who shoveled my sidewalk this morning?" she called out.

Isaac sent Rafe a sidelong look. He was obviously dying to confess.

"Somebody shoveled your walk? That was nice of them," Rafe said, with a warning look to his son not to spill the beans.

"So very kind. If I only knew who it was, I might repay them with some of my chocolate chip cookies."

"I bet whoever did it loves chocolate chip cookies a lot," Isaac said in a wistful tone that gave away the whole game.

Delores chuckled and Rafe couldn't help joining her.

"Well, thank you," she said.

"You don't have to repay us with cookies, Mrs. Parker. We were happy to do it."

"And did I see you helping our Amanda, too? Good. She spends too much time taking care of everyone else. It's nice to see someone helping her out for a change."

Maybe they had helped her a little bit, clearing the snow away, but then he had added more chaos to her life by that kiss she had not asked for or encouraged.

He still didn't know what had come over him, other than the pure sweetness of unexpectedly finding himself in a cozy kitchen with a lovely woman he couldn't seem to stop thinking about.

"I like Mrs. Parker. She's funny," Isaac said as they tromped up to the porch of their house, which Rafe was slowly renovating. "And she makes really good cookies, too."

Apparently that was a true sign of character, as far as his son was concerned.

"We're lucky to have such good neighbors, aren't we?"

Isaac nodded solemnly. "And I really like Amanda. She's pretty and smells nice and that bacon was the best I ever had."

He could not disagree, though he of course did not mention that her mouth tasted far better than the bacon ever could.

AFTER A SUCCESSFUL FIRST DAY OF THE SHELTER SPRINGS
Giving Market, Amanda had hoped every subsequent day at the
market would go as smoothly.

Nope.

The moment she walked into the convention center after fixing breakfast for Rafe and Isaac, then spending a few hours at
her downtown store, several people rushed over to her, brim-
ming over with problems for her to solve. They ranged from a
concern over the distant assigned parking available to vendors,
a sliding window that was jammed in one of the kiosks and a
large puddle on the floor in the corner of the convention hall
that needed immediate attention.

She handed the parking and window questions over to various committee members but decided to check out the puddle
herself.

"It's grown bigger even since I first noticed it about ten minutes ago." Victor Reed, who had a stall featuring his handworked leather items, gazed at her with wide, worried eyes.

"Looks to me like the roof is leaking. I hope it doesn't start leaking on my booth. Everything will be ruined."

Since his booth was more than thirty feet away from the leak, she doubted that would happen. But she also knew Victor, who had served on her committee for the past two years, tended to stress about every detail.

"Don't worry. I'll ask the maintenance crew to put down some buckets for now and let the convention center team know so they can have someone come in to check out the roof tomorrow while we are closed. I'm so glad you brought this to my attention, Victor. Thank you."

"I knew you would be able to handle it. You're so good in a crisis, Amanda."

"That's very kind of you to say," she said, meeting his wide smile with a much more restrained one of her own. Lately, Victor had started making a few comments that left her feeling awkward and uncomfortable. She had a feeling he might be trying to flirt with her and she wasn't quite sure how to respond.

Victor was a very nice man but he was also in his late fifties and had never married, was balding and paunchy and had lived with his mother until three years earlier, when she went into a nursing home.

"How were your sales yesterday?" she asked politely.

"Okay. Not as good as last year's first day, according to the data I've collected, but I'm hoping the few extra days of the market will make up for that. How about yourself?"

"I haven't had the chance to do a day-by-day comparison to our sales of last year but they seemed pretty brisk. We were busy all day."

"I hope this gamble of yours pays off," he said, his tone shifting from flirtatious to doubtful.

Victor had been one of those in town who had argued against expanding the market, a small but vocal contingent that claimed the market had grown large enough. To handle the increased attendance, they should start selling tickets ahead of time.

She knew there were pros and cons to that option. Selling tickets would provide a new revenue stream to the foundation's fundraising efforts but it might also be cost prohibitive for some families and seniors on fixed incomes who liked to come back to the market again and again.

After a few more moments of conversation, she was able to extricate herself. She found buckets and towels to mop up the mess and then talked to the maintenance crew about the problem. Later, she headed back to her booth to continue adding fresh inventory to their display before the doors opened.

She was rearranging a few items for better visibility when she saw Rafe walk in, moving with his usual determination.

He wore navy blue cargo pants, a white polo shirt with the fire department insignia and a red fleece jacket. Amanda couldn't help noticing she wasn't the only woman who watched him make his way to the first aid station.

Right before he reached to unlock the door to the small room, he shifted as if he felt her looking at him, and their gazes met before she could quickly turn away.

Amanda felt heat soak her cheeks. She had to hope he couldn't see it from twenty feet away. Sometimes she really hated having red hair and a pale complexion that tended to show all her emotions.

She forced a smile and waved, then quickly shifted her attention back to rearranging the display, mortified that he had caught her staring.

She sensed his approach a few moments later, some stir in the atmosphere before she saw him. When she turned, she found him standing a few feet away, watching her with a look she couldn't interpret.

"Is there anything I can help you do before the market opens?" he asked.

She shook her head. "I'm almost done. But thank you."

"I have to tell you, breakfast was a big hit with Isaac. He hasn't stopped talking about you and your bacon all morning long."

She gave him a careful look to see if he was annoyed that she and his son seemed to have established a friendship. He didn't look put out, only amused.

"You know what they say. The way to a six-year-old's heart is through his stomach," she said.

"Well, you certainly found your way to Isaac's heart."

"Have you finished your Christmas shopping for him?"

"Not quite. I have a few more things I wanted to pick up. He hasn't given me any hints about what he really wants so I've mostly had to guess. I have a feeling there's something big. I'm hoping if he stops by today to talk to Santa, I can take a break so I can eavesdrop on the conversation."

"Smart. I guess parents must pick up those little tricks along the way."

"Believe me, I'm no expert when it comes to parenting. I'm figuring out my way as I go along."

"From what my friends who have children say, that's what everybody does."

"Some make it look so easy, though. Joe and Crista have two kids, yet they juggle everything without a problem."

She thought of her friend McKenna and her husband, Travis, who had been in a rough place the previous Christmas. "That might only be your perspective from the outside. You never really know what people might be struggling through within the walls of their own home."

"True enough."

"Anyway, Crista and Joe can tag team when one of them needs a break or is doing something else, like Crista here at the market with her stall. You're going it alone. Give yourself a break, Rafe. I think you're doing a great job. Your son is sweet and kind and seems well-adjusted, despite everything the two of you have been through."

He studied her for a long moment, then gave her a warm smile. For one wild moment, she thought he wanted to kiss her again. Something bright and sparkly flashed in his dark eyes and he even took a slight step forward.

Fortunately—or unfortunately, depending on her perspective—Scarlet returned from refilling her coffee thermos in the hospitality room outside the convention hall that had been set up for vendors.

"Are you guys ready? We've got throngs of people lined up outside, eager to come in. Looks like the doors are about to open."

Amanda glanced at her watch and saw it was nearly noon. Where had the morning gone?

"Ready or not," Rafe said. "I better head back."

She waved at him with one hand, then hurried to gather the boxes she had used to carry in the inventory and tucked them under the counter.

"That man is fine," Scarlet said after Rafe had walked away.

Amanda frowned at her employee. "And too old for you. He has at least twelve or thirteen years on you."

"Maybe I'm looking for a hot older man who can take care of me. I suspect Rafe would definitely take care of a woman, if you know what I mean."

Amanda must have looked as shocked as she felt. Scarlet laughed. "I wish you could see your face right now. Don't worry. I'm just kidding. For now, I'm fine with all the cute little puppy dogs who are my age. Anyway, I think that particular hot firefighter might be interested in someone else."

She was relieved when the doors to the market opened at that moment and shoppers rushed in, saving her from having to ask what Scarlet meant.

Throughout the day as she dealt with shoppers and market problems alike, Amanda tried not to gawk at him every spare moment, though she found it ridiculously difficult. As she helped customers or worked to troubleshoot market administrative problems, she was constantly aware of Rafe out of the corner of her gaze.

Several hours after they opened, her feet ached and a tension headache seemed to grab hold of her skull with sharp talons. She was finishing the process of checking out a couple of customers, best friends who said they drove over from Boise specifically to shop at the market, when she heard a young-sounding voice calling her name.

"Hey! Amanda! Amanda!"

She looked up to find Isaac Arredondo running toward her. As was becoming his habit, he wrapped his arms around her waist. Her headache seemed to lift in an instant and she felt a funny little lurch in her chest at his bighearted affection.

She hugged him back. "Hi. There's my favorite snow shoveler."

He beamed at her, shoving up his glasses. "I'm here with *Ito*. My grandpa. He brought me so I can go see Santa Claus."

"That's what you said you wanted to do this morning. How exciting."

"Have you talked to Santa yet to tell him what you want for Christmas?" he asked, studying her closely.

Amanda thought of her quiet Christmases of the past few years, where she exchanged a few gifts with her grandmother and Griffin, when he was home. She would usually have a video call with her mother, and then try to order herself something special online that she wouldn't normally purchase.

"Um. No. Not yet."

"Do you want to come with us to see Santa?"

"I don't think I can leave my store right now."

"Sure you can." Scarlet gave her an encouraging nod. "I can hold down the fort. Things have slowed down a little bit after the big rush of earlier. Go see Santa Claus with your friend here."

"My name is Isaac," he said cheerfully to her.

"Hi, Isaac. Nice to meet you. I'm Scarlet."

"I have a friend named Scarlet, only she is six, like me, not a grown-up. She's in my class."

"Is that right?"

"Yeah. And she doesn't have blue hair, either. She has dark hair like me."

He looked around as if making sure there was no one there to overhear, then lowered his voice to a whisper. "Once, she tried to kiss me under the table while we were having art class and both of us dropped our colored pencils at the same time."

"Oh wow. Your Scarlet sounds fun."

He grinned. "She is. When I told her not to kiss me, she wasn't even mad. She just laughed and told me a funny joke. Do you want to hear it?"

He looked straight at Amanda and she nodded. "Sure. Go ahead."

"Why is it so cold at Christmas?"

"Why?" She played along.

"Because it's Decem-brrrr."

He laughed uproariously at the joke and both Scarlet and Amanda laughed in response.

"That's a great one," Amanda said. "I'll have to remember that."

"My little nieces will love that one," Scarlet said. She gave Amanda an encouraging look. "Go ahead and take a break. You've been working hard for hours, without even a bathroom break. You need to at least stretch your legs."

She had a feeling Scarlet wouldn't let up until she agreed. "Okay," she agreed, taking off her embroidered store apron. "Let me grab my coat."

The market Santa Claus was outside this year, set up in a

charming small wooden chalet adorned with icicle lights. After she put on her parka, Isaac grabbed her.

"We have to get my dad. He and my *ito* want to come see Santa, too."

Amanda instantly felt awkward and out of place. This was a family moment and she was only in the way. "Maybe you should let your father and grandfather take you without me."

"Why? I want *you* to come, too."

"Go ahead," Scarlet urged with a not-so-innocent smile. Outnumbered, Amanda sighed, wishing she had time to freshen up her lipstick—an impulse that appalled her. She reached for the boy's outstretched hand and walked with him across the way to the first aid station.

They found Rafe chatting with his cousin Izzy, wearing a matching paramedic uniform, and his father, Alberto, whom everyone called Al.

She saw Al and Izzy exchange a look while Rafe blinked with surprise. "Oh. Hi."

"Dad. Can Miss Amanda come with us to see Santa Claus? She really wants to."

Amanda gave Isaac a startled look, fully aware she had not said anything of the sort. Defending herself would only make her sound ridiculous, though.

Rafe looked at his son with a mystified expression. "Um. Sure. She can come with us."

If she could have found a little magic Christmas sparkle dust in that moment, she would have happily used it to fly away from the noisy market and the entire Arredondo family.

"You sure you'll be okay?" he asked his cousin.

Izzy gestured around the empty area. "I have no idea how I'll handle this crowd all by myself."

Rafe chuckled as he pulled on the red fire department fleece jacket she had seen him wearing earlier.

"I think I'll stick around here and give you a hand, Isabella," Al Arredondo said after a moment. "When we walked past earlier, there was a pretty big line for Santa. You might be a minute."

"Are you sure?" Rafe frowned. "I know how much you enjoy watching the grandkids go see Santa."

"I'm fine. Take some good pictures for me."

Amanda felt heat rise from her neck to her cheeks. She knew exactly why Al didn't want to accompany his son and grandson—because she was there and he didn't want to be around her.

No matter how hard she worked to make Shelter Springs a better place—accepting every single committee assignment she was offered and spending long hours in boring meetings when she would rather be hiking or kayaking on the lake or working in her store—she would always remain Dennis Taylor's daughter.

Certain families in town couldn't seem to get past that connection, no matter how hard she tried to prove she wasn't anything like her father.

How could she blame them, really? Her father's actions had destroyed so many lives.

Four young people had died because her father had chosen to get behind the wheel while under the influence.

Amanda had known every one of those teenagers.

Rafe's cousin—Izzy's brother, Alex—had been a standout high school athlete with a basketball scholarship to a Florida university. He had been driving. Next to him had been his girlfriend, a cheerleader, Harper Peterson. She had been strikingly pretty, with big blue eyes and a wide smile. More than that, she had been genuinely kind, the sort of girl who was nice to everyone.

With them had been another couple, Alex's friend and fellow athlete Wyatt Johnson, along with his date, Fatima Ali, who had been Amanda's good friend and a fellow member of the swimming team and on track to graduate as the valedictorian of Amanda's class.

All that promise. All that potential. Four young people who would never have the chance to see any of their own dreams—or their families' dreams *for* them—realized. Because of Amanda's father.

She didn't know that anyone actively blamed her for the accident. Why would they? She had been a teenager too, wrapped up in her own pain from her parents' divorce and the many years of bitter unhappiness in her home that had preceded it.

They might not actively blame her but *she* blamed herself. She could have tried to stop her father somehow. Hidden his keys, maybe, or called the cops to find him and pull him over.

Amanda had known he was spiraling out of control. She might have been the only one to see it. Griffin had been off to college, her mom was living in an apartment in Haven Point and Birdie had stopped talking to her son-in-law years earlier.

Instead, Amanda had seen him grab his keys, suspecting that he had already finished off a six-pack of beer. She hadn't said a word as he drove off.

By that point in her life, she knew it was pointless. What could she possibly say that she and her mother and Griffin hadn't already tried to say a thousand times before?

She should have tried one more time. Maybe that would have made the difference. Instead, her father had walked out the door, had driven to the liquor store and had sat in his car overlooking the lake for the next hour, drinking an entire bottle of Jack Daniel's.

"I really don't have to go with you," she said now in an undertone to Rafe, pushing away the dark past.

He sent her a swift look. "You don't," he agreed. "I'm sorry Isaac dragged you into something you don't want to do."

"That's not what I meant. I thought it was sweet that he invited me and I would love to go. But I didn't think about how uncomfortable that might make things for your father."

His forehead furrowed in confusion. "What are you talking about?"

"I know how your family must hate me."

"Why would they?"

"Because I'm a Taylor. Because my father killed your cousin."

She saw memories and old pain in his expression at the reminder.

"They don't hate you. That's absurd."

She sighed. "You're right. *Hate* is probably too strong a word. But I know that seeing me causes them pain. I'm a reminder of what happened to Alex. Of all the misery and grief my father left behind."

"You shouldn't think that. You were just a girl yourself. My family understands that."

She did not want to argue with him, but it seemed suddenly important that he understand her perspective. "Intellectually, maybe. But I'm sure there's some sort of instinctive reaction. Like muscle memory. I can't blame them. I'm the same way. Whenever I see someone from your family or the other families who were so tragically impacted, I can't help but remember everything that happened."

"Even when you see me?" he asked, watching her out of those intense dark eyes.

She swallowed. "Not as much as I used to," she admitted. "Now I tend to think about…other things when I see you."

She had not meant to confess that particular tidbit of information. She regretted it as soon as the words escaped, especially when his gaze intensified and heat seemed to glitter to life between them.

Isaac, walking between them, tugged on his father's hand. "Is that the line for Santa Claus?" he asked.

Rafe blinked a few times, then looked down at his son. "Looks like it, kiddo."

Amanda was deeply grateful for the cold air, hoping it could ease the color in her cheeks she knew must be there.

What had she been thinking to blurt out something like that? He was going to guess correctly that she had a ridiculous crush on him. She had kissed him that morning as if she was suddenly in need of mouth-to-mouth, for heaven's sake.

She wanted to figure out some way to backpedal, but nothing came to mind. To her relief, Isaac was chattering away to his father about the Christmas movie he had watched that afternoon with his grandfather and how Al had fallen asleep at the best part.

She was almost relieved a few moments later when Al Arredondo joined them in the queue.

Rafe looked surprised but pleased to see his father. "Papi. I'm glad you joined us."

"Your cousin said I was getting in the way," he said, his tone grumpy.

"Look, *Ito*. The line isn't as long as you said it would be!" Isaac said in a gleeful tone.

"Lucky for us," Al said. "Otherwise, my toes might get frostbite."

Six or seven families were ahead of them in line. She recognized a few of them but not everyone. Unfortunately, one of the people she recognized was Lily Peterson Davis, whose older sister Harper had been killed in the accident.

She stood with her husband as well as their twin girls, whom Amanda thought were four or five years old. They were adorable, both wearing beanies that had two sparkly pom-poms that looked like ears.

Lily gave Rafe and Al a warm greeting. Her smile dimmed slightly when she spotted Amanda, though she greeted her cordially enough.

See what I mean? Amanda wanted to say, fighting the urge to give Rafe a meaningful look as she returned the greeting.

"We're gonna see Santa Claus," the twin with the purple beanie announced.

"And Mrs. Claus," her sister said.

"So are we," Isaac informed them. "I know what I'm going to ask him. Do you?"

The girls tripped over each other to talk about some of the things on their list. Isaac, Amanda couldn't help but notice, stayed quiet about his list.

The men chatted easily and she remembered that Lily's husband, Blake, must know Rafe and Al from the fire department. While Rafe was a full-time employee, Al had been a volunteer until he retired, and Blake was a volunteer now, working as a financial planner when he wasn't driving one of the fire engines.

Amanda shifted in the cold line, feeling awkward and wondering again why Isaac had insisted she come along with him.

"The market is really lovely this year," Lily said after the silence began to drag out uncomfortably. "I love that you moved some of the booths outside. It really brings a magical feeling to the season, especially when there is a light snow like this evening."

Amanda looked around at the bustling shoppers, the small wooden shops and the Christmas tree that dominated the entire scene. "Thank you. It's an experiment. I was worried people would mostly want to stay inside to keep warm. We went back and forth about where to put Santa and Mrs. Claus and we finally decided outside would be better."

"I can see why. Keep the overexcited children away from all the fragile items inside."

That definitely had been part of the discussion, but the main argument for moving the chalet outside had been for crowd control. It did add to the festive mood, though.

"Let us know how you like it out here. There should be

suggestion boxes around the market or you can always email through the website. We're always looking for input."

"I'll try to remember," Lily said as a new group joined the queue.

Amanda saw with relief it was McKenna, Travis and their three children. Travis wore Austin, bundled up against the cold, in a baby carrier against his chest, and the boy beamed at everyone around him, his eyes sparkling with color from the lights on the Christmas tree.

McKenna hugged her. "What are you doing out here? Don't tell me you want to sit on Santa's lap, too."

Travis grinned. "What's your wish? Let me guess. You want a few more town committees to serve on."

Amanda rolled her eyes, though she could feel herself flush. One of these days, she needed to learn how to say no.

"I'm not sure why I'm here, to tell you the truth." She gestured ahead of them in the line. "My little neighbor Isaac asked me to come out with him. Scarlet persuaded me I needed a break and should breathe some fresh air."

McKenna caught sight of Lily ahead of them and the two women also greeted each other with hugs.

The children obviously knew each other as well. "This is my friend Hazel," Isaac announced. "She goes to my school."

"Except we're not in the same class because I'm in kindergarten."

"And I'm in first grade," Isaac said.

"We do get to sing together when we practice our school concert."

While the conversation flowed around her between neighbors, friends and schoolmates, Amanda wanted nothing more than to slip away. She didn't belong here. All of these people were part of a shared club, families with small children.

She thought again of her quiet holiday celebrations. She loved her family but sometimes she longed for something…more.

If her life had turned out as she had once planned as a teenager in love, she and Jake might have been here with these other parents, watching their children bubble over with holiday excitement.

They had both wanted four children and had planned to start their family as soon as they each graduated from college. She had even come up with names for them.

That girl who had so many dreams seemed like another person sometimes. Life had changed her irrevocably.

She was thirty-one now with no prospects of making a family with anyone, having children of her own.

She released a breath, pushing away the sadness. She was fine. Better than fine. She had picked up the charred remnants of the life she had once planned and had rebuilt it into a happy, productive existence.

She had a business she loved, she was slowly renovating her grandmother's charming cottage, she had dear friends and her spare time was filled with volunteer work.

Instead of focusing on all the things she didn't have, the dreams that were snatched away in the blink of an eye, she should direct her attention to the many things she loved about her life.

The reminder rang hollow even to her as she stood alone in the midst of a crowd of excited families, waiting for their turn to hand over their wishes to Santa.

15

THOUGH HE KNEW HE SHOULD BE WHOLLY FOCUSED on his son and this fun holiday tradition, Rafe couldn't help watching Amanda out of the corner of his gaze.

She was uneasy and he wasn't sure why.

Though she smiled as she chatted with her friend McKenna and with Lily Davis, Rafe couldn't miss the slight, subtle shadow in her expression.

He doubted anyone else could see it. He wasn't sure why *he* could tell, yet to him the hint of sadness was unmistakable. He wanted to pull her against him and tell her everything would be all right. That was silly, wasn't it?

As the line moved slowly forward, she seemed distracted, her expression flitting from the other women to the children and back again.

"We're almost there!" Isaac looked almost giddy at the prospect of taking a turn on Santa's lap.

"What are you going to ask for?" Rafe asked.

"I'll tell Santa Claus when I get there," Isaac insisted, with aggravating stubbornness.

Rafe wanted to grind his teeth. Isaac had been oddly close-mouthed this year about the main thing on his wish list. No matter how hard Rafe tried to convince him to spill the beans, Isaac insisted he only wanted to give the wish to Santa.

None of Rafe's family members had any clue either, so the kid truly must want to keep it to himself.

It was enough to make a dad want to pull out his hair. How could he make his son's wish come true if he had no idea what he wanted?

Finally, they neared the wooden chalet where he could see Eugene and Flora Murphy dressed in their Santa and Mrs. Claus costumes they had been donning since *Rafe* was a kid, waiting to sit on their laps to tell them about the iPod he wanted and the new baseball glove and the skateboard with the flared kicktail.

At the gesture from the elf assistant, Isaac raced over to Eugene-slash-Santa, beaming.

"Hi there," Mrs. Claus said kindly, smiling back at the boy. "Your name is Isaac, isn't it?"

Isaac's eyes widened. "How do you know that?"

"Santa tries to know the names of all the children," she said. "And if he isn't sure, I do my best to help him."

She met Rafe's gaze and gave a barely perceptible wink. He had to respect the couple's dedication to play the role for two generations now.

"Come over here, young man," her husband urged behind his big white beard. "Tell me about yourself."

Isaac hopped onto his lap and Rafe and his father both pulled their phones out to take pictures. He noticed Amanda was hanging back behind his father, looking as if she wished she were anywhere else at the market but here.

"My name is Isaac Arredondo and I'm six years old. I have a dad named Rafe and a grandpa named Al and a grandma named Louise. Me and my cousins call them *Ito* and *Abi*. And my *abuelo* is named Paolo."

"I believe I know your family. You have a good one, don't you?"

He nodded vigorously. "My Al takes me fishing and my *abi* Louise makes the best PB and J sandwiches and *Abuelo* gave me a remote control car that goes superfast."

Aware of the other children waiting impatiently for their turns, Rafe made a go-ahead gesture to his son.

"Tell me what you would like Santa to bring you this year," Eugene finally said kindly.

Isaac sighed. "I have a lot of toys so I really don't *need* anything. But if you have room in your sleigh, I would like a new Star Wars LEGO set and some new cars to drive on my carpet that looks like a road."

Whew. At least Rafe had somewhere to start. He had already picked up a couple of basic beginner Star Wars LEGO sets and several new Hot Wheels cars.

"Can I ask for another thing?" Isaac asked with a furtive look at Rafe. "It's a secret."

"Of course, son." Santa leaned down, and Isaac whispered to him for a moment, hand cupped over his mouth as if afraid someone would try to read his lips.

Rafe strained to hear but the noise of the crowd was too intense. He saw Eugene's eyes widen behind his glasses and he sent a startled look at Rafe and then another one at Amanda, several paces behind them.

"I'm not sure about that. I can't carry that in my sleigh, can I?" Eugene murmured, his voice low.

"Maybe not. But that's what I really, really want," Isaac said, his small voice vibrating with emotion.

"That isn't up to me, I'm afraid. It's not up to you, either."

"But I've tried to be good this year, even when it was *so hard*. I practice reading out loud and I pick up my toys before I go to bed and I brush my teeth for two whole minutes in the morning and two whole minutes at night."

"That's a good start." Eugene's voice was everything calm and patient and kind. "That thing you asked for might happen someday but there's not much you or I can do about it, I'm afraid. I'm sorry."

"Okay." Isaac sounded dejected.

"I will see what I can do about the other things on your list. Now why don't you give your dad and your grandpa one more great big smile so they can get a good picture?"

Isaac gave a smile that looked fake. Rafe almost thought he saw tears threaten, but his son blinked several times and they were gone by the time he hopped down from Santa's lap.

"Dad, do you want to sit on Santa's lap?"

Rafe cleared his throat. "That's only for kids your age. I'm way too big."

"He might still be able to bring you what you want for Christmas."

For some wild reason, Rafe's thoughts strayed to Amanda and it was all he could do not to look at her.

"I'm good."

"Who's next?" Eugene asked. "Miss Amanda, how about you?"

Rafe could see she looked startled. "I'm fine. Really."

"You have to tell him or he won't know what to bring you," Isaac said, all earnestness and childlike faith.

"I will. I'll come back another time, okay? There are lots of other children who would like their turn and I don't want to make them wait in the cold any longer."

Isaac looked as if he wanted to argue, but after a moment he sighed and slipped his hand in hers as they walked out the other door of the chalet. "I asked him for something I really want but he said he can't bring it."

"What is it?" she asked. "Let me guess. A giraffe?"

He snickered. "No. The reindeer couldn't carry a giraffe on the sleigh. Plus, my house isn't big enough for a giraffe. Unless maybe it was a baby giraffe."

He sent a questioning look at Rafe, who quickly shook his head.

"Even a baby giraffe wouldn't fit, I'm afraid," his father said.

"Is it a new car?" Amanda asked.

He giggled with glee at that, any trace of tears forgotten. "I can't drive. I'm only six!"

"Oh right. I forgot."

"I can't tell you, anyway. It's a secret."

The exit to the Santa chalet led straight to the Christmas tree, at least twenty feet high and brightly lit against the night sky. Amanda's cheeks were flushed, her eyes bright and so lovely he wanted to kiss her all over again, right there in front of the whole town.

"I should probably get back to the store," she said with an apologetic tone.

"And I need to go back inside for a moment and make sure Izzy has everything she needs for the evening shift."

"Dad, can I get a hot cocoa?" Isaac asked. "My friend named Hazel said they're super yummy."

"I can take you," Rafe's father told him. "Hot cocoa sounds great to me, too. I hear they can even add Baileys to it."

"What's Baileys? Is it good? Can I have some?"

Al grinned. "Probably not. That's a special hot cocoa for grown-ups. You wouldn't like it."

"How about you get the one with marshmallows? I hear they have marshmallows shaped like snowmen," Rafe suggested.

"I guess."

Al took Isaac's hand and with a nod to both Rafe and Amanda, the older Arredondo led his grandson toward the hot cocoa stand.

"Thank you again for coming with us. It meant a lot to Isaac," he said to Amanda.

"I'm not sure why," she said, her brow furrowed. "Do you have any idea why he wanted me there?"

Rafe suspected, but he wasn't sure he wanted to share that nugget of info with her.

Isaac had been asking more questions lately about his mother. Why wasn't she in his life? What happened to her? Why had she left?

Did he do something wrong to make her leave? Or worse, did she not love him enough to stay?

Rafe hated those questions, though he tried to answer as honestly as possible to a young child with a limited understanding of the nuances concerning someone who struggled with addiction.

He gently explained that Caitlin had loved him very much, as much or more than any mother loved her boy. She had loved being his mother, but she had been sick and she had to go away for a while to try to get better. And then, sadly, she had died while she was gone, before she could make it back to them.

It wasn't a lie, though Rafe was aware the explanation glossed over many of the darker points. He wasn't about to tell a six-year-old boy the hard truth.

Rafe would have given anything to be able to give him another reason for Caitlin's absence from his life. Cancer, a car accident, a sudden brain aneurysm. All would have been tragic and hard to explain to a child but without the undercurrent of guilt that Rafe still felt at not being able to help the woman he had loved.

Amanda was looking at him expectantly, seeking an explanation for Isaac's request. He couldn't be completely honest with his son but he would try with Amanda, he decided. No matter how awkward.

"Over the past few months, he has begun to notice that our family is a little…nontraditional. He sees his friends with their moms and their dads and has asked me why he doesn't have a mother. He hardly remembers Caitlin. I very much suspect that might be what he talked to Santa about. Bringing him a mother."

She frowned. "What does that have to do with me?"

He sighed, wishing he hadn't started this. "Isaac likes you.

He has talked about you a lot since that day his remote control car tripped you up at the Shelter Inn."

He saw the pieces click into place as her expression shifted from confusion to astonishment. "And you think he wants *me* to be his mother? Why on earth would he want that?"

"Who knows exactly what goes on in the head of a six-year-old boy? Not me, certainly. But you've been kind to him. You are warm and nice and...pretty."

He wanted to say breathtakingly lovely, but decided this was an awkward enough conversation. "I think he might have a little crush on you. I suspect he wanted Santa to meet you so he could know what to bring on Christmas morning."

When she was emotional, embarrassed or upset about something, her cheeks turned the color of his mother's favorite pale, delicate roses. Now they were even brighter, like two bright, flaming red Christmas ornaments.

"That's ridiculous. Impossible. You can't just ask Santa for a mother!"

For one contrary moment, he wanted to argue with her. Was it *completely* impossible?

He couldn't say that, of course.

"Obviously."

"You have to tell him he can't ask Santa to bring him a mother for Christmas. It doesn't work that way. I hate the idea of him waking up disappointed on Christmas morning when he doesn't find someone under the tree who will...will make him cookies and tuck him in at night."

Rafe knew he shouldn't find that image so very appealing. Not so much the making cookies part, but the idea of someone being there for both him and Isaac.

Of not being quite so alone on this parenting journey.

"I'll try to have a word with him. I'm sorry about this. It's been a rough few years and we're only now beginning to find our way."

She started moving through the market on her way to the store.

"You have no reason to apologize. He's a darling boy and any woman would be lucky to be his mother. Stepmother, anyway. But obviously, we both know that woman is not going to be me."

Rafe again was a little astonished at how much he wanted to argue with her.

"I will talk to him. You have to admit, it's a little sweet, though. Right? I'm not sure anybody has ever asked to find *me* under their Christmas tree."

She sent him a sidelong look, eyebrows raised in a skeptical way that made him want to smile. Amanda Taylor made him smile far more often than any woman had in a very long time.

"It is very sweet. I'm touched that he seems to like me. But he needs to know a...a mother can't magically appear along with a LEGO set and new bike on Christmas morning."

"I'll talk to him," he promised. "Thanks again for going outside with us."

She shrugged. "It was nice to see how the queue for Mr. and Mrs. Claus worked from the perspective of the children awaiting their turn. I might suggest a few changes for next year."

"Will you be the market coordinator again next year?"

"I haven't decided. I'm still trying to make up my mind. Either way, I'll leave extensive notes for those who might be coming after me."

That was the kind of person she was, he thought as they continued walking.

In addition to being kind to his son and lovely as an April morning, Amanda was generous with her time and deeply invested in making their town better.

She was the exactly the kind of woman his son deserved for a mother.

16

AS THEY CONTINUED WALKING THROUGH THE MARKET ON the way to the first aid station and The Lucky Goat kiosk, Amanda could feel the heat in her cheeks and sincerely hoped Rafe didn't notice.

She was fiercely aware of him walking beside her, lean and muscled and gorgeous. She could see other women notice him as he walked through, with those broad muscles and his dark good looks.

Goodness. His son had asked Santa Claus for *her* to be his mother. She didn't know how she was supposed to respond to that, especially when her thoughts felt as jumbled and tangled as last season's Christmas lights. She had this vague sense of embarrassment, as if she had done something wrong.

More than that, she was suddenly aware of a deep ache of longing.

This was only a young child's foolish Christmas wish. Completely unattainable. Like all those years when she had prayed and wished for her father to stop drinking, for a "normal" family like her friends had.

They were passing the Shelter Inn booth when she noticed her grandmother and Paolo working together again. Birdie was saying something that made Paolo laugh. As Amanda watched, the man put his hand over Birdie's, looking down at her with so much clear affection, it made Amanda stop in her tracks, that weird feeling in her chest again.

Amid all the chaos of the market opening and organizing her shop, she had almost forgotten about the Birdie-Paolo dilemma.

Their relationship wasn't going away. The two of them seemed closer than ever.

Rafe didn't seem to notice she had stopped until he had taken a few more steps. When he saw she wasn't beside him, he turned with a quizzical look.

"What's wrong?"

She gestured to the Shelter Inn booth. He followed her gaze, his expression confused. When he spied Birdie and Paolo holding hands, he smiled.

"Looks like things are getting a little more serious. Maybe I need to have The Talk with Grandpa."

She didn't want to hear this. "Someone needs to talk some sense into both of them," she muttered.

"Why does it bother you so much? Don't you want Birdie to be happy?"

"She *was* happy. Since my grandfather died, Birdie has become the strongest, most independent woman I know. Even after she started to lose her sight, she insisted on staying at Rose Cottage for several years on her own, until I finally moved in with her. She has built a wonderful life for herself. This just feels so...out of character for her."

"I guess true love can make a person do things they would never consider doing otherwise."

She frowned, wondering if he was mocking her somehow.

"Can you tell me you're completely comfortable with your grandfather dating Birdie, less than a year after your grandmother died?"

"He's seventy-six years old. He has buried his wife, a daughter and a grandson. If Birdie makes him happy for the remaining years he has left, who are we to argue?"

She knew he was right and she wanted to celebrate this new relationship in her grandmother's life. She wanted nothing so much as to see her grandmother happy, but she had never considered the possibility that Birdie might suddenly start dating again, after twenty years as a widow. It was taking her time to adjust to the idea.

Before she could respond, Paolo spotted them and called out. "Hello, Amanda. Hello, Rafael."

Rafe waved at his grandfather and started to head over to say hello. Amanda sighed. She needed to get back to The Lucky Goat kiosk but her grandmother would be hurt if she didn't at least stop by for a few moments to chat.

The Shelter Inn booth was bustling with customers, as well as several other residents of the retirement community who were helping out.

"Hi, Grandma," she said. "It's Amanda."

She leaned in to kiss her grandmother's wrinkled cheek that smelled of lavender soap.

Birdie reached for her hands. "Oh!" her grandmother exclaimed. "Your fingers are freezing! What have you been up to?"

Amanda hesitated, not quite sure how to respond.

"My son, Isaac, wanted to see Santa Claus," Rafe answered after a pause. "We went along as his paparazzi."

She could only be grateful he didn't add his suspicions about Isaac's reason for inviting Amanda along.

"How fun. I remember taking my own children to see Santa." Birdie's smile held years of fond memories. "This was when George Keller used to dress in the red suit and set up at the five and dime over on Lakefront Street. Do you remember that store?" she asked Paolo.

"Oh yes. I remember. I used to work there stocking shelves and unloading the deliveries."

"The whole store smelled of peppermint sticks and dried apples. I can almost smell it."

"As if it were yesterday," Paolo said with a warm, affectionate smile that seemed to exclude everyone else in the entire market convention hall.

She couldn't deny that her grandmother seemed happier than she had in a long time, more energetic and vibrant. Rafe was right. Paolo and Birdie were certainly capable of making their own decisions. She didn't know his grandfather well, but Birdie at least was as sharp as she had ever been.

Maybe she should just trust they knew what they were doing.

"Amanda. Hi!" Liz Cisneros Shepherd, Natalie and Mc-Kenna's maternal aunt—and new stepmother—stepped forward and gave her a bright smile.

"Hi, Liz. How's married life?"

Liz beamed across the stall at her husband, who was busy helping a couple of young boys looking at the vast wooden car collection. "Lovely. Truly lovely."

It still seemed more than a little odd for Amanda to see the two of them together.

Steve had been a devoted husband to his wife, Jeanette, Liz's older sister. He had nursed her through two years of cancer therapy. After she lost the battle, Steve had been more than a little lost, too. He had left his teenage children to live off-grid in Alaska.

His father's desertion had been one more blow to Jake. In his anger at his father and his grief over losing his mother, he had partied hard, sinking into the oblivion of alcohol and marijuana. Amanda had tried to help him through it, certain their love would be strong enough to help him weather the pain.

It hadn't.

She hadn't been strong enough. As the months wore on and Jake showed no sign of easing off, Amanda had finally accepted she couldn't stand by and walk the same path her mother had.

As the child of someone with an addiction disorder, she had seen firsthand the damage he had done to those who loved him. She hadn't been willing to accept that kind of future for herself.

I love you and always will, she had said through her tears as she handed him back her engagement ring. *But I can't stand by and let you destroy both of us.*

A week later, Jake had died in that avalanche.

While she was happy for her friend Liz and her newfound happiness with Steve, Amanda still struggled to forgive the man for surrendering to his own pain instead of staying to help his children grieve the death of their mother.

"I've been meaning to stop by The Lucky Goat booth to say hello and give you kudos on an amazing market this year," Liz said. "I'm loving the new outdoor space and the extended time frame. At first when you told me you wanted to add four more days, I wasn't so sure our residents would be able to make enough items to last us two full weeks but everyone really came through. We're already on track to have our biggest sales year ever."

Barring the previous year when she had been recovering from knee surgery, Liz always organized the entire booth for the retirement community, including the coordination of volunteers who would work there each day.

"I'm glad. I haven't had a chance to talk to many of the other vendors. It's great to hear positive feedback."

"If I had my way, you would be the permanent market director. You're brilliant at it."

"Thank you, Liz. That means a lot."

Liz and McKenna had both worked with her for years on the market committee. No one worked harder than they did.

"We're only in our second day but everything has been wonderful," Liz said. "I look forward to seeing how the rest of the market goes."

"Keep your fingers crossed we don't have any more crises."

Liz held up both hands with her pointer and middle fingers crossed. "I'm sure you can handle anything that comes along," she said, before returning to help another customer at the booth.

Amanda wished she shared her friend's confidence.

She certainly couldn't seem to handle her growing attraction to a man she could never have or keep her heart safe from his adorable son.

OVER THE NEXT WEEK, AMANDA WAS TOO BUSY TO worry much about either Birdie and Paolo or her own growing feelings for Rafe.

Between her downtown store and her market responsibilities, she didn't have a spare second.

During the day, anyway.

At night, when she should have been collapsing into a dreamless, exhausted slumber, her subconscious seemed to want her to focus almost exclusively on Rafe and Isaac.

She dreamed of them nearly every night.

Sometimes her subconscious relived that stunning, fleeting kiss she and Rafe had shared, and she would wake up with the sheets tangled around her and her body aching.

She could understand that. She hadn't been this attracted to anyone in a long time. Maybe not even since Jake.

Weirder, though, were the dreams where she, Rafe and Isaac weren't doing anything exciting, simply the ordinary activities of life. Washing dishes together, doing yard work, blowing out birthday candles.

Either way, she awoke each day with a strange ache in her chest, a loneliness she didn't want to face. Instead of dwelling on it, she invariably tried to jump straight into the chaos of the day, determined to push them both out of her head.

In reality, she rarely saw Rafe over the next several days. They did not have another conversation longer than a passing hello. They certainly did not share more of those stirring, spellbinding kisses.

Now that she was fairly certain most of the kinks of the market had been ironed out, she chose to split her time more evenly instead of spending all day at the market. She still worked at the kiosk for several hours, mostly in the evenings after she had worked at her downtown store.

She was fully aware Rafe worked almost the exact opposite schedule. He had told her that was the plan. Still, Amanda would never have admitted to anyone else that the reason she was so willing to turn over more responsibilities to her market kiosk team during the day might have something to do with the very sexy paramedic working across the row at the first aid station.

Finally, after the market had been open a week, she came in around five, expecting him to be gone.

Instead, almost the first thing she saw when she arrived was Rafe at the first aid station with Kelli Child, a woman several years younger than Amanda who sold her locally produced honey products at her kiosk several rows over.

Rafe's dark head was bent over the other woman's hand, turning it back and forth as he examined it.

Kelli was pretty, curvy, vivacious. Everything Amanda wasn't. She sighed, annoyed with herself.

The young woman was also obviously interested in Rafe. Amanda wasn't close enough to hear their conversation, but she could see the way Kelli angled her head just so and leaned her body closer to his big, muscular frame.

Amanda had heard rumors a few weeks ago that Kelli had recently broken up with her longtime boyfriend. Some kind of spat over credit card bills.

Rory owned a landscaping business and played in a band on the weekend. He was also ten years older than Kelli. Apparently she had a type, since Rafe was at least that.

Kelli said something and then laughed, a tinkling, delicate laugh that seemed to shriek like a fire alarm in the crowded hall. Rafe said something in response, giving Kelli a slow, amused smile that made Amanda shiver, even from the end of the row. Not her business. If he wanted to smile at a notorious flirt like Kelli Child, he was completely entitled. Kelli might be young but she was an adult, despite her surname.

Unfortunately, Amanda had to walk directly past them on the way to her shop. She could always go down the next row and walk halfway back up to The Lucky Goat stall, but that would just be silly, wouldn't it?

She drew in a breath, hitched her messenger bag over her shoulder and walked casually toward her shop.

Unfortunately, she had only taken a few steps when he spotted her.

"Amanda. Hi."

She widened her eyes, as if she had just noticed him. "Oh. Rafe. Hi. Hello, Kelli."

The woman clearly didn't look thrilled at the interruption. She glowered slightly before pasting on a fake smile.

"Hi, Amanda."

"I didn't expect to see you here this evening. I thought you were mostly working at the first aid station during the day."

As soon as her words were out, Amanda regretted them. He would likely sense—correctly—that she had been thinking about him entirely too much.

"That's right. Afternoons usually work better with Isaac's school schedule but the medic who was covering the first aid station tonight called in sick and Izzy already had plans, so I'm pinch-hitting. Isaac is spending the night with his grandparents. I believe they're going to watch the Lights on the Lake parade."

"Is that still going on?" Kelli rolled her eyes. "It was so lame the last time my friends and I went. Who wants to stand outside in the cold to watch a bunch of stupid boats go past?"

Amanda adored the festival that was one of the only joint activities between Shelter Springs and the neighboring town of Haven Point.

When she was a girl, she and Birdie and Griffin used to go every year, bundled up in their warmest coats, and hold their own judging contest. They would rank the boats that traveled between their marina and the one in Haven Point and back, choosing the rig with the best lights, the most unique decorations, the silliest, the most beautiful.

It was one of her favorite childhood memories about the holidays. She would much rather be wrapped up in a blanket on a lawn chair next to her grandmother, laughing and drinking hot cocoa while they watched festively lit boats go past under the stars.

Instead, she was here at the market, which was sure to become even more hectic with shoppers looking to come inside and warm up the moment the last boat sailed from Shelter Springs to make its way down to Haven Point.

"It's not lame if you're six years old and love boats," Rafe pointed out.

"I suppose that's true," Kelli conceded. "And it's always fun to go down to Haven Point and visit their little festival."

Amanda knew the early organizers of the Shelter Springs Giving Market originally started it as competition for the Haven Point Lights on the Lake Festival. Instead of holding a fair over only one night, as Haven Point did, Shelter Springs could have one that lasted an entire week. The event had steadily grown over the years until it was now a two-week-long extravaganza.

"I'm sorry you couldn't join Isaac and your parents to watch the boats," Amanda said.

"I'll survive. I'm sure he will tell me all about it tomorrow, in vivid detail. At least it will give him something else to talk about besides his visit to Santa a week ago."

She caught her breath at the reminder of the boy's wish for a mother for Christmas. A mother who wouldn't be her.

"In my limited experience, I don't believe Isaac must ever lack for something to talk about."

"True enough," he said with a smile before turning back to Kelli, finishing his work wrapping an elastic bandage around her wrist using his right arm as well as the one in the cast.

"There you go. That should help keep down the swelling if it's sprained, though you definitely want to have your doctor take some X-rays as soon as you can."

"Thanks."

"How did you hurt your wrist?" Amanda asked.

Kelli withdrew her arm with clear reluctance from Rafe's. "My stupid landlord didn't salt the steps again after the storm last night. I slid on the ice as I was walking to my car after I ran home for lunch to grab my phone charger."

At least her injury hadn't happened here at the market. Their liability insurer would appreciate that.

"It's been killing me all afternoon and I finally decided I should do something about it."

Amanda strongly suspected she had probably waited until Rafe came on duty.

Kelli examined her wrist from various angles. "Thanks. Great job. You're good at that."

"Um. Thanks."

"So good at it, in fact, I might ask you to wrap it again for me tomorrow."

"That might be a little tough since tomorrow is Sunday and I won't be here."

She made a face. "I forgot the market was closed tomorrow. I still think we should have stayed open every day. By closing on Sundays, we're missing half the weekend shoppers."

Amanda did not really feel like explaining all the reasons again to Kelli. Over the years, the organizing committee had experimented with staying open on Sundays but data showed they actually saw half the traffic on that day as other days of the week. Since many of the vendors ran one- or two-person operations, the decision had been made to remain open only six days of the week so that those hardworking merchants could have a chance to breathe.

"As you are so passionate about it, you should definitely write that comment in the suggestion form we've asked everyone with a booth to fill out. That helps us figure out what to do in the future." She gave a polite smile. "Also, you could always volunteer to be on the market committee next year."

Kelli grimaced, clearly not enamored with that idea. "Maybe. Between my YouTube videos, TikToks and Instagram, I don't have a lot of free time for this kind of thing, like you do."

Amanda wasn't exactly overflowing with empty hours she needed to fill, but she decided there was no point in responding to Kelli's barbed comment.

"I should get back," the other woman said after a moment. "My sister is filling in for me and she said she had to leave at five thirty."

Which had been at least twenty minutes earlier, Amanda thought rather sourly.

Kelli hopped up from the chair and placed her wrapped hand on Rafe's arm in an unmistakably proprietary gesture.

"Thanks again, Rafe. You're the sweetest."

He raised an eyebrow at her enthusiastic gushing but only gave her a slight smile in response. Kelli gave a little finger wave to Amanda and headed through the crowd toward her stall, which was on the other side of the convention hall.

"Are you planning to stay until the market closes, or will you have a chance to make it to any of the boat festival activities?" Rafe asked.

"I'm here for the duration, until closing. Later, actually. Our security guard will be a little late since he was going to the festival with his family, so I told him I would do the final walk-through to make sure all the vendors have locked up their stalls and everyone is out of the building."

"Is security for the event really a major concern?"

"Not normally but we caught a couple of kids hiding out in the bathrooms earlier in the week, waiting until everyone was gone so they could cause mischief and raid any unlocked shops. Apparently somebody at school dared them."

"I'm surprised it wasn't one of those lame social media challenges."

"It might have been, as far as I know. Anyway, we are trying to be extra vigilant now so I said I could stay after closing."

"Do you have someone staying with you?"

"No. I'm fine. The security guard should only be about half an hour later than normal, but that's long enough for someone up to no good to cause trouble."

"I'm not sure that's a great idea. You should have someone with you, especially if you've already had problems with trespassing kids."

"I'm not worried."

"Good for you. I am. As I said, Isaac is staying overnight at my parents' house after the boat festival. I'll stay with you when the market closes so there are two of us to do the final walk-through."

She instinctively wanted to argue, to tell him she was perfectly capable of handling the responsibility on her own. The truth was, though, while she was certain she could handle a

few juvenile delinquents, she would be grateful to have someone else here.

Amanda was embarrassed to admit that she didn't like being
alone in the huge convention hall. She found it more than a little spooky. Something about the empty rows of closed-up shops
that were usually bustling with activity seemed eerie, unnatural.

It seemed silly to argue with him when she would truly appreciate his presence. "Okay. If you're sure you don't mind,
thank you."

"I'll find you after the market closes."

She nodded and hurried on her way to The Lucky Goat
kiosk, where she donned her apron again, put on her most
cheerful smile and did her best to convince herself she had no
reason for this buzz of anticipation.

18

THREE HOURS LATER, AFTER THE MARKET OFFICIALLY closed and the few remaining merchants and shoppers made their way to the exits, Rafe was still asking himself why he had volunteered to spend even more time with Amanda Taylor.

He should have been coming up with a better strategy to stay away from the woman. Instead, he jumped at the first excuse to extend their time together. Worse, they would be alone here at the market, with only the empty stalls and darkened holiday decorations as company.

He had a vague feeling of dread, that he had made a huge mistake, but knew he couldn't back out now. He wouldn't, even if he managed to figure out a way.

He truly wasn't comfortable with the idea of her being here alone. He could only imagine someone with nefarious intent lurking around a corner, ready to attack her as soon as she was alone in the hall.

Yeah. He probably read too many thrillers. This was Shelter Springs. While the town certainly had its share of crimes, those were usually petty. Vandalism, theft, shoplifting. Kids who hid out in a bathroom on a dare. That sort of thing. Violent crimes were rare—but certainly not impossible.

Even if he hadn't volunteered to stay with her, Amanda most likely would be perfectly fine here until the night watchman came on duty.

He still didn't like the idea, and he would be able to sleep better that night knowing he had done his best to keep her safe.

After checking to ensure all the first aid supplies were locked away in the cabinets and making a quick note on his phone about the few items he and the other EMTs had used up the past few days so he could replenish stores for the following week, Rafe locked the door to the small room behind him and walked out into the hall. The lights had been dimmed in all the nearby stalls except one. The Lucky Goat.

He could see Amanda inside, illuminated by the glow of the Christmas lights that lined her shop. Her auburn hair seemed to glow in the lights, reflecting them like a halo around her head.

She was lovely, a vision of warmth in the midst of darkness.

She looked up as he approached, and he caught a fleeting expression in her eyes he couldn't immediately identify. "Oh. Hi."

"Hello. How was your evening? Your shop seemed busy, especially when the crowds came in after the boat festival."

"We had a good night. I've been thrilled with our first-week sales numbers. The market will still be open all this week and we already have almost matched last year's total numbers."

"That's great. Good work."

She gestured to him. "You really do not have to stay with me, Rafe. I'm sure you're anxious to get home to rest your arm after your long day."

Most of the time, he felt fine but sometimes his arm ached like somebody had come along and banged it against a brick wall for a few hours. He wasn't about to admit that to her, though.

"I don't mind at all," he said. "What's another half hour?"

She sighed. "You're not going to budge on this, are you?"

He shook his head, his expression firm.

She sighed. "Fine. I need to finish up here and close down the shop, then we can do the final walk-through."

"Anything I can do to help?"

"I'm only trying to refill the shelves so Scarlet, who is working first thing Monday, doesn't have to worry about anything but unlocking the store. I'm sorry to make you wait for a moment. I wanted to finish this earlier but, as you said, we were too busy for me to do anything but deal with customers."

"How can I help?"

"If you want to hand me items out of the box, I can put them in their designated spot."

They fell into an easy rhythm as he pulled out various scented soaps and lotions that she shelved in the appropriate slot. She clearly had a system and knew where everything belonged.

"What made you open a soap business?" he asked after a moment.

She gestured around the aromatic little wooden shop. "I sell far more than just soap, as you can see. The Lucky Goat offers natural lotions, skin care products, candles, lip balm. We also sell safe and organic cleaning products and certain carefully curated handmade items."

He smiled at the unmistakable note of pride in her voice. "What led you in this direction? I mean, you could have opened a shoe store or a candy shop or a clothing boutique. Why this?"

Her brow wrinkled as she pondered the question.

"I guess you could say I sort of fell into it. After college, I had two good friends in the area who were interested in augmenting their family incomes with something they could do around the schedules of their small children. They started experimenting with soaps and lotions. They wanted to sell their items at farmers' markets and festivals in the area but neither had the time available for a weekly commitment. I was working an online marketing job with a flexible schedule so I volunteered to handle their retail sales."

She returned the lid to the container and slid it out of sight under the counter. "Through that experience, that summer of traveling around the area going to fairs and markets, I realized there was a huge community out there of people looking for natural products to use in their homes and on their skin. On the other side of the equation, there were also many people, mostly women, who were making those products and trying to gain traction by selling on Etsy and other marketplaces like that. But it's hard to choose a scent from an online description, so I decided to fill both needs."

She glowed with enthusiasm when she talked about her store. Rafe was fascinated by the whole thing. Though he had taken a few business classes in school, he had never really been interested in commerce. Still, he respected the hell out of those willing to hustle to build something worthwhile that they enjoyed.

"It's not a huge moneymaking venture but that doesn't really matter to me. It's fun and rewarding and I'm surrounded by good people and lovely fragrances all the time. There are certainly worse ways to make a living."

Rafe could not disagree, though he expected his hands would smell like lavender for the rest of the weekend.

"What about you?" she asked, turning the tables. "What led you to a career as a firefighter and paramedic?"

He considered all the choices, good and bad, that had carried him to this place in his life. "While I was working on my degree, I spent summers fighting wildfires around the country."

"Were you a smoke jumper?"

"Hotshot."

"Sorry to be dense but what's the difference?"

"Smoke jumpers do exactly that. They parachute into a fire. Hotshots, on the other hand, hike up to remote areas carrying their gear. Both of them are badasses, though."

Her smile was slow and sweet and adorable. "And you were… a badass?"

"Still am," he deadpanned.

Her smile widened and he had to fight the urge to kiss her right there in the darkened market.

He cleared his throat. "I fought fires for a few years after I graduated from college while I was working as a volunteer fire-fighter and EMT here. I found the calls I enjoyed the most were the medical ones. I liked feeling like I was helping people. It seemed a natural progression to become a paramedic, especially since Shelter Springs had a big need."

"I'm sorry to sound stupid again but what is the difference between an EMT and a paramedic?"

"Mostly training. Paramedics have to undergo more extensive training in lifesaving methods. We can still do all the things EMTs can do, plus we can intubate, start IVs, read EKGs, etc. It took another two years of training."

Her eyes widened with surprise. "Wow. With all that training, you still fight fires?"

"I'm technically a firefighter paramedic. Chief Bennett and I are the only two here in Shelter Springs, though a few others are working toward it."

"So that means Shelter Springs is now down to one, at least until your arm heals."

He made a face. "A few more weeks and I'll be back on the job."

"The whole town will be better for it."

She grabbed her coat from a hook in the corner of the stall, and he stepped forward to help her into it, trying not to notice that she smelled far better than anything else found in her shop.

He helped her close up and lock the wooden stall tightly. When she had double-checked the locks, she stepped back.

"Where do we start?" Rafe asked.

"I guess we walk through row by row to make sure everything is secured for the night and there are no stragglers. We definitely need to check the restrooms."

"Do we need to check the outside section of the market as well?"

"Yes. Probably. I know the security guards walk through it

every so often. Let's work through the inside first, though. By then, Walt should be here."

They walked together in a comfortable silence for a few moments before she spoke in a low voice. "I don't think I have said this before but I'm very sorry about Caitlin. She used to come into the shop after she had Isaac. I liked her a lot. I was sad to hear what happened to her after she...she left town."

Rafe didn't like talking about the pain and loss and guilt associated with that time, but he was also grateful when people didn't try to pretend that part of his life had never happened.

"Thank you. I'm never quite sure what to say when people express their condolences to me. By the time she overdosed, I hardly recognized her. The woman I once loved had been lost somewhere along the way."

"That doesn't mean you don't miss the person she was before she gave in to her addictions," she said, her voice quiet.

"Yeah. I do." He paused. "It's hard not to blame myself. I knew she was struggling with her depression and anxiety and self-medicating with alcohol. When that no longer helped, she turned to other things. I tried to get her help. I tried to persuade her to go into rehab. I talked to various professionals about what steps I could take to help her. Nothing worked."

That feeling of helplessness those last few months of his marriage had been torture, dealing with Isaac basically as a single father by that point while trying to be the husband Caitlin had needed—compassionate and loving while walking the fine line between enabling her behavior.

Amanda stopped walking and turned to him, her features soft with compassion in the vast hall lit by only a single row of lights near the entrance. "You can't blame yourself, Rafe. I'm sure you tried everything you could. A person struggling with addiction needs to sometimes hit bottom before they can claw their way out."

She understood, he realized. Few others did, but Amanda had lived through the same thing from a child's perspective.

Everyone in town had known Dennis Taylor drank to excess—and that he was a mean drunk. It had been a poorly kept secret. He had to wonder what her life had been like, growing up under those circumstances.

Isaac had only been two when Caitlin started drinking more heavily, three when she left. Even then, as young as he had been, Rafe knew his son had suffered. During that time, Isaac had become anxious, irritable, prone to tantrums one moment and inconsolable tears the next.

Amanda had lived with an addict for a father throughout her childhood and her teen years. How difficult that must have been for her. After Dennis died in the fiery crash that killed four innocent teenagers, she had been forced to bear her own grief as well as the pain of knowing what her father had done.

Not long after that, she had lost her boyfriend when Jake Shepherd had died in that avalanche.

He had been under the influence, too. Rafe had definitely smelled alcohol on him while he had been working with Amanda's brother to resuscitate him.

Thinking of that teenager she had been, scarred by so much pain, made his heart hurt.

"You are a remarkably strong woman, Amanda."

She gazed at him, color suddenly tinting her cheeks. "Why do you say that?"

"You've been through trauma most people couldn't endure. The accident, your dad's death, Jake. Despite that, I've never seen you be anything other than generous and compassionate with everyone. Even those in town who aren't necessarily as generous and compassionate to you in return."

She flashed him a quick look, then glanced away. "I understand that sometimes people act without thinking, out of pain."

"A pain you had nothing to do with, other than being your father's daughter."

"That's more than enough reason."

"Can you honestly tell me it doesn't wound you when people don't come to your shop or refuse to serve on a committee with you because of your father?"

She released a heavy sigh. "It hurts," she admitted. "But I try to give grace where I can."

"Like I said. Remarkably strong."

She looked up at him, her expression a tangled mix of emotions. She hitched in a little breath, only a tiny puff of air, and her gaze shifted to his mouth for only an instant before she quickly looked away.

Rafe caught his breath and took a step toward her, framing her face with his hands.

"Remarkable," he murmured. A woman he simply couldn't resist.

He shouldn't be doing this. Even as he touched her soft skin, lowered his head, Rafe knew he was about to make a massive mistake.

Days after their previous kiss, he still hadn't managed to get it out of his mind. He remembered the scent of her, the softness of her skin, the taste of her, like maple syrup and coffee and heaven.

What was it about Amanda Taylor that seemed to burrow under his skin? That strength he was talking about, yes. Most definitely. But there was also vulnerability about her, a soft sweetness that made him want to shield her from anything rough happening to her ever again.

He had it bad for her.

He wasn't sure how it happened but he had begun to ache for this woman with the kind eyes and the generous heart. This certainly wasn't going to help, he thought in the instant before he lowered his mouth to hers.

Her mouth was everything he remembered and more. This time she tasted of hot cocoa and marshmallows with a little hint of cinnamon. She hesitated for only a moment, her body tight in his arms before he felt a small sigh against his mouth. Her hands slid around his neck and her mouth softened and he was lost.

EVEN BEFORE HIS MOUTH BRUSHED AGAINST HERS, IN that instant when the world seemed frozen, Amanda knew they should not be doing this.

She should ease away now, before everything between them became even more complicated.

How could she, though, when she felt as if she had been reliving their previous kiss all week long.

She was only vaguely aware of curling her fingers into his shirt, of angling her mouth just so. She didn't want to stop. Not now, not in a few moments, not for the rest of the night.

Maybe not ever.

She was falling for this man, with his slow smile and his hard strength and his adorable son. Despite a hundred reasons she knew she shouldn't and the certain knowledge that she was barreling headlong toward disaster, she still couldn't break away.

For now, this moment, she did not want to listen to the strident voice telling her all the reasons she should end the kiss.

As he deepened the kiss, she surrendered. When was the

last time she did something solely for herself? Right now, in this moment, she wanted to kiss him more than she could remember wanting anything else, ever. She would deal with the consequences later.

For long, glorious moments, she lost track of everything but how very right and perfect this felt, worlds better than any of her fragments of dreams over the past week. They might have continued indefinitely if she hadn't suddenly heard a door opening in the vast hall, then the echo of a man's voice calling her name.

"Amanda? Are you still here? It's Walt. I made it back a little earlier than I planned."

She froze, her heart pounding and her breathing ragged. Walt. Walt Randall, the retired Shelter Springs police officer who worked as the security guard for the town convention center.

Amanda wrenched her mouth away from Rafe's and took a shaky step backward, grateful when she backed into the rough wooden wall of one of the shops. She stared at Rafe, whose dark eyes looked almost as stunned as she felt.

She had to say something but she couldn't seem to make the connection work between her brain and her voice. She opened her mouth, closed it again, then tried once more.

"Yes. I'm here." Her voice sounded ragged, rough, and she cleared it again. "We're here. Row four, near Gingerbread House Gifts."

Her friend Barbara did a very thriving business selling beautiful one-of-a-kind gift baskets filled with hand-selected items she collected from various sources throughout the year.

Were Amanda's lips as swollen as they felt? Would Walt be able to guess what he had interrupted?

A moment later, the security guard walked around the corner and headed toward them.

"Hey, Rafe," he said in surprise. "I didn't know you were here, too."

Rafe gave a tight nod, his eyes hooded now. "I stayed to help Amanda do the final walk-through."

"We're not quite done," she admitted. *We both were distracted.*

"We only made it this far and we haven't checked the restrooms yet. Do you want us to continue?"

Amanda was quite proud that her voice didn't wobble like she suspected her knees were doing.

He waved a hand at them. "Not at all. I've got this. You're both probably ready to go home. You've already had a long day, I imagine."

Oh, he had no idea.

"Are you sure?" Rafe asked. "We can absolutely finish what we started."

At his phrasing, she sent him a swift look. He responded with a sidelong look that told her it was completely intentional.

"You want the truth, I'm looking forward to my shift tonight. Look what I had my grandson bring me when he came over today."

With a wide grin, he held out an electric scooter.

"I figured I'd try this bad boy out tonight on my rounds."

Amanda's head suddenly filled with images of Walt crashing into everything, falling and conking his head. The man was in his late sixties. He shouldn't be anywhere near a scooter, should he?

"Are you sure it's safe?" she asked.

Walt gave a deep-throated laugh. "Not at all. That's half the fun, right? I did practice with my grandkids earlier. They gave me some great tips. I only fell once."

That information didn't particularly make her feel any better.

"Promise me you'll be careful."

"I will. Don't you worry about me. Now go on. Get some rest, you two."

"Thank you."

She was touched when he gave her a little hug and a kiss on the cheek. Walt had always been kind to her. His daughter Erin, who now taught at the elementary school, had been one of Amanda's close friends growing up. Amanda had spent many happy hours at their house, especially on the elaborate backyard play set and zip line course Walt had built for his children.

The Randall family had been one of those who had stood by her after her father's fiery accident and she would always be grateful for it.

"Be careful," she admonished again, then she and Rafe headed for the exit.

"I don't have a great feeling about leaving Walter Randall by himself with an electric scooter and a great expanse of concrete floor," she said.

He gave a small laugh. "Right? What could possibly go wrong?"

"I hope he keeps his cell phone handy so he can call somebody for help if he falls down."

"Maybe I should alert the guys at the fire station to stand by, just in case."

"That might be overkill. He should be fine."

She hoped, anyway.

They walked through the convention center doors to the large brick plaza that held the outside stalls. The stalls were dark, though colored lights still sparkled from the large Christmas tree. A few snowflakes fluttered down in the moonlight, creating a scene straight out of a holiday movie.

"Where's your car?" Rafe asked. "I can walk you to it."

"I walked here from my house, actually. Downtown parking is such a mess during the market and I knew it would be even worse with the Lights on the Lake Festival underway."

At her words, he looked toward the dark expanse of Lake Haven, beyond the downtown area, where Amanda could still see a few splashes of color, brightly decorated boats making their way back to the Shelter Springs harbor.

"Smart," he answered. "I can give you a ride, if you want. I left my truck parked at the fire station, which is right on the way. It will save you a couple of steps, anyway."

She could see the recently renovated historic fire station from here, at the end of the block. After a moment's internal debate, she nodded. What was the point in arguing, when she likely wouldn't win anyway?

"Thank you. I would appreciate that."

They walked in silence as more soft snowflakes swirled around them. She knew they needed to talk about what had happened a few moments before, that unbelievably intense kiss.

She had no idea where to start. "Rafe," she started, then lapsed into silence again, not sure where to go after that.

"You don't have to say anything," he said, before she could form her thoughts into words. "I know we shouldn't have kissed again. Here's the problem, though. I like kissing you. If I had the chance, I would do it again."

Despite the snowflakes and the temperature only a degree or two above freezing, the December night suddenly felt warm. She had a wild impulse to stop right there, in the alcove of the garden supply store, and kiss him until no more words were needed between them.

"Well, you can't," she said, feeling childish and petulant.

He looked down at her. "Is that a challenge? Because I am more than willing to take you up on it."

Amanda curled her hands into fists and shoved them into the pockets of her parka. "We both know that's not a good idea."

"Do we?"

She flashed him a quick look and found his expression unreadable.

"Yes. Neither of us is…is in a good place for a relationship right now. Things are already complicated enough between us.

We're neighbors. That's not likely to change anytime soon. I love my house and don't intend to leave."

"Same. I just signed my life away in a thirty-year mortgage."

She swallowed, imagining the years stretching ahead of them with the unsettling knowledge that he and Isaac were only down the street.

"There you go. We are stuck as neighbors for the foreseeable future. Maybe years. I don't want to screw that up by...by making things between us messy."

"Hate to break it to you, Amanda, but things are already messy."

"All the more reason we should give our best effort at damage control."

He was silent for a few more steps. "Okay. If that's what you want, I understand."

The problem was, she didn't know what she wanted. When she was with him, all she wanted to do was kiss him again. When they were apart, she could only think about all the reasons she couldn't afford to take that kind of risk.

They reached the fire station parking lot and his pickup truck a moment later. Rafe unlocked it with a key fob and the lights flashed. He moved around to the passenger door and opened it for her.

She looked at the door and then at the night, with the snowflakes drifting lazily around them. "I really don't mind walking."

He frowned at her. "Get in, or I'll pick you up and toss you onto the seat."

She was almost certain he couldn't do that one-handed. "That would be kidnapping. And in the fire station parking lot, too. If you think the city threw a fit about you working at the first aid clinic with a broken arm, imagine what would happen if you have a kidnapping charge against you for an incident on city property. Also with a broken arm."

"I'm willing to risk it."

She didn't doubt it. For all his talk, she knew he wouldn't throw her into his truck. Since she had no good reason to refuse, though, she stepped up onto the running board and climbed into the passenger seat that smelled like him, clean and masculine.

He closed the door and moved around to the driver's side, started the truck and backed out of the space.

When he pulled onto Huckleberry Street, she almost suggested he park at his own house and she would walk home the rest of the way but she didn't want to push him. Instead, she kept her mouth shut as he drove four houses down and pulled into the driveway of Rose Cottage.

She somehow wasn't at all surprised when he climbed out of his truck, walked around the vehicle and opened her door.

He held his hand out to help her down. After a brief hesitation, she reached for it. The vehicle was high off the ground and she had a grim image of what might happen if she didn't take his hand. She would likely end up falling at his feet.

His hand was big and warm and she had to force herself to let go.

"Thank you for the ride."

"You're welcome. I'll walk you up."

His concern warmed her as much as his hand had. It was nice to have someone besides Birdie and Griffin care about her well-being.

"I like your Christmas tree," he said.

Her small artificial tree gleamed a cheery welcome through the front window, set on a timer to come on each evening at dusk.

"Thanks, but it's pretty bare. I can't leave many ornaments on it or the cats will knock them all off."

"It's still nice. We just put ours up the other night."

"I usually set up mine before Thanksgiving, since I know I'll be too busy once the holidays start in earnest."

He studied her. "Do you ever get a little tired of all the Christmas fuss? I would imagine you probably work on the market year-round. By the time the holidays arrive, aren't you ready for the whole thing to be over?"

"No, to be honest. Thanks to the market, I can actually tolerate Christmas. Otherwise, I would probably skip the whole thing and go to Hawaii or something."

He stared in surprise. "Did the Queen of the Shelter Springs Holiday Giving Market really say just say she would consider skipping Christmas? Why?"

She gripped the keys she had fished out of her bag, wishing she hadn't said anything. Now that she had started the conversation, she didn't see how she could avoid answering him.

"I don't have the greatest memories of the holidays from my childhood. My parents fought a lot about my dad's drinking and the holidays always seemed to heighten the tension in our home."

His dark eyes lost their teasing glint, filling with compassion instead. "I'm sorry. That can be rough on a kid."

She unlocked her front door, not looking at him as she moved forward slightly into the warmth of her entryway.

"And then Jake died a few days before Christmas. For a long time, I didn't want anything to do with the holidays."

"Yet now you're the fearless leader of the biggest holiday event in town."

"I wouldn't exactly say *fearless*." An understatement. If she were fearless, she would step forward and kiss him again without thinking at all about the consequences to her fragile heart.

"How does somebody go from wanting to completely avoid the holidays to taking the helm of something as relentlessly festive as the Shelter Springs Giving Market?"

She made a face. "I decided a few years after I opened the

store that I was tired of my annual holiday pity party, so I signed up for a stall at the market."

"What happened?"

"I loved it so much that the next year I volunteered for the committee. Being involved with the market helped me connect to the core meaning of the holidays. Peace, joy, renewal. Helping others. Caring about your fellow humans, who are all walking this tough road together."

His gaze softened into something almost...tender. "So you did it again the next year."

She nodded. "And the next. And the year after that I became the chair of the committee."

"And you haven't looked back."

She shrugged. "You have to look back sometimes, right? If only to see how far you've come."

His eyes were warm, with a light that almost looked...tender. "You're remarkable, Amanda."

She flushed. "Remarkably cheesy, you mean. Maybe I should be writing greeting cards."

He reached for her hand. "I think you're doing exactly what you were meant to do. Making the holidays brighter for everyone in town, visitors and residents alike."

His words sent a soft warmth seeping through her. "Thanks. I don't save lives like you do, though."

"My job might be to save lives. But you help make those lives have meaning."

"And now who's being cheesy?" she said, though his words touched her.

"Not me. I'm completely sincere."

They gazed at each other for a long moment, and she knew he wanted to kiss her again.

I like kissing you. If I had the chance, I would do it again.

He lowered his head slightly and she held her breath, waiting. Before he could kiss her, an orange blur leaped across the window next to the door and Amanda jumped before she realized what it was.

"Sorry. That's Willow. She's probably annoyed that I haven't paid her enough attention today."

As he gazed at her for a heartbeat, she almost thought he would pull her into his arms, anyway. Instead, he only leaned in to kiss her cheek.

"Good night, Amanda."

He waited until she slipped into her house, then headed down the walk toward his truck again.

She didn't watch him drive away. He wasn't going far, anyway, only a few houses away, and she didn't want him to see her gazing after him like some kind of lovesick teenager.

This wasn't love.

She simply refused to let it be.

20

AS MUCH AS SHE ADORED THE HOLIDAY MARKET, AMANDA
was always happy when it was nearly finished for the season.

She was running low on product for The Lucky Goat kiosk,
and a few of the shelves were empty. Her employees were
equally depleted of energy and enthusiasm for dealing with the
seemingly endless crowds of shoppers.

All week long, she had only been able to come to the market in the evenings. She told herself it was by necessity, since
she was so busy with holiday shoppers at her store as well, but
she knew the truth.

She was doing her best to avoid Rafe.

Yes, she was being a coward. Unfortunately, she had absolutely no willpower where the man was concerned. Despite
knowing all the risks and dangers, she was rushing headlong
into disaster, her feelings for him growing stronger every time
they were together.

After that last kiss between them, it had been easier to avoid him than to deal with the awkwardness of seeing him again or confronting this deep ache inside her for more.

On the Saturday before Christmas, the final day of the market, she had no choice but to spend the afternoon and evening at The Lucky Goat stall. She was shorthanded, with a few of her employees leaving early for the holidays to spend time with family out of town.

She not only had to deal with details of wrapping up the market from her position as the organizer but she also had to take down her products and decorations so the wooden stall could be disassembled after the holidays and stored with all the others in a vast warehouse on the edge of town.

She rather hoped Rafe wouldn't be there since it was the final day of the market. No luck. She saw him as soon as she turned the corner to head toward her kiosk. He stood just inside the first aid room.

For a fleeting moment, she thought about sneaking past him unseen, hiding herself among a quartet of women obviously out for a girls' day. She wouldn't be *that* cowardly, though. Instead, she drew in a breath, braced herself and moved toward him.

When he spotted her, his gaze seemed to brighten. "Amanda. Hi."

Oh, she had missed him. She hadn't realized it until this moment, standing in front of him again. How ridiculous was that? He wasn't hers to miss.

"How are you, Rafe? How's the arm?"

He held it up and she saw he now had a black brace instead of the old-style cast. "It's fine. I've transitioned to a removable cast, which is much more convenient. I don't have to wrap it up in plastic to take a shower."

She didn't want to think about the words *Rafe* and *shower* in the same sentence.

"Where's Isaac today?"

"Spending the day with his grandfather again. I think they plan to knock off some last-minute shopping."

"On the final Saturday before Christmas? Your father is brave. You know that's the busiest shopping day of the year, right? People usually think it's Black Friday. They're wrong. As a small business owner, I can tell you that I always have far more customers in my store today than on the day after Thanksgiving."

"Better my dad than me, I guess."

She managed a smile and gestured to the first aid station. "I imagine you're happy to be almost done with your assignment here. When will you be able to go back to work?"

"After the holidays. Working here hasn't been as bad as I feared. We didn't have to perform any dramatic rescues with the jaws of life but I've enjoyed the people watching. And I'm not as sick of Christmas music as I expected to be."

She smiled. "Maybe we'll see you back here next year, then."

"I wouldn't go quite that far."

"Here's hoping," she said.

They were interrupted by one of the vendors from out of town asking Rafe if he had any ibuprofen for a headache. With a wave, she left him to his duties and hurried the rest of the way to her market stall.

Throughout the day as she chatted with all the customers taking advantage of the last day clearance sales, she was aware of Rafe across the way.

She noticed when he attended to an older woman with a walking frame who seemed to be having a dizzy spell. When he helped Janet Pell from the crepe stand, who apparently had a small hot oil burn, when he rewrapped Kelli Child's wrist, which seemed to be taking an extraordinarily long time to heal.

She was trying not to stare as he chatted with a couple she didn't know when Cat Lewis spoke over her shoulder.

"He's mighty fine, isn't he?"

She jumped, caught unawares. "Who is?" She feigned ignorance. "I don't know what you're talking about."

"Don't you?" Cat gave her a knowing look. "I've seen those sneaky little peeks you've been taking at the town's sexiest paramedic. I can't say I blame you. The man should be on one of those smokin' firefighter calendars."

Amanda hoped Cat couldn't see her color rise. "I'm not looking at anyone," she lied. "Don't be ridiculous."

"Aren't you?" Cat's expression turned shrewd. "That's too bad, since that particular sexy firefighter in question keeps sneaking looks over here, too. Somehow I don't think married old me is the person who has caught his eye."

Despite the sharp thrill the words sent through her, Amanda forced herself not to react.

"Coincidence," she said promptly.

Cat looked disappointed. "I was really hoping I was sniffing a new romance in the air, along with all the peppermint and hot cocoa."

"Rafe and I are friends. That's all. He's been enormously helpful at the first aid station, even with his broken arm. I've also grown fond of his son, Isaac."

"He's a cutie," Cat agreed. "The two of them make quite an irresistible package. Too bad I'm not in the market for a sexy paramedic with a cute kid."

Neither was Amanda, she reminded herself. She spent the rest of the afternoon and evening doing her best to avoid even accidentally glancing in that direction.

Finally, after what felt like an endless day, the last shoppers wandered out of the convention hall, the food concessionaires started cleaning their grills and other merchants began packing up their wares.

"Well, looks like we survived another market."

She smiled at Cat. "It's been a record-breaking event."

"How long before you have to start planning for next year?"

her friend asked as she pulled out boxes from under the counter and began filling them with their few remaining unsold items.

"Not yet, thank heavens. Give me a few months to catch my breath first."

She and Cat quickly packed up the rest of the inventory and worked together to pull down their sign and the brightly colored Christmas lights from the facade of the shop.

She picked up two boxes to carry out to her SUV. With a tired sigh, Cat did the same. "I've got this," Amanda said. "Go home and take a rest. You've earned it."

"I don't mind helping."

"I know, but you're dead on your feet. This won't take me long."

Cat looked as if she wanted to argue but she finally sighed. "You're as tired as I am, but you definitely beat me in the stubborn department. All right. I'll take off. I'll carry what I can to my car and drop it at the store on Monday."

If her arms were not loaded with boxes, she would have hugged her friend. Instead, she could only nod as she turned toward the exit nearest where she had parked. She only made it a few steps when Rafe joined her, reaching for the boxes. "Here. Let me carry that out for you."

"You don't have to do that. You have a broken arm."

He raised an eyebrow. "Which doesn't stop me from carrying a few light boxes."

If she was stubborn, Rafe was positively intractable.

"Thank you, then," she said with as much graciousness as she could muster. She grabbed another two boxes and followed him out the door.

She led the way to her SUV, where she popped the hatch with her key. He slid in the boxes he carried, then took the other two from her so he could place them in as well.

"Are you clearing everything from your kiosk out tonight?"

She nodded. "I find it's always better to take care of it the night the market closes rather than drag it out through the weekend, like some of the vendors prefer to do. When it's over, I want to be done."

"I can understand that. I'll help you finish up."

"I would appreciate that, if you're sure you don't mind. Cat was more than willing to help me, but she was dead on her feet and ready to go home."

"No problem."

They made several more trips, loading up every inch of her vehicle, from the cargo area to the back row of seats and even the passenger seat.

They had picked up the final trio of boxes when they bumped into Isaac and his grandfather.

The boy beamed with delight. "Hi, Amanda!"

"Hello, Isaac. Mr. Arredondo."

"What are you guys doing here?" Rafe asked. "I was planning to come pick Isaac up at the house after I finished helping Amanda load up."

"We figured we would drop by and see if your mom and Crista might need help taking down their booth."

Guilt flashed across Rafe's features, as if he had only then remembered his mother and sister-in-law would also be carrying boxes out of the convention center.

"Right. Let me take these last few boxes out to Amanda's car then I'll come back and help Mom and Crista."

"Can I help you?" Isaac asked Amanda.

She set down her boxes on the counter and handed him the smallest one from the top.

"Here's a box that's just Isaac-size," Amanda said. "Is that one too heavy for you?"

"No. I'm not as strong as my dad but I still have muscles."

From what she knew of the man, Amanda could think of few people as strong as Rafe.

"I'll head over to find your mom and Crista, then," Al Arredondo said.

Rafe nodded. "We'll be there soon."

Together, he, Amanda and Isaac carried the rest of her boxes out to her SUV and managed to find room on the floor of the passenger seat.

"Thank you," she said as they returned to the convention hall. "You helped shorten a job that would have taken me another hour."

"My pleasure," Rafe said, with a slow smile that made her toes curl.

"Hey, Amanda." Isaac skipped along beside them. "Guess what? Christmas Eve will be here in only three more sleeps!"

"I know. Isn't that exciting?"

"And yesterday was my last day of school. And tomorrow is my concert."

"Oh. You're having a Christmas concert?"

"Not just Christmas. It's our December concert for all the holidays. The whole school is in it."

"That sounds great."

"It will be," he said with complete confidence. "Anybody can go see it. Do you want to come?"

"Um. I would think the concert is for the families of the students who are performing."

He shook his head vigorously, his dark curls flopping. "Not *only* for family. Miss Watson said our friends can come to see us if they want. You're my friend, aren't you?"

She sent a helpless look at Rafe.

"This is a hectic time of year for people," he said gently to his son. "Amanda is extra busy. She's been working hard here at the market for the past few weeks and she's also got her store in town. She might not have time to come to a school show, especially since she doesn't have any kids performing in it."

Amanda let out a breath. She had once wanted a house full

of children but fate had other plans for her. She fought down the instinctive sadness over something she couldn't change.

Her circumstances didn't mean she had to stay at home and feel sorry for herself.

"You know what?" she said suddenly. "I would love to see your concert. You said it's tomorrow? On Sunday? Are you sure?"

Isaac's eyes lit up with excitement. "That's right. We're doing it that day so more people maybe can go, like grandmas and grandpas from out of town. It starts at six o'clock, but you should probably be there a little bit early if you can. My teacher said it's going to be packed and there might not be enough seats for everyone. Do you know where the elementary school is?"

She smiled. "I actually went to that same elementary school a long time ago."

It had been rebuilt since then but at the same location.

"My dad went there, too," Isaac said, eyes bright. "Did you know my dad when he was a kid like me?"

She and Rafe again exchanged looks. "I did, actually. I didn't know him very well. He was older than me by a few years and he was one of the boys who always played basketball or football out in the playground. But I definitely remember him."

Rafe gave her a sidelong look, his eyes sparkling as much as his son's. "I hope I wasn't mean to you or something."

"I never saw you be mean to anybody." She plucked a sudden memory from the depths of her subconscious. "Once, I fell on the playground and scraped my knee. I was crying and upset, thinking my mom was going to be so mad at me for ripping my jeans. I remember you helped me to the office and made sure I got a bandage. I guess you were in training to be a first responder, even back then."

"My dad is one of the helpers," Isaac said proudly.

"I know. Aren't we so lucky to have him?"

Rafe looked embarrassed as he opened the door to the convention hall for them. "I don't remember that. I'll have to take your word that it really happened."

"It did," she answered, just as Mr. Arredondo came toward them, carrying a couple of boxes.

"I can get those," Rafe said, but his father held them out of his reach.

"I'm good. They're not heavy."

"How many more boxes does Crista have?"

"A few, plus the display easels and racks."

"We'll head there now," Rafe said.

"I would be happy to help them take the booth apart, especially after you and Isaac helped me," Amanda offered.

Always try to pay it forward. That was one lesson Birdie had tried to teach both her and Griffin.

To her relief, Rafe didn't argue. "Thank you," he said and headed toward Crista's stall.

Isaac didn't release her hand as they walked, chattering about his program and his friends and how he couldn't wait for Christmas. She had no idea why the boy seemed to like her so much, but she was too charmed by his sweet affection to question it too much.

Crista's booth seemed bare and rather forlorn without all of her beautiful watercolors on display and with only a few of the hand-painted wooden ornaments and Nativity figures that Amanda had always found lovely and detailed.

"Hi, *Abi*. Hi, Aunt Crista," Isaac called out as they approached.

Louise looked up with a bright smile for her grandson. As soon as she spotted Amanda walking beside her son, her smile faded like cocoa left to cool too long.

She gave Amanda a rather stiff nod that she tried to return with more warmth.

"We came to help you carry stuff outside," Isaac announced. "Good thing I have big muscles, huh?"

She gave her grandson an affectionate pat on his curls. "Yes. It's a very good thing."

Louise turned back to Amanda. "Don't you have your own market stall to take down?"

"I'm done, actually. Your son and grandson were kind enough to help me. I'm happy to help you."

"Thank you, but we can handle it ourselves," Louise said, her voice firm. She wasn't overtly rude but she also made it clear as fresh ice that Amanda was not welcome within her family circle, even in something as benign as helping them take down their booth.

Under other circumstances, Amanda might have nodded politely and walked away. But Rafe had been kind enough to help her and she felt compelled to help his family in return.

Whether his mother liked it or not.

"I don't mind," she said calmly.

She picked up an empty compartmentalized box and gestured to the wooden ornaments hanging on pegboards. "Do these go in here?"

Crista came forward. "Yes."

"Would you like them wrapped in paper or anything?"

"No. They should be fine in the box," his sister-in-law said with a smile. "Thank you."

Amanda nodded and went to work, trying her best to focus on the task at hand instead of Louise's coolness and the reason behind it.

21

RAFE ADORED HIS MOTHER, BUT SOMETIMES SHE COULD
be more stubborn and unreasonable than he was.

It made him hurt for Amanda, for the stigma she bore with
some in town simply because her father had been Dennis Taylor.

She didn't seem to be bothered by his mother's obvious reluctance to accept her help, though he knew it must sting.

Instead, Amanda simply went to work helping load the remaining merchandise into boxes and taking apart the shelving
units and pegboard. She listened to Isaac's nonstop chatter, she
was cordial to his father, she talked easily with Crista, who apparently served on a library committee with Amanda.

When his brother, Joe, and their two kids showed up to help,
she seemed easy and comfortable with them, too.

She didn't even seem to notice that his mother's spine was
straight as a frosty tree branch, about to snap.

Finally, when everything had been packed away, he saw that
Amanda's mouth was tight with fatigue. He wanted to pick her

up, tuck her against his chest and carry her out to her SUV. If not for his stupid broken arm, he might have tried it.

She stayed at it until they had carried the last display piece out to Joe's truck, then gave them all a polite smile.

"I'll take off, then. Thank you for all your hard work making the market a success," she said to Crista. "I hope you'll think about coming back next year. Your paintings and ornaments have always been a huge hit."

Crista shuddered. "It's hard to think about next year at this point, to be honest. Right now if I never see another watercolor brush again, I won't mind at all. I just want to get through the holidays and make it safely to Utah next week to see my family. But I expect I'll be back again next year. I love doing it."

"I'm glad to hear that. Good night, everyone."

Rafe did not like the idea of her walking to the car by herself. "I think we'll take off, too," he said quickly. "I can come over to the house if you need me to help you unload the truck."

"Not necessary," his younger brother said. "I'm going to park the truck in the garage and unload after the holidays."

Rafe hugged his mother and sister-in-law, nodded to his dad, then grabbed Isaac's hand. His son was tired as well. Rafe could see the signs, confirmed when Isaac didn't protest at having to leave before his cousins did.

The two of them headed out behind Amanda, reaching her as she walked out of the convention hall to the parking lot. She looked up in surprise when she sensed their presence. "Oh. I didn't realize you were leaving as well."

"Yes. It's been a long day for Isaac. We're parked right by you," he pointed out.

"Oh. Of course."

"Bye, Amanda," Isaac said, giving her another of his generous hugs that always seemed to take her by surprise.

"I'm sorry about my mom," Rafe murmured. "I'll talk to her."

She shook her head with vigor, looking alarmed. "Don't. She didn't do anything."

"Maybe not overtly. But we both know she wasn't very gracious, when you were only trying to help."

She shoved her hands in the pockets of her parka. "My presence upsets her. I understand that. The pain of losing your cousin is still fresh and I'm a reminder of that."

"She can't hold you responsible for something that was not your fault in the slightest," he pointed out again.

"Look! It's snowing," Isaac exclaimed, interrupting their conversation. He stuck his tongue out to catch a snowflake, which made Amanda smile and lose some of her fatigue.

"Good night," Rafe murmured. "I hope you have a restful day tomorrow."

"I plan to sit on my sofa and do absolutely nothing except cuddle my cats, read a good book and maybe wrap a few presents."

"You're going to come to my concert, though. Right?" Isaac said anxiously.

She smiled. "I'll be there. A delightful December concert will be exactly what I need to put me in the holiday mood."

"I wish we had a cat," Isaac said. "Can I come visit your cats?"

"Sure. Whenever you want, as long as your dad says it's okay."

"We'll see."

He sure hoped Isaac didn't become a nuisance. His son could go after what he wanted with a single-minded determination he only could have inherited from Rafe.

"Good night. It's been fun hanging out across the row from you for the past two weeks," he said.

She gave him a doubtful look. "Why don't I believe you?"

"Maybe under all those cute holiday sweaters, you're a big skeptic."

"Possibly."

"Good night," he said again, leaning in to kiss her cheek, savoring the scent of cookies and strawberries and Amanda.

He would have liked to give her another real kiss but it was snowing and the parking lot was filled with people, including his son.

She had told him he couldn't kiss her again. That didn't stop him from wishing for something he couldn't have.

Rafe found the chance to talk to his mother about Amanda the next day when he and Isaac decided on impulse to drive to the Shelter Inn retirement apartments to visit Paolo the afternoon before Isaac's school performance.

They had just walked inside the building, Isaac running ahead, when Rafe spotted his parents coming toward them from the other direction.

"Well, hello," Louise said with delight, hugging Isaac. "This is a nice surprise. What are you doing here?"

"We made chocolate pretzel logs today and thought *Abuelo* might like some," Isaac informed her. "We have red ones and green ones and some that are red *and* green. They're soooo good."

"I'm sure he will love them. That's very nice of you," she said with raised eyebrows at Rafe.

"I had a wild hare," he said with a shrug. "We made some for our neighbors and had some extras. I had to come up with something to keep Isaac entertained today. He's been awake and going hard since six and is a little jacked up for his show tonight. And for Christmas in general, I guess."

She chuckled. "Boy, can I relate to that. You always loved the holidays. You had enough energy all through the month of December to light up the whole town's Christmas lights."

"Sorry I was such a pain."

His ADHD had seemed like a curse when he was younger, until he figured out strategies to deal with it, like staying physically active.

"You were never a pain," his mother declared, giving him a fond smile. "You just had a big personality trapped in a child's body."

"Well, thanks for putting up with me."

She shook her head. "I would do it all over again a hundred times if I had the chance."

"Can I go see *Abuelo*?" Isaac asked, clearly impatient with the conversation and eager to give their treat to his great-grandfather.

"Yes. Go ahead."

"Do you think he'll let me play with the remote control car while I'm here?"

"I wouldn't be at all surprised."

Isaac grinned with delight and raced toward his grandfather's apartment, carrying the plate of pretzels they had made.

"I'll come with you, *mijo*. I think I forgot my hat," Rafe's father said.

It was the perfect opportunity to talk to his mother, one he couldn't pass up.

"Have you been visiting *Abuelo* all afternoon?"

"No. Only a few minutes. I made green pozole today and you know how much he likes it, so we decided to drop some off for him so he doesn't have to fix dinner before the concert tonight."

"That's nice of you." His mother was usually kind to everyone, which made her coolness to Amanda stand out in stark contrast.

"I'm actually glad to have the chance to talk to you."

"I'm always glad to talk to you too, son," she said with a smile.

He hesitated, remembering that Amanda had asked him not to talk to his mother. He decided he needed to do it, anyway, even if he did feel more than a twinge of guilt at overriding her wishes.

"I wanted to ask you something."

"Oh?"

No other way to do this than to be straight. "Why don't you like Amanda Taylor?"

She visibly tensed, suddenly wary. "Who said I don't like her? She's a lovely woman."

"Yes. She is. Yet you hardly ever exchange even a handful of words with her."

"Sure I do." Louise looked startled. "I talk to her all the time. I chatted with her last night while she was helping us take down your sister-in-law's booth at the market."

"No. You didn't. When you couldn't avoid her completely, you spoke in monosyllables."

She gave him a sharp-eyed look. "Why should it matter to you whether I talk to Amanda? Are you interested in her?"

He wasn't prepared for his mother to turn the questions back on him, though he should have been. That was one of her favorite tactics to catch her children off guard. Follow a question with a question.

"We're friends," he said, grateful he didn't blush or he would be fiery red in this moment. "We happen to be close neighbors now, and for reasons I don't quite understand, Isaac suddenly adores her. Beyond that, she works tremendously hard for the town of Shelter Springs."

His mother was still eyeing him with growing interest, making him wish he had never brought up the topic.

"There's more to it, though, isn't there?" Louise said.

He could never seem to fool his mother. Even when he had been an unruly teenager, into trouble with his cousin and his brother, Louise had somehow always known. She used to tell them she had spies everywhere.

They had believed her. How else could she have such an uncanny knack for finding out all the dumb things they used to do?

"Amanda is a kind woman who has endured a great deal of tragedy in her life. She's also innocent of anything her father did. It's not her fault Dennis Taylor climbed behind the wheel while under the influence. It's not fair to blame her for Alex's death."

"I don't," she protested.

"On some level, I think you do. Why else would you be so cool to her? You're always friendly to everyone else except Amanda. It's a stark contrast, obvious to everyone."

His mother looked horrified. "If that is true, I'm sorry," his mother said after a long moment. "I didn't mean to hurt her. I wasn't aware I treat her any differently than anyone else or that anyone else could sense my...turmoil."

"She can see it. It cuts her. For what it's worth, she blames herself, not you."

His mother closed her eyes. When she opened them, he saw they were filled with sadness. "You're right. When I see Amanda, I'm reminded of her father and that dark time, as fresh and raw as if it happened yesterday. When I see her, I somehow feel like we have lost our Alex all over again, right at the time of his life when he was on the brink of amazing things. It makes my heart hurt."

"Mom. I miss him, too." Alex had been far more than just a cousin. He had been Rafe's best friend, as close to him as Joe and their sister. "But imagine for a moment how hard all of this has been for Amanda over the years. She was only a teenager too, yet for all this time, she has been forced to carry the weight of her father's choices."

His mother pressed a hand to her mouth and he saw tears forming in her eyes. "That poor girl. She must hate me."

"No. She doesn't hate anyone. She only feels sorrow for us and the pain our family and all the other families involved have endured. I'm afraid some part of her feels like she has to pay penance for what her father did."

"She most certainly does not. Oh, that breaks my heart. How do I make it right? I should talk to her. Apologize."

He considered that. If his mother talked to her, Amanda would know he had gone to Louise despite her wishes. She would likely be angry with him. He decided that was a small price to pay if it eased some of her pain.

"You could talk to her, if you feel it's necessary. Or you can simply try to treat her from now on with the same warmth and kindness you show to everyone else. I think that would make a big difference for her."

"I will definitely do that," Louise vowed. She gave him a careful look, and Rafe tried to keep his expression impassive and bland.

He apparently didn't succeed.

"You *do* like her, don't you?"

He frowned, feeling his face heat again. "I told you. We're friends and neighbors."

Louise chuckled again and reached up to touch his cheek. "I know my son. I suspect there is more to it than that. But you don't have to tell me right now."

He hesitated, then plunged forward. "Would it bother you, given all the history between our families, if Amanda and I did start to…have a relationship?"

He couldn't quite believe he was actually considering the possibility—or that he was talking to his mother about it. But somehow over the past month, Amanda had started to work her way into his heart.

"Absolutely not," Louise assured him, looking delighted. "If she makes you happy and treats you and Isaac in a loving, kind way, that's all I want for you. Especially after everything the two of you have been through."

"Thanks." He hugged his mother, grateful for her constant support. He suspected her feelings toward Amanda wouldn't change in an instant, but he knew that now Louise was aware her reserve was hurtful, she would do everything possible to change it.

His mom would be on board. Now he only had to persuade Amanda to give them a chance.

He expected that to be a much harder sell.

22

FEW THINGS MADE AMANDA FEEL MORE OUT OF PLACE than attending an event where she was a lone woman surrounded by happy, enthusiastic families.

As she walked through the doors of Shelter Springs Elementary, Amanda wondered again why she had agreed to attend the school concert.

Yes, Isaac had invited her. It wasn't a command performance. She could have refused or simply stayed away. Right now, she could be at home on her sofa with a cat on either side of her, a bowl of popcorn on her lap and one of her favorite Christmas movies playing on her television.

Instead, she stood outside the auditorium while a swell of noise and excitement seemed to ripple out from the children and their families.

This would be fun, she told herself. A big burst of holiday cheer to carry her through Christmas.

She walked inside and looked around for a seat. The auditorium was part of the major school rebuild that had been

done a decade earlier. Before that, in her time, all school performances and events had taken place in the gymnasium that
also served as the dodgeball arena, the volleyball court and the
school cafeteria.

Now the elementary school had a dedicated auditorium that
could host community events as well as special school assem-
blies and cultural performances.

The room was filled to capacity with parents, grandparents,
siblings of the students. Apparently the evening would be split,
she had learned by talking to her friend McKenna. In order
to accommodate students in all grades, the younger students
in grades kindergarten through second would be performing
their concert first. After they finished, the students in grades
three through five would take the stage.

Family members could be free to leave after their students
performed, though some attendees would attend both shows if
they had children or grandchildren in multiple grades.

Amanda had already decided she would only stay for Isaac's
turn, then would slip away again so that someone else could
take her seat.

She was searching for an empty spot when she spotted Mc-
Kenna waving at her from three rows ahead.

"Amanda! Come sit here! We saved you a seat."

She looked down the row and saw McKenna's family as well
as Griffin and Natalie. Travis Dodd sat next to McKenna with
their youngest daughter, Nora, beside him. Amanda's brother,
next to Travis, was holding the Dodds' son that he had helped
deliver a year earlier on Christmas Eve.

"Are you here to see Hazel?" Nora asked when Amanda sat
down in the empty seat on the row, next to Natalie.

"Definitely. Along with the other children."

"I wish I could be in the show," the girl said with a pout.
"Hazel gets to wear reindeer antlers and a red nose like Rudolph."

"You will be," her aunt Natalie assured her. "Next year. You'll be in kindergarten with all your friends. I know you'll sound amazing."

Nora seemed content with that.

"Let's see your sweater today," McKenna ordered. Amanda unzipped her parka to reveal one of her favorites, with a cat twisted in tangled Christmas lights and the words *Meowy Christmas*. The sweater was a wild explosion of color, as if someone had let a reindeer loose on a knitting machine after a few too many eggnogs.

"I love it," Nat exclaimed. "Where on earth do you find them?"

"I order a few online and search boutiques for them. Thrift stores are also great places to find ugly sweaters. I even have suppliers to my store who find them for me."

While they waited for the concert to begin, they all chatted easily about her sweater collection, about their holiday plans, about the charitable proceeds from the market. Somehow in the course of the conversation, Amanda ended up holding little Austin, who seemed fascinated by the colors on her sweater.

She was laughing at a story McKenna shared about the girls trying to make sure they stayed on the nice list at all costs when she caught sight of a familiar figure.

Rafe sat in the section next to them, two rows ahead, with his mother and father and his brother and their children. Also on the row, she saw to her surprise, were Paolo and Birdie. Her grandmother looked particularly festive with a gold-and-green headband that somehow complemented the purple streaks in her hair.

Birdie seemed completely comfortable with the Arredondo family, as if she had belonged in their midst her entire life.

Amanda frowned, trying to ignore the niggling worry for her grandmother. She truly hoped Birdie wasn't headed for heartbreak but had to trust her grandmother knew what she was doing.

Austin apparently didn't like her frown. He fretted and Amanda quickly turned her attention away from her grandmother's romantic life to nuzzle his neck until he beamed and giggled at her.

When she looked up again, she found Rafe watching her, dark eyes glittering with an intense expression that made her feel hot and jittery.

"Are you going to the Shelter Inn potluck tomorrow?" Natalie asked.

With effort, Amanda forced herself to look away from him and focus on her dearest friend. "I haven't decided. I'll be working at the store until at least six and the potluck starts at seven. That doesn't give me much time to make anything to share, unless I find time tonight."

"You can buy something on your way," Nat answered. "Or not. That's fine, too. You don't have to provide anything. No one will care. It's about family and community and being together, not about whatever food you take. I know Birdie would want you there."

"I will have to see how things go tomorrow," she answered. "How are the wedding plans?"

Nat rolled her eyes. "I haven't thought about it for longer than about five minutes. I've been so busy trying to wrap up a couple of articles about our trip to Guatemala that everything else has sort of fallen by the wayside."

"I'm here to do whatever you need. Let's plan to meet after the holidays with Kenna so we can make some concrete plans."

"We'll have to squeeze it in, since I'm leaving in mid-January for the Netherlands."

She admired the busy life Natalie had created for herself as a digital nomad, writing travel articles, freelance editing and caring for other people's houses and pets.

Natalie had literally seen the world, while Amanda rarely even traveled thirty miles away from Lake Haven.

She was about to address Nat's concerns when the school principal, a frequent customer of The Lucky Goat and one of Amanda's favorite people, walked onstage and the crowd went silent.

"Welcome to the Shelter Springs Elementary School holiday concert," Elizabeth Williams said with a bright smile. "All of our students, teachers and staff have worked so very hard to bring you this show in hopes of adding to your holiday spirit. Without further ado, let's welcome our kindergarten class."

The curtains opened to reveal an adorable group of children standing on risers.

The children looked giddy with excitement, all but vibrating with it as they waved with glee to their parents and friends.

"That's my sister," Nora said loudly, clapping as hard as anyone in the room.

On her lap, Austin seemed startled by the loud applause, then threw his own chubby little hands together with an enthusiasm that made her smile.

The show was delightful. The four kindergarten classes sang a few classics like "Jingle Bells," "Rudolph the Red-Nosed Reindeer" and one Amanda didn't know about Santa Claus.

Hazel Dodd sang her little heart out, her face screwed up with intensity as if she were performing an emotional opera in front of an audience of thousands.

They finished to thunderous applause and bowed several times before the curtain closed. After a noisy few moments when they could hear children's loud voices behind the curtain, it opened again to reveal the first graders.

Again, the new group of children waved to their family members. She spotted Isaac easily with his glasses and curly dark hair. To her delight, the boy waved to his family and then, spotting her in the crowd, he waved just as vigorously to her.

His grade sang four songs with as much glee as the kinder-gartners. Isaac waved to her twice more.

"You certainly have a fan in little Isaac Arredondo, don't you?" Natalie murmured after the curtain closed on his grade.

She remembered how Isaac had told Santa he wanted a mother for Christmas. She certainly couldn't tell that to Natalie.

"He's an adorable kid. I don't quite know why, but he has decided I'm his new best friend."

"I mean. The kid would be cute enough on his own. Throw in his hot dad and the two make quite a package."

She wanted to say she wasn't interested in Rafe, but the words seemed hollow, patently false, so she merely smiled.

After the first graders left, the curtain opened again on the second graders. She decided to wait until they were finished before leaving. When the first concert ended, she quickly said goodbye to her brother and Natalie as well as McKenna and Travis, who all planned to stay for the next concert. Amanda made her way to the hall outside the auditorium. Her hopes for a quick exit were dashed when Isaac came bolting over to her as the children were led inside to rejoin their families.

He threw his arms around her waist. "Did you hear me, Amanda?"

"I sure did," she said, hugging him back. "Those were some wonderful songs."

"Which one did you like the best?"

"Um. That's hard to pick. I liked them all."

"Dad, which one did you like?"

She looked over her shoulder to find Rafe coming out of the auditorium. He seemed struck to find her with Isaac.

"Amanda's exactly right. That's too hard to pick. You knew all the words to every song, though. I didn't see you miss a single line. Way to practice, kiddo."

Isaac beamed at his father and Amanda felt warmth seep through her. She couldn't help contrasting Rafe's fathering style to that of Dennis Taylor, who had either been distant to her and Griffin, too busy with his practice to pay them much attention, or hostile and angry and drunk.

Rafe was a wonderful father, doing his best to provide his son all the love and care the boy couldn't receive from his mother now.

"Thank you so much for inviting me," she said to Isaac. "I enjoyed it very much."

"You're welcome. I waved at you. Did you see?"

She smiled. "I did. I waved back. Did you see me?"

He nodded just as Rafe's parents emerged from the auditorium.

"There's our darling boy." Louise Arredondo swept Isaac into a hug. "You sang so beautifully. I was so proud of you."

"Thanks, *Abi*."

Amanda wanted to slip away as the family talked about the concert and the songs they liked best, but to her vast surprise, Rafe's mother stepped forward and slipped an arm through hers as if they were old and dear friends.

"Amanda. Lovely to see you again. How nice of you to come and watch the school concert."

She almost stared at the woman, agape at her friendliness. Gathering her composure, she smiled. "It was my pleasure. I was honored that Isaac invited me."

Louise looked down at her grandson, who was busy telling his grandfather and father about all of his classmates.

"He is certainly fond of you," she said in a low voice. "He talked about you nonstop this week, every time he came to see us at the market. How pretty you are. How nice you are. I think he has a bit of a crush on you."

Amanda felt distinctly uncomfortable, as if she had done something wrong. "I'm sorry. I don't understand it myself. I'll try to talk to him."

"Why? It's very sweet." Louise looked around and then lowered her voice even further. "I'm not sure he's the only one. I think my son might feel the same way."

She felt hot, suddenly, like a teapot left too long on the stove. "Mrs. Arredondo. I assure you, Rafe and I are...we're only friends. You don't have to worry about anything."

"Worry? Why should I worry?" Louise smiled.

"I know I'm probably the last person in town you would like to see involved with your son. I understand that. I would never want to do anything to bring more pain to your family."

To her shock, Louise hugged her arm more tightly. "Rafael and I had a talk earlier today about you. You should know how concerned he was for you. He made me see that I have not treated you as kindly as I should have since...since our Alex died. I haven't been able to stop thinking about what he said. I've been unfair to you and I'm very sorry for that. I hope you can forgive me, Amanda."

Amanda didn't know what to say. She glanced over at Rafe and found him watching her and his mother, his expression veiled. She wrenched her gaze back to his mother.

"You've done nothing wrong. Nothing. You were grieving your nephew. I completely understood. My father is the only one to blame here."

"Exactly. Your father. Not you. You were a child, Amanda. A *child*."

Tears welled in the other woman's green eyes, so different from her son's warm brown but somehow no less comforting.

"Your father was an addict. He had an illness. Do I wish he had been able to get help for it? Yes. Do I wish he had never climbed behind the wheel that night? Of course. But he did. It happened and the ripple effects have impacted all of our lives. Maybe especially yours."

Louise gave her a full hug now, and Amanda felt tears gather in her own eyes as she felt years of guilt lift from her shoulders.

"I love that my grandson enjoys being in your company so

much. And if my son does as well, I'm delighted with that, too. He has seen too much sadness in his life. Both of you have."

In light of Louise's sudden kindness, Amanda did not have the heart to reiterate that she and Rafe were only friends.

Yes, they were friends who had exchanged a few very heated kisses, but that's all they would ever have.

She was spared from having to answer when Elizabeth's voice came over the sound system in the hallway.

"Those of you who are staying for the second concert, we would ask you to begin taking your seats again."

Louise smiled. "We're going in to watch our other two grandchildren. You're welcome to join us, if you would like. We have an extra seat."

She knew the woman was offering a sturdy, reliable olive branch. For a moment Amanda was tempted to pretend she was part of their big, loving, boisterous family.

She wasn't, though. They might have embraced Birdie as one of their own, but Amanda had no role in the Arredondo family.

"Thank you, but I need to go," she said.

"I understand. We'll talk again soon," Louise promised.

Amanda nodded, then hurried away, wishing she could outrun her tangled emotions as easily.

23

RAFE WATCHED AMANDA RUSH OUT OF THE ELEMEN-
tary school as if she were being chased by *El Cucuy de Navidad*,
the bogeyman his cousins used to tell him roamed the streets
at Christmas looking for naughty children to punish.

What was that about? She had been speaking with his mother
one moment, the next she had rushed away as if she couldn't
go fast enough.

What had his mother said to her? They seemed to have been
conversing amicably enough but maybe he had misinterpreted
the discussion. Had his mother been cool again to her, despite
their talk earlier that day?

Louise bustled back into the auditorium before he could
ask her.

"Dad, can we watch the rest of the concert? I want to hear
the older kids sing."

He wanted to chase after Amanda, to make sure she wasn't
upset about something his mother had said. Right now, his son
had to be the priority.

"Sure. Let's go support your cousins."

They made their way back to the crowded auditorium, where they found two empty seats near Birdie and Paolo.

"Can we sit by you, *Abuelo*?" Isaac asked his grandfather.

"Of course. Sit down. Sit down."

"Is that Isaac?" Birdie asked. She managed her world with such ease that Rafe sometimes forgot she had low vision.

"Yes," his grandfather responded. "Isaac and Rafael."

She smiled brightly in their direction.

"Paolo said my granddaughter was here earlier," she said. "What a surprise. She doesn't often come to many school events. I have a feeling the two of you might have something to do with her presence here."

"Amanda is my friend," Isaac said. "I invited her so she could hear me sing."

"Oh, how nice."

"It was very kind of her to make the effort," Rafe said.

Despite the principal's admonishment for everyone to be seated, the second concert still hadn't yet started. He could hear rustling behind the curtain and assumed the next grade of children were moving into position.

"You know," Birdie said in an undertone, "I worry for that girl."

"Who? Amanda?"

She nodded. "She was always such a sensitive girl. She couldn't bear raised voices. Growing up in that home was a nightmare for her. She internalized everything."

Rafe didn't know what to say, saddened to think about Amanda struggling through her difficult childhood.

"I love my daughter," Birdie went on. "I only wish she had found the strength to walk away from her husband years earlier. They all would have been much better off."

"It can be tough to give up hope on someone you love." Even up until he found out about Caitlin's overdose, Rafe had hoped she would be able to find the strength to overcome her struggles.

"Amanda jumped into a relationship with Jake Shepherd, I think because she was so very desperate to remake her unhappy childhood into something better. I thought she was much too young to even think about marriage, but she wouldn't listen to me. Jake was her refuge, especially after the accident. She was engaged straight out of high school. And then...everything happened afterward."

"It was rough, wasn't it?"

"She didn't smile for a long time after Jake died. I wasn't sure she ever would again. She withdrew into herself, dropped all her friends, fell behind in her college coursework. She was in a really dark place. I worried about her. I was afraid she would one day decide she couldn't bear the pain anymore."

Caitlin had struggled through pain that dense and difficult.

His wife had never known her father, and her mother was also an addict. Caitlin had ended up in foster care for several years before she had been taken in by a reluctant aunt and her husband, who had been neglectful, bordering on abusive. In high school, she had dabbled in drugs, had made poor romantic choices and had been a victim of domestic and sexual abuse from a series of men.

Caitlin had fought through it all to try to have a happy life. After going to college and earning her associate's degree, she had finished cosmetology school and had taken a job at his mother's salon, where Rafe had met her.

She had been deliriously happy after Isaac had been born and he thought they were in a great place. They might have stayed there, adding to their family and building their life together in Shelter Springs, until she had received word her estranged mother had died and for reasons he still didn't quite fathom, that information had sent her spiraling.

His beautiful, bright, courageous wife had turned into someone else almost overnight, slipping back into destructive patterns and leaving him feeling helpless and sick with worry for her.

Perhaps she still yearned for her mother's love or maybe she didn't feel she deserved happiness and had deliberately sabotaged herself. He didn't know. But eventually, Caitlin had left town, ostensibly to go through rehab and therapy so she could work on overcoming her difficult past once and for all.

Only a few months later, he received a call from the Portland police department, telling him his wife had died at a party of a drug overdose.

Amanda wasn't Caitlin.

Yes, she had endured hard things but she hadn't turned to destructive habits, hadn't tried to dull her pain with anything she could find.

Instead, she reached out to others. She brought meals to wounded neighbors, she cared for her grandmother, she volunteered to lift those in need.

"Please take your seats," Elizabeth Williams said into the microphone.

Birdie held her gnarled, wrinkled hand out and Rafe grasped it, not sure what else to do. "Amanda is lonely. She won't admit it to anyone, but there it is. She has so much love to give the right person, if only she can learn to trust her heart again."

He wanted to ask Birdie why she was telling him this, but the curtain opened and the next group of children began to sing about joy and peace and goodwill.

As he listened to their sweet voices, Rafe couldn't seem to think about anything except the woman he had begun to care about deeply.

24

"I CAN'T BELIEVE CHRISTMAS EVE IS TOMORROW. THIS holiday season went by so fast!"

Amanda finished bagging ten small bottles of lotion for her friend, the gifts Holly planned to give her neighbors.

"Every year it feels like the month of December whips by faster and faster," she answered.

"Santa's coming tomorrow night." Lydia's mouth worked carefully around each word.

"I know. Isn't it wonderful?"

"I been very, very good."

"I don't doubt it for a minute. You're *always* very, very good."

Lydia beamed at her, fifty pounds of joy.

"Thank you for these," Holly said. "We wanted to make some cookies to take around to the neighbors but I've been so busy with work, I haven't had a chance. I was panicking about it, until I remembered you always have the best neighbor gifts."

"I'm glad you found something."

"These are perfect. What are you doing for Christmas? Are you spending it with Birdie?"

"That's the plan. I wanted her to come stay a few days with me at Rose Cottage like she has in the past but she wants to stay at the Shelter Inn this year."

"Oh, that's right. I heard Birdie has a boyfriend there." Holly grinned.

"She doesn't have a boyfriend. They are only friends."

She sounded cranky, but Holly only gave her an amused look. She was one of Amanda's oldest and dearest friends, who had grown up with her twin across the street from the Taylors. She and Hannah both knew Amanda entirely too well.

"Fine. She has a gentleman companion. I love Paolo. His restaurant made the best Mexican food in the whole county. It's still good, but not like it used to be when he and his wife were running it."

"Yes. Paolo is very nice."

McKenna Dodd, who had stopped in to purchase a last-minute gift for a friend from out of town coming in unexpectedly for the holidays, joined the conversation.

"They are so cute together," she said. "I just love to see them in the evenings, playing games in the recreation room with some of our other residents or swimming in the pool. Paolo adores her."

At least their affection seemed to be mutual. That went a long way toward allaying her worry for Birdie.

"You're coming to dinner tonight, aren't you?" McKenna asked.

"I still haven't decided. I have a little bit of wrapping to do. And to be honest, after all the chaos of the market, I'm not feeling very social."

"I get that. But you can't miss it. Birdie will be so disappointed. Griffin and Nat are planning to stop by. Many of the residents have invited their extended families."

Including Rafe and Isaac? That was yet another reason she ought to stay home.

Maybe if she tried to regain a little distance between them, she could start figuring out how she would go on without them after the holidays were over.

"What's happening tonight?" Holly asked with interest.

"We are hosting our second annual Shelter Inn potluck dinner for the holidays, a tradition that was started by necessity after the big blizzard last Christmas shut everything down."

"That's this little guy's first birthday, right?" Amanda gestured to Austin, on McKenna's hip. The baby gave his wide grin.

McKenna made a face. "Oh yes. We can't forget that. We'll have a cake for him, too. In case you're wondering, I do not recommend having a baby unexpectedly at home during a blizzard on Christmas Eve. It was the weirdest holiday season ever."

"But also one of the most wonderful," Amanda said. "Look what came out of it!"

McKenna hugged her son. "Absolutely. If you remember, when the storm hit last year, many people couldn't travel in or out of town. Our residents were upset about not being able to see their families, but Liz and Natalie saved the day by coming up with the idea to throw a big potluck dinner. Since everyone already had food prepared for their family gatherings, no one had to do any extra work and they all had a wonderful time. Except for me, anyway. I was in labor. Not my finest hour."

"Unfortunately, I had to miss the fun too since I was still down with Covid," Amanda said. "I didn't want to give it to Birdie or any of the other residents, so I had Christmas Eve all by myself enjoying chicken noodle soup and watching Hallmark movies."

"I mean, that's not the worst way to spend Christmas Eve," Holly pointed out.

"True enough." Amanda smiled.

"The residents enjoyed the potluck so much, they decided they wanted another one this year. Sort of our community holiday celebration. We wanted to save Christmas Eve for people to spend with their families, so that's why we're doing it tonight. The night before the night before Christmas."

"This is Christmas Eve Eve," Lydia informed them.

"Exactly!" Amanda beamed at her. "This is Christmas Eve Eve."

"If you would like to come, you and Lydia are more than welcome," McKenna said. "The potluck is open to everyone, not only our residents and their families. Besides, you feel like one of the family. I know how much everyone at the Shelter Inn loves you and Lydia whenever she comes over to swim with Nora and Hazel."

"Nora and Hazel are my friends," Lydia said.

"Yes they are. Aren't we lucky," her mother said, smiling at her daughter with such tenderness it made Amanda's heart hurt. Holly and Lydia deserved far better than they had received from Holly's ex.

"There should be plenty of food," McKenna added. "Please come."

"We'll have to see." Holly held up the paper bag of small items. "We need to take these last-minute neighbor gifts around this afternoon. If we can finish that, maybe we'll try. Lydia loves any chance to go to the apartment building, not only because all the residents spoil her but she also loves seeing all the inflatable decorations you put up."

"My girls love them, too. We talked about skipping them this year but there was a huge outcry from Nora and Hazel, as well as several of the residents. I guess we're stuck with them now."

Every year, Amanda knew, Liz and McKenna chose at random a dozen inflatables to decorate the grounds from the vast collection the apartment building's residents had brought with them when they downsized and moved in.

"You still haven't said whether you're coming," McKenna pointed out to Amanda.

She really didn't know how she could wriggle out of it, since Birdie also had specifically asked her to attend. For all she knew, Rafe and Isaac would not even go. If they did, surely she could spend one more evening with them, then do her best to make a clean break.

"I can give you an unqualified *maybe*," she said. "I will have to see how the rest of my day goes."

"If I end up making it, we will see you there, then," Holly said.

Before Amanda could answer, her cell phone rang from the counter beside her. Thinking it must be Birdie, who was almost the only person who preferred to communicate with her via phone calls instead of texts, she looked down at the caller ID and was shocked to see Rafe's name.

Why on earth would he be calling her?

"Hello?"

"Amanda. It's Rafe. I'm so glad you picked up."

The urgency in his voice sent alarm bells clanging through her. She had never heard that particular tone from him before.

"Is… Is everything okay?"

She heard an overlong pause on the line, as if he were trying to find words. "No," he finally said. "I'm so sorry to be the one to tell you this but there's been an accident. It involved your grandmother."

Panic clutched at her. "What kind of accident?"

"My *abuelo* was driving with Birdie to Haven Point today, I guess. A tourist who was going too damn fast crossed the median and was about to hit them head-on. At the last minute, Paolo swerved off the road to avoid him and they ended up hitting a guardrail."

Amanda sank down on the stool behind the counter, limp

suddenly, as if all her bones and muscles had dissolved. No. Not Birdie. She could not lose her grandmother!

"Are they—" She couldn't finish the unthinkable phrase.

"They're both hurt. I don't know how badly. I know they're both on their way to the hospital. That's all I can tell you at this point. The first responders called me as soon as they recognized Paolo. I'm on my way there. I'll give you more information when I arrive at the hospital. I wanted to wait to talk to you until I found out more, but I also knew you would want to know as soon as possible."

"Yes. I... Yes. Thank you."

She hung up without saying goodbye and stared blankly around the store for a long moment.

"What is it?" McKenna demanded, her features suddenly serious. "What's happened?"

Amanda couldn't seem to think as fear and shock and dismay battled within her.

"It's Birdie. She and Paolo Arredondo were in an accident. They've both been taken to the hospital. Oh!"

She felt dizzy suddenly, weak, her breath coming in sharp gasps. She lowered her face to her hands, trying to regain composure. In an instant, both Holly and McKenna were at her side.

"Breathe, Mandy. You have to breathe," McKenna urged.

"Breathe," Lydia echoed, her eyes round with concern.

Amanda forced herself to inhale and exhale to the count of five, just as Birdie always taught her, to help find calm when she was stressed.

"Here. Have a drink," Holly urged, pulling Amanda's water bottle from beside the cash register.

She sipped obediently, feeling numb yet somehow ice-cold.

"I have to go." She rose to unsteady feet. "I have to go to the hospital."

"Of course you do." Cat was already ahead of Amanda, handing over her coat and her purse.

Her friend must have come back from her lunch break just in time to see Amanda fall apart.

"I'm sorry to leave you alone when we're so busy."

"Don't give it another thought. We'll be fine. I'll call in Scarlet. Go be with your grandmother."

"Thank you. All of you." She was so deeply grateful for good friends.

"Let us know how she's doing. How they're *both* doing." McKenna's features were tight with worry. "If there's anything we can do, just reach out. We're here. I'll send out a text to all of our residents right away so they can start a prayer chain."

"Thank you."

With one more quick hug for her friends, she rushed outside. In her panicked state, it took her a moment to remember where she had parked. She was in the employee lot of the inner block, she remembered, a few moments' walk away.

She raced for it and quickly started driving toward the hospital, still feeling frozen with shock.

Her windshield wipers beat against a light snow that she scarcely registered as she drove out of Shelter Springs toward the hospital that had been built several years ago between Shelter Springs and Haven Point.

As she pulled into the visitor parking lot for the emergency room, her phone rang again.

She tensed, almost afraid to pick it up. When she looked at it, she saw her brother's name on the caller ID.

"What's going on?" she asked, her tone urgent. "How is she?"

Griffin paused for a few seconds. "I was calling to tell you Birdie was in an accident, but it sounds like you already know."

"Rafe called me a few moments ago. I've just arrived at the hospital but I haven't gone in yet. What is happening? Have you seen her?"

"Yes. I've seen her. My friend Michelle, Dr. Okita, is the attending in the ER right now. She's excellent. She called as soon as she saw my name listed as one of the emergency contacts for Birdie. She is conscious and talking. They're running tests to look for internal injuries."

"Oh no."

"It was a bad accident, sis. She had to be extricated and she blacked out for a little while, which is always a concern. Especially at her age. She has quite a few cuts and abrasions but so far they haven't found any broken bones."

"Are you staying at the hospital or do you need to head back to your clinic?"

"I've canceled the rest of my afternoon appointments. I only had a few, nothing urgent. I'll stick around until we at least know if they're going to admit her."

The next day was Christmas Eve, Amanda suddenly remembered. As much as her grandmother adored the holidays, it would be extra difficult for Birdie to be in the hospital over Christmas.

And the poor Arredondo family. They were still grieving the loss of Rosita less than a year ago. How tragic it would be for them if they lost their beloved grandfather as well.

"How is Paolo?"

"About the same as Birdie. Banged up, but no obvious broken bones. They're both lucky to be alive. He managed to minimize the impact as much as possible by turning off the road and hitting that guardrail, but I believe he is still racked with guilt that Birdie was injured while a passenger in his car. He's worried about her, she's worried about him."

"Give her my love. I'm on my way inside now."

"Okay. I'll see you in a few moments then."

They ended the call and she rushed straight to the emergency department. The clerk behind the desk, she saw, was a friend who served with her on the same committee with Crista Arredondo.

"Amanda. Hi." Pam Mitchell's expression softened into one of sympathy and concern. "You're here to see Birdie."

"Yes."

"Let me check with her nurse to see if she can have visitors."

Amanda wanted to burst through the doors to the examination rooms, regardless of what might be allowed or not, but she forced herself to wait patiently while Pam paged a nurse.

She could only hear one side of the conversation but saw her friend nod after a moment.

"Yes. I'll tell her." Pam hung up the phone, then turned back to Amanda.

"She's having an MRI right now, but her nurse said you are welcome to go back and wait in her room, if you would like. She's in exam room twelve."

She pressed a button on her desk and the security doors leading back to the emergency department opened, allowing Amanda to hurry through with a grateful nod to Pam.

The hospital was modern and well equipped for a facility that served a population of less than a hundred thousand people in the region.

It smelled of some kind of citrusy cleanser mixed with the sharp tang of bleach.

Before she could reach her grandmother's room, she saw her brother talking to several other medical professionals who were gathered at a nursing station in the center of the emergency department.

He looked serious and professional in a dress shirt and tie, with a stethoscope and an ID badge around his neck. An undeniable air of authority clung to him. To her, Griffin still usually seemed like the teasing older brother who used to hide her favorite toys and complain to their parents when she tried to hang around with him and his friends, but she was suddenly deeply grateful for his years of education and his passion to his vocation.

Griffin had made it his life's goal to be the sort of hardworking, dedicated family physician their father should have been.

Amanda hadn't wanted him to come back to Shelter Springs to open his family medicine practice. She knew well the opposition he would face as Dennis Taylor's son and that he would never be wholly accepted in some circles. Right now, in this moment, she could be nothing but grateful he had insisted he wanted to help the people of their hometown.

He spied her at the same moment, broke off his conversation with his colleagues in midsentence and hurried toward her, sweeping her into his arms.

"Hey, sis. Birdie is having an MRI right now."

"That's what Pam Mitchell just told me."

"She should be back soon."

She gripped his hands in hers. "Tell me the truth. How is she really doing? What are the big concerns?"

He hesitated, obviously choosing his words carefully. "In any vehicle accident like this we worry about internal bleeding, of course. She definitely sustained some degree of head trauma, most likely a moderate concussion, but she was talking coherently before they took her down to radiology. She was even teasing the staff."

Amanda exhaled a long, heartfelt breath.

"I can't tell you more than that. It's too soon to say. I was just talking with the attending physician. Dr. Okita told me that even if everything checks out, she's going to talk to the hospitalist and recommend admitting her for observation, at least overnight."

"What is she most worried about?"

"Her age, mostly, as well as the possibility of swelling on the brain."

She would focus on the positive, that Birdie was whole and talking. "Better to be safe than sorry, I suppose, but she's going to hate having to stay over. Especially during Christmas."

"Definitely. It can't be helped. If she puts up a fuss, I'll tell her the same thing she used to say to us. Remember, you can do hard things."

For the first time since Rafe had called her at the store, Amanda managed a semblance of a smile as she remembered all the times her grandmother said that to both of them.

"Where is Paolo?"

Griffin gestured to the room next to Birdie's, where she saw the number eleven on the door. "He wanted to stay close to her. It's sweet, actually. He's pretty torn up about the whole thing. He shouldn't be. If not for his quick thinking, neither of them would be here."

She couldn't help thinking that if not for Paolo, Birdie wouldn't have been on that road at all.

"You can wait in her room," Griffin said. "There are a couple of visitor chairs in there. She shouldn't be long."

She nodded and pushed open the door. The room seemed empty without a hospital gurney. Two visitor chairs, a few treatment trays and a rolling stool were the only other furniture pieces, along with a bag containing what she assumed were her grandmother's personal effects hanging on a hook by the door.

Amanda took a seat, her stomach still twisted with nerves. She wouldn't be comfortable until she had seen Birdie for herself. Maybe not even then.

She was texting an update to her friends at The Lucky Goat when the door opened and a couple of hospital workers in scrubs pushed a hospital bed through. Birdie lay against the white bedding, her purple streaks a bright, incongruously cheerful contrast to the pillow.

She had a huge bandage on her forehead, with a few drops of blood still clinging to her hair, and another bandage along her chin. She also had dark bruises on one eye and cheek.

Any reassurance she might have received from speaking with Griffin seemed to disappear when confronted with the hard reality of Birdie's physical status. Her grandmother rarely seemed frail but she did right now.

"Oh, Grandma."

Birdie looked toward her, though she knew her grandmother couldn't see her. "Amanda! Hello. How did you know where to find me?"

Her voice sounded weak and thready but as cheerful as ever as one of the hospital workers bustled around the bed, hooking her back up to monitors.

"You're the talk of the town. First Rafe called to tell me you and Paolo were in a crash, and then Griffin called with the same news. I'm so sorry this happened to you."

"Isn't this a mess? I keep telling these nice people that I'm fine and they're making a fuss about nothing, but nobody seems to be listening."

When the two medical workers left the room, Amanda pulled a visitor chair next to her grandmother's bed and took the hand that didn't have an IV line in it.

"What happened? Where were you and Paolo heading?"

Birdie gave a tremulous smile. "He ordered some tamales from his restaurant for the potluck tonight. We were on our way to pick them up in Haven Point. I probably won't make the party, will I?"

Amanda squeezed her fingers gently, feeling their slight tremble. "I wouldn't plan on it. Don't worry. There's always next year."

She gave a wordless prayer that Birdie would be around the next year.

Her grandmother closed her eyes and Amanda pushed a strand of hair away from her bandage. "Go ahead and rest. I'll be here."

Birdie opened her eyes, spearing her with an intense expression. "I need you to do something for me." She whispered the words, though they were the only two in the room.

"What's that?"

"I need to know how Paolo is. How he *really* is. Your brother won't tell me anything. Some nonsense about privacy laws. I just need to know Paolo will be okay. I trust you to tell me the truth. Can you go check on him for me?"

"I don't want to leave you, Grandma." She realized how rarely she called Birdie that but it seemed appropriate in this setting.

"I'm fine. I'm not going anywhere. They won't let me, even if I wanted to or had a way out of here. I'll be fine. I have to know how he is."

She recognized the obstinate set of her grandmother's jaw. More than that, she saw the raw fear in Birdie's eyes.

Amanda still didn't know for sure about Birdie's own condition. She wouldn't until she had a chance to talk to her doctor and until more test results came in.

Meantime, she could at least try to set her mind at ease about Paolo, if she could.

With a sigh, she leaned forward and kissed the top of her grandmother's head. "Fine. Griffin said his room is next door. I'll go check on him. I'll be right back."

"Thank you, my dear. He saved my life, you know. If not for him turning at the last moment we wouldn't be here."

"I'll go check on him."

She left the room, moving toward the room next door, where she knocked softly.

"Come in," a low male voice answered.

She pushed open the door, expecting only to find Paolo or perhaps Louise and Al. Instead, Rafe stood just inside, leaning against a sink.

He looked big and solid and reassuring and she wanted to fly into his arms.

He gave her a small smile that didn't hide the worry in his eyes. "Hey there. I wondered if you might be here."

"I only arrived a few moments ago. Birdie has sent me on an urgent errand to find out how your grandfather is. I'm not sure she will be able to rest until she knows something."

"They just took him for an MRI."

"The radiology techs must have picked him up as soon as they took Birdie back to her room. Is he in a lot of pain?"

"He says he's not, but I suspect he's running on adrenaline. He's been so upset about your grandmother. I had to practically tie him to the bed to keep him from going over there to check on her."

He genuinely cared about Birdie, as she did for Paolo.

"Not quite the Christmas any of us planned, is it?"

He shook his head. "No. But it could have been so much worse."

"That's what everyone is saying. That seems a small consolation prize, though, when my grandmother looks like she literally got run over by a reindeer."

A slow smile lifted his features and for some reason this, above everything else, made her throat tighten and tears burn behind her eyes. She fought them for a few seconds, then one spilled out and dripped down her cheek.

"Hey. Don't cry. They're going to be okay."

"I was so scared," she said, her voice small and strained. "I can't lose her."

He was next to her in an instant, his arms reaching for her. She wanted to press her face into the crook of his neck and weep. Instead she wrapped her arms around him, deeply grateful for his reassuring strength.

As she rested her cheek against his chest, feeling his steady heartbeat against her skin, Amanda relived that moment when she had opened the door, when for an instant, all the fear had fled and she had only been deeply grateful he was there.

She was in love with him.

The knowledge seemed to sear through her, burning away any remnants of self-delusion.

Completely in love.

Oh, what had she done?

She allowed herself to glean a few more moments of comfort from his embrace before forcing herself to step away.

"Thank you. I didn't mean to cry all over you."

"Not the first time a woman has cried in my arms and probably won't be the last."

He gave that lopsided smile she had come to adore and she swallowed hard, wondering how she could have ignored all her own warning signs and let herself fall headlong into love with him, even knowing it would only end in heartbreak.

"I should get back to Birdie. I told her I would only leave her for a moment to see about your grandfather."

"So far everything is checking out. They're talking about keeping him overnight. We will have to wait for the MRI results but he seems okay."

"Oh, that's good. She'll be so relieved."

"What is Birdie's status? I know *Abuelo* will want to know everything."

She told him what little she knew so far, all while hoping he couldn't see the truth about her feelings for him on her features.

"Keep me posted," he said.

She nodded, then escaped as quickly as she could to her grandmother's side.

25

"I DON'T GET IT. WHY CAN'T WE STAY FOR DINNER? I'm so hungry."

Rafe glanced in the rearview mirror at his son in the back seat of his crew cab pickup.

"We're only dropping off the tamales Grandpa ordered for the party at the Shelter Inn."

"What if I want to eat a tamale? I love tamales."

"You love everything, kiddo."

"I don't love radishes. Or chocolate candy with the fruity guts inside."

Rafe had to admit, he wasn't a big fan of crème chocolates, either. Give him a good toffee or chocolate-covered almond any day.

This errand seemed fairly superfluous to Rafe, but Paolo had insisted. After he had been assured that Birdie was doing fine, Paolo hadn't been able to focus on anything else but the tamales.

"I promised everybody I would take tamales from the restaurant to the potluck. I don't want to disappoint them," he had said firmly.

"I'm pretty sure people will understand. A bad car accident is a great excuse not to deliver on a tamale promise," Rafe had told him.

Paolo had been unconvinced. "Your cousin went to all the trouble of making four dozen tamales and I've already paid for them. They're just going to go bad if someone doesn't eat them. You know how I hate to waste food."

"Yeah. I know."

"It would mean a lot to me if you would pick them up and take them to the Shelter Inn for me, but you don't have to, if it's too much bother."

Rafe had rolled his eyes. His grandfather was excellent at delivering guilt trips. It was hard to say no to a man in a hospital bed with bruises and cuts all over his face.

So here he was some hours later, driving to his grandfather's senior apartment building with four dozen tamales in aluminum serving trays on the passenger seat next to him, sending out their delicious aroma and making his own stomach growl.

He should have ordered some for himself while he was picking these up from his family's restaurant. Handmade tamales had always been among his favorite things about the holidays, though he expected that had more to do with his memories of everyone gathered around his grandmother's kitchen. They would all work together, laughing and telling stories while spreading the masala dough on the dried corn husks, topping with the filling, rolling them up carefully then boiling.

He cherished those memories even more, now that his grandmother was gone.

"We can stop and grab something on our way home," he told his son now.

"Can I have a Happy Meal?"

"We'll see," he said as they parked in front of the apartment building. Fast food was, unfortunately, a much more likely option than him spending three hours making his own tamales from scratch.

As soon as he walked into the building, his arms loaded with the four serving trays, it was obvious a party was in full swing. He could hear Christmas music playing on the sound system of the recreation room just beyond the lobby, and a trio of women were setting out food items on long tables. At least a dozen more round tables with chairs took up the large meeting space, covered with red tablecloths decorated with miniature Christmas trees.

It seemed to Rafe that all the residents of the senior apartment facility were already gathered, though he didn't think the party was supposed to officially start for another twenty minutes.

The first person to see him was Liz Shepherd, who ran the retirement community with her niece McKenna. She rushed over to him. "Oh, Rafe. Such terrible news about your grandfather and Birdie. How are they? Any updates?"

"They are okay. Both of them are banged up, with cuts and bruises. My grandfather's back is pretty sore and he might have whiplash. No broken bones, as far as the X-rays show. The doctors decided to keep both of them for observation until the morning but if all goes well, they should be back here causing trouble for Christmas Eve tomorrow."

She closed her eyes and almost sagged with relief. "Thank heavens. We have all been so worried. We thought about canceling the dinner, but McKenna and I suspected that would be the last thing Birdie or Paolo would want us to do."

"Exactly right. I doubt they would take kindly to finding out anything was canceled because of them. Paolo even sent me to pick up the tamales he ordered from Rosita's."

"They smell delicious," her husband, Steve, exclaimed.

"I know," Isaac chimed in. "I'm *so* hungry."

"You must both stay for dinner." Liz's expression was firm. "We have tons of food."

Isaac tugged at his hand. "Can we, Dad? They even have cupcakes!"

He gazed down at his son. Isaac was hungry. While Rafe didn't really feel like socializing, he had to admit that after a stressful afternoon in the emergency room, he would much rather have a couple of his cousin's tamales than fast food. Okay, and maybe a cupcake.

While the demographic skewed toward the senior citizens who lived in the apartment, there were also plenty of younger people, likely family members of the residents. They wouldn't be out of place among them.

"We could probably stay for a while and grab a plate, if you're sure there's enough. Everything looks delicious."

"Oh yay." Liz touched his arm. "Trust me, there's plenty! Find a seat wherever you would like. We should be starting in only a few moments."

"Can I go see my friends?" Isaac asked, gesturing toward McKenna Dodd's two cute daughters, who were sitting on the floor in one corner, petting Birdie's dog, Dash.

"Sure, as long as you stay in this room. You can't leave to go run around in the halls. Got it?"

Isaac nodded vigorously. "I promise."

As his son rushed off, Rafe looked around for a seat and spotted Travis Dodd, whom he considered a good friend. As he made his way over to his table, Rafe was stopped several times by people asking after Birdie and Paolo, all with genuine concern on their expressions.

Moving here had been good for his grandfather. He had made new friends, reconnected with old ones and seemed to be surrounded by a community that cared about him. Rafe knew it had not been easy for Paolo to sell his home and downsize here after Rosita's death but he could see now it had been a wise decision.

Birdie, especially, had been good for his grandfather. Her warmth and kindness had helped him slowly find his way through his grief.

Paolo definitely cared for the woman. If Rafe had any doubts about their growing relationship, they had been erased that afternoon as he witnessed his grandfather's deep concern for her.

His thoughts naturally shifted from Birdie to her granddaughter, though Amanda never seemed to be far from his thoughts these days. At random moments throughout his day, he would think of that little sprinkle of freckles across her nose, of her vast collection of festive sweaters, of her soft smile that could appear out of nowhere.

As soon as she had walked into his grandfather's hospital room, Rafe had felt relief and peace, an odd, unaccustomed assurance that as long as she was there, he could find the strength to handle anything that came along.

He remembered that moment when she had sagged into his arms, clasping him tightly as if he were her life preserver in a turbulent sea.

He needed her in his life. Over the past few weeks, Amanda Taylor had become integral to him. She had woven herself into the very fabric of his existence.

"Hey, Rafe," Travis said in a low voice, holding his sleeping son on his lap. "Sorry to hear about your grandfather. How is he?"

He took a seat at the table, giving the same answer he had offered to Liz and everyone else.

Staying to eat here had been a good idea too, Rafe thought later as he finished his second tamale, then took his last bite of a delicious brisket that apparently James Johnson had smoked on the patio of his apartment unit.

The food was tasty and plentiful, and the company was somehow calming. Most important, Isaac was enjoying himself and now Rafe wouldn't have to worry about figuring out what to feed him that night.

He stood up to take his paper plate to the garbage can Steve Shepherd had brought out and was considering a cupcake when his attention was drawn to a woman who had just entered the apartment building foyer, outside the recreation room.

His heart seemed to give a little kick of recognition even before he saw for certain that the newcomer was Amanda. She stood at the entrance to the recreation room, looking a little lost until Natalie Shepherd and McKenna Dodd both hurried out of the room to hug her.

He was thinking how glad he was that she had good friends to help her through hard times when Isaac jumped up from the table and ran over to her.

"Hey! It's my friend! Hi, Amanda."

Her features softened and she knelt down to hug him. Rafe rose from his chair, intending to retrieve his son, but Amanda seemed in no hurry to let the boy go, as if she needed his sweet-natured comfort.

She stood up as Rafe joined the group. Isaac clung to her hand, as if afraid to let her go.

Yeah. I know how you feel, kid.

As Amanda met his gaze, she appeared for a moment as if she wanted to sink into his arms again. He almost held them out, but then she seemed to draw in a breath and returned to the conversation with her friends.

"I didn't expect to see you here tonight," McKenna was saying. "I thought for sure you would be staying at the hospital with your grandmother."

"That is the plan. The nurses said they could pull in a sleep chair for me so I can stay with her overnight. I don't feel good about leaving her alone even for a moment, but she was worried about Dash and asked me to come check on him and to pick up a few of her things for the night. Her CPAP, her own nightgown, some headphones so she can listen to her audiobook. That kind of thing."

"Dash is fine," McKenna assured her. "The girls love having him as a houseguest. They have been fighting over who gets to sleep with him tonight."

"Oh, that will put Birdie's mind at ease."

"Have you had dinner?" Liz asked, ever the nurturer. "You should grab something while you're here."

Amanda looked torn. "I should hurry back to the hospital."

The older woman frowned. "Squeezing out ten more minutes for yourself so that you can eat won't make any difference to your grandmother but definitely will help *you* feel better. You have to take care of yourself in order to take care of her."

That was apparently exactly the right argument. After a moment, Amanda nodded and moved toward the table arrayed with a wide selection of food, Isaac still holding her hand.

"Son. Let Amanda grab some food," Rafe finally interceded.

"You can sit by us," Isaac told her in a rather bossy tone.

She agreed before Rafe could tell his son that perhaps Amanda would prefer to sit with her friends.

"I will. Give me a moment, okay?"

Isaac nodded happily and returned to his chair, leaving Rafe to do the same.

A few moments later, Amanda took the empty seat at their table, between Isaac and Travis. She had added some fruit to a plate, a small slice of turkey and one of the tamales from Rosita's, he was happy to see.

"How was your grandmother when you left?" he asked. He had left the hospital as soon as his grandfather had been moved to a regular room. By then, his parents had arrived to stay with Paolo, and Rafe had to go pick up Isaac from his sister's house.

He was also tending his brother's dog while Joe and Crista

drove out of state to spend the holiday with her parents, so he had to make a stop at his house first to let Sophie out.

"She's been sleeping most of the afternoon," Amanda answered. "The doctor says it's normal from the adrenaline crash and some of the pain medication they gave her. She says she feels fine, but I'm still worried."

"Naturally."

She took a drink from her red plastic cup. "I didn't expect to see you and Isaac here."

He gave a wry smile. "It's been a whole thing. *Abuelo* insisted I pick up the tamales he ordered from the restaurant in Haven Point. Once we got here, it was tough to say no to all this good food."

She smiled, though her eyes still looked exhausted. He wanted to rest her head against his shoulder and let her sleep.

She stayed at their table for ten minutes, talking mostly to Travis and McKenna. He did notice she only ate a few bites of the turkey, about a third of the tamale and a few strawberries.

Isaac lasted about half as long, finishing his plate in a rush, then hurrying over to once more play with Dash and the Dodd girls.

Finally, Amanda pushed away from the table, picking up her plate.

"I should be going. I still need to go to Birdie's apartment to grab her things, then I need to head back to the hospital."

McKenna jumped up and hugged her again. As Amanda embraced her friend, her chin wobbled slightly. She was keeping up a brave front but was ready to crack at any moment.

He sat for a moment after she took her plate to the garbage, then finally stood himself.

"Would you mind keeping an eye on Isaac for me, just for a few moments?" he asked McKenna and Travis. "I'm going to see if Amanda needs help carrying anything."

McKenna exchanged a look with her husband that Rafe

didn't quite understand, then she smiled and made a shooing motion with her hand. "Go. That's very kind of you. Isaac will be fine. We will watch over him."

He nodded his thanks and left with a strange prickle of unease. He suspected her friend was trying to matchmake and he wasn't sure how to feel about it.

Were his growing feelings for Amanda that transparent?

Yeah. Probably.

Pushing away his discomfort, he hurried down the hall. He caught up with Amanda as she used a key fob to unlock Birdie's door, with its holiday wreath and a cheerful snowman decoration standing sentinel.

As he approached, Amanda looked up with surprise. "Hello," she said, clearly confused about why he had followed her.

"I thought you might need some help carrying things out to your car."

The explanation sounded lame, even to him, but she either didn't notice or was too well-mannered to mention it.

"Thank you. I'm sure I'll be fine but it was nice of you to think of it."

She opened the door to the apartment that smelled of cinnamon and sugar. He saw the reason when he spotted two cooling racks full of cookies on the countertop.

"Birdie wanted me to take the snickerdoodles she made earlier out for the potluck but they seem to have plenty of dessert. I'll put some in a bag for you and Isaac. He can eat a few and put a few out for Santa Claus."

She reached into one of the drawers and pulled out a bag, then started putting cookies in it. Amanda liked to help people. He suspected that was the way she dealt with her own emotions.

"I can put cookies in a bag," he told her. "Why don't you work on gathering the things that would bring Birdie comfort?"

"Okay. Thank you."

"I can also drop a few cookies in a bag for you to take to the hospital with you. Maybe the nurses would appreciate it."

"Birdie would like that. Thank you."

She moved past him and he thought how taut she suddenly seemed, as if the thin outer covering of her control was starting to crackle.

A few moments later, she emerged from the bedroom with a large tote bag full of items and a rueful expression. "I started with the things on her list and then kept thinking of more. Slippers, some lotion that she likes, clothing for her to wear home tomorrow."

"Good idea."

"I wish I could do more for her. She seems so frail in that hospital bed. Every one of her eighty years and then s-some."

Without warning, Amanda suddenly burst into tears. She dropped the tote and covered her face with her hands. Not knowing what else to do, Rafe reached her side in two steps and wrapped his arms around her.

"I'm sorry. I think it must be a d-delayed reaction or something."

"Understandable. It's been a rough day. She's okay, though. They'll both be okay."

She cried for a moment, then eased away, reaching for a tissue from a box on the counter adorned with Nutcracker soldiers.

"I'm such a mess."

If she was a mess, she was a beautiful one. The most lovely mess he had ever seen.

She wiped at her eyes. "I love her so much. I can't bear thinking about what might have happened."

"She's okay," he repeated. "I have no doubt that in a few days, your grandmother will be back to her same feisty self."

She gave a watery smile. "I hope so."

"She will be. Birdie is tough. Something she passed along to her granddaughter."

Her short laugh sounded rough with disbelief. "I am far from tough. The exact opposite. I've been a complete wreck since you called me with the news about the accident."

"I'm sorry I had to break it to you that way. I didn't have time to come in person and I figured it would be better to tell you quickly over the phone so you could get to the hospital as soon as possible."

"No, it was good. You were very sweet. Thank you."

She gave him a tremulous smile that seemed to reach right in and punch him in the chest. Unable to help himself, Rafe brushed a strand of auburn hair from her face. She gazed up at him, her green eyes wide. He couldn't help himself. He leaned down and kissed her forehead.

"You are not a mess," he murmured. "You're the amazing Amanda Taylor. You've got this."

She sighed against him, her eyes closed. Tenderness soaked through him and he couldn't help himself. He gently pressed his mouth to hers, a whisper-soft kiss.

That was all he intended to do but when he lifted his mouth away slightly, intending to break the kiss, she made a tiny sound and leaned closer, her mouth moving under his.

For the first time since Mike had called to tell him about Paolo and Birdie, Rafe felt as if he could breathe again. Here, with Amanda, he finally felt peace.

He needed her in his life. Not just for his son but for himself. Because she was the best thing that had happened to him in a long time and he didn't want to let her go.

He didn't think the kiss lasted a long time, but in that fleeting moment, Rafe knew for certain he was in love with her. This wasn't an infatuation or a fleeting attraction. It was a deep, abiding love that had taken root in his heart and his soul.

He pulled her closer, needing her warmth and her softness. He trailed his lips from her mouth to her cheeks so that he could kiss away the salty remnants of her tears.

She gazed at him, her eyes a murky green, then she suddenly blinked several times as if coming out of a spell.

"Stop. Please stop."

The tremor in her small, distressed voice pierced through to him and he immediately broke away. "What's wrong?"

"This!" She stepped away, nearly stumbling in her haste. "I don't want this, Rafe. I can't want this."

He refrained from pointing out that she had kissed him like someone who very much wanted whatever "this" she might be referring to. He had only intended a small kiss of comfort. She had been the one who deepened the kiss, who clutched him to her and slid her arms around his neck and pressed her soft curves against him.

He would never, ever argue with a woman who didn't want him to kiss her, but he also needed to be clear about his feelings.

He stepped away from her and faced her. "I'm not sure what it is exactly that you don't want, but I have to tell you something. I might be falling in love with you."

The word sounded trite and not at all adequate to convey his feelings so he tried again.

"Actually, there's no *might* about it. I *am* falling in love with you. I have been for some time."

She stared at him, eyes huge with shock. He couldn't tell, what she might be thinking and suddenly realized he had picked a lousy time to do this, when she was already on an emotional roller coaster about her grandmother.

He couldn't help that now. There was no way he was going to backtrack.

He took a chance and reached for her hand, feeling her fingers tremble in his.

"Amanda, you have to know. I haven't let myself care about anyone since Caitlin. I didn't *want* to care about anyone. Life seemed easier that way. Safer. But somehow you have worked your way into my life. Into my heart."

She closed her eyes for a heartbeat. When she opened them, he saw a myriad of emotions there, too tangled together for him to identify them all except fear, tenderness and a sorrow that instantly filled him with dread.

She slid her fingers from his and curled them into her palms. "I care about you too, Rafe. You and Isaac both. How could I not?"

She inhaled sharply and then let her breath out in a rush. "I have...feelings for you. But it's not enough. I don't want this. I don't want to...to love you."

He would not have expected the caustic pain that howled through him at her words—pain and loss and anger at himself for revealing his soft underbelly of vulnerability for her to gouge and claw at.

"You don't want love at all?" He had to ask. "Or you don't want to love *me*?"

She closed her eyes again. When she opened them, they were clear and emotionless, anything she might be feeling hidden away from him.

"Both. I've lost too much, Rafe. I am not strong enough to go through this again."

"Through what?"

She looked away. "I don't have a good track record at love. I was engaged once to the man I thought was the love of my life, a man who died because of his own recklessness. I was nearly engaged a second time to a man who decided he was still in love with his ex-wife. The first time nearly destroyed me. The second hardened something inside me, I think."

Of course he knew about Jake. He had been there and had fought to keep the man alive. The other one was a surprise.

"What happened with the second guy?" he had to ask.

Her mouth compressed into a tight line. "Ben had two children I adored and an ex-wife who suddenly decided she wanted him back. For the sake of his girls, we both knew they had to try again."

"I'm sorry."

She made a dismissive gesture. "He still loved her. Some part of me knew that, but I wanted a family so much that I ignored the warning signs."

She swallowed, looking away again. "I don't miss Ben. Not really. But I have grieved the loss of those girls. I haven't seen them in two years but they're still here," she said, tapping her chest.

She must have been heartbroken. He thought of her kindness with Isaac and the bond the two of them already seemed to have formed.

"I already adore your son," she went on, confirming his thoughts. "If I truly…let myself care about him and about you, if I allow myself to start dreaming about a future with the two of you and then it…it somehow doesn't happen, I don't think I would have the strength to make it through."

How could he argue against her instinct for self-preservation? He understood it better than most would. He had been fighting the same thing, refusing to give someone else the power to walk away again.

Yet he had given his heart to her, and now she seemed to be confirming everything he had worried about. She was walking away from him, too.

"You won't even give us a chance?" he asked, his voice gruff.

"There is no *us*, Rafe. We're neighbors. I hope somehow we can remain friends. But that's all. Thank you for your help. I need to go back to the hospital."

Words flew through his mind, jumbled arguments and pleas, but somehow he sensed in that moment that none of them would do any good. Left with no choice, he pivoted and walked out of the apartment.

She followed him, the tote bag firmly over her shoulder.

She wouldn't even give him the chance to help carry the bag. Before he could take it from her, before he could say anything else, she hurried out the nearest side door to the parking lot.

For a long time after she left, Rafe stood in the hallway feeling worse than he had in a long time.

He wasn't ready to talk to anyone yet, until he had a moment to absorb the pain of her blunt rejection, her refusal to accept anything from him beyond friendship.

When Caitlin had left him, she had given in to her addiction. Amanda was surrendering to her own fears.

He was a tough firefighter and paramedic, used to rushing headlong into dangerous situations where he didn't know what to do and had to act out of instinct and experience.

His arm ached suddenly in the brace, reminding him of Pearl Barnes, stuck on that rooftop after Thanksgiving, too afraid to climb back down to safety. She had only moved after Rafe had talked to her with soothing words, calming her enough that she could find the strength to let him harness her into the bucket so she could be hoisted down.

He couldn't talk his way through this with Amanda. She was rejecting everything he had to offer, refusing to allow him to take her hand and help her find safety and peace.

She had to find her way through on her own.

He didn't know if she could do it or was even willing to try. By every indication, she was closing that door firmly between him, shutting him out.

He only knew his priority had to be Isaac. His son had been through enough, losing his mother. Rafe couldn't afford to risk his emotional well-being more than he already had.

He would have to let her go, no matter how hard it would hurt.

26

SHE WAS A COWARD AND A FOOL.

With tears dripping down her cheeks, Amanda rushed out to the parking lot.

Despising herself for her weakness, she climbed into her car and started the engine. The cold steering wheel made her fingers ache but she didn't want to take the time to pull out her gloves. She had to get away.

She quickly pulled out of the parking lot and drove off through the dark night, the moon obscured by inky clouds that held the portent of snow.

Knowing she needed to compose herself before she arrived at the hospital or she would upset Birdie, she decided to run home so she could change from her work clothes to yoga pants, which would be much more comfortable to sleep in at the hospital.

A few more moments likely wouldn't make any difference to her grandmother.

Her Christmas tree glowed with cheerful welcome in the window, the exact opposite of how Amanda felt right now. She wanted to climb into her bed, pull the covers over her head and pretend that this horrible day hadn't happened at all, starting with that phone call from Rafe.

When she unlocked the door to Rose Cottage, Oscar and Willow wandered out to greet her, long tails swaying, and she sank to the floor for a moment, needing the comfort of their warm softness.

Willow, the more affectionate one, nudged her arm with her head. Even Oscar patiently let her pick him up. To her dismay, she felt more tears well up as she petted them.

I am falling in love with you. I have been for some time.

When she thought of tough and hard-edged Rafe Arredondo baring his heart to her, more tears slipped down to drop into Oscar's fur.

After a moment of indulging the tears, she pushed them away and drew several deep, cleansing breaths. She had been right to push him away. She had always known they could never be together.

She was fine being alone. She had her friends, her store, her volunteer work and her cats.

Okay, maybe some part of her longed for something else. But at what cost?

Love was fragile. Ephemeral. Those she loved could be gone in an instant, either by fate or by choice. Birdie's accident had certainly reinforced that.

She hurt too much now, when she and Rafe had only shared more than a few fleeting kisses. If she allowed herself to love him and Isaac wholly and without reservation, she could very well end up completely wrecked if things didn't work out.

"I'm fine, dear. You don't need to fuss over me."

"What if I like fussing over you?" Amanda said with a smile the next afternoon as she tucked a blanket around Birdie more securely, making sure her grandmother was warm and cozy in her favorite recliner in her apartment at the Shelter Inn, with Dash watching protectively over her from the floor.

Birdie touched Amanda's hand, her own clearly showing the bruise from the IV line that had been removed earlier that afternoon. "I should be taking care of you. I don't like having our roles reversed."

Amanda kissed the top of Birdie's head. "It's about time you let me help you then, isn't it? Now you relax and take a nap while I fix our Christmas Eve dinner."

Birdie sighed. "I feel like all I have done for the past twenty-four hours is sleep."

"That's perfectly fine. Your body is telling you that's what it needs."

"I wish my body would shut the hell up sometimes," Birdie muttered.

"Can I help you find something to watch, then?"

"Sure. Find a good Christmas movie for me. The more romantic, the better."

Amanda selected a movie from one of the streaming services that she had saved in her own profile to her grandmother's device. Soon the opening credits were playing, and Amanda headed to the kitchen to find the ingredients for their dinner.

By the time she gathered everything for the lasagna they had already planned to make together, Birdie's eyes were closed and she was snoring softly.

Her grandmother looked fragile as a paper-thin petal trembling in the wind, especially with her bruises and that stark white bandage.

After a night spent in the hospital with nurses and aides and doctors interrupting her sleep every time she closed her eyes, Amanda wanted to curl up on the sofa next to her grandmother's recliner and nap for a few days.

Birdie was much tougher than she was. Her grandmother had endured the comings and goings without complaint while

Amanda had wanted to march out to the hallway and post a big sign on the door that said Do Not Disturb. Healing in Progress.

She was chopping onions for the lasagna when someone knocked softly on the door. After quickly washing her hands and swiping her watery eyes with a tissue, she crossed the room to answer it.

Her brother stood on the other side. "I came to check on you two," he said in a hushed voice when he saw Birdie sleeping from the doorway. "How is our girl?"

Amanda walked out into the hall with him so they could speak without disturbing her rest. "She says she's fine but I don't know. She's exhausted."

"I'm not surprised. Hospitals are lousy places to get a good night's sleep."

Yes, she had learned that lesson well the previous night.

"You should be resting, too," her brother said and she knew he must be seeing the circles smudged under her eyes and the lines of fatigue around her mouth.

"I'm fine. I'll rest after I prepare our dinner."

"Are you making Birdie's famous lasagna?"

"Of course. It's our Christmas Eve tradition, isn't it? It won't be as good as hers but there will be plenty of leftovers for you later tonight when you're here."

They had agreed that Griffin would keep his prearranged plans to have Christmas Eve dinner with Natalie's family at Steve and Liz's house. He would then take the overnight shift to watch over their grandmother.

"Yum. I'll be back here as soon as we're done with dinner."

"Are you sure you wouldn't rather spend Christmas Eve with Nat? I can sleep on the sofa."

He frowned. "You spent last night on an uncomfortable chair at the hospital. You don't need to have another one on the sofa. No. I'm fine staying here. Nat and I have the rest of our lives to spend Christmas Eve together."

His words stung like hand sanitizer on an open wound. She hadn't let herself think about either Rafe or Isaac since she had rushed away from the building the day before. It hurt too much to imagine how colorless and drab her world would be without them in it.

Some of her emotions must have shown on her face. Griffin gave her a careful look. "Are you okay?"

She blinked away the pain, forcing a smile for him. "Yeah. As you said. I'm tired. And I was chopping onions."

"We won't be late. According to McKenna and Travis, we have to be done with all the festivities early so they can get the kids to bed at a reasonable hour."

"I wish her luck with that, knowing Hazel and Nora."

"Right?" He smiled and Amanda spent a moment imagining all the noise and chaos and wonder.

Thinking of the girls drew her thoughts back to Isaac again. She truly hoped he was not too disappointed when his Christmas wish did not come true and he did not find a new mother wrapped with a ribbon under his tree.

"Take your time," she said. "We'll be fine."

After he left, she returned inside to the apartment to find Birdie still asleep.

Her grandmother awoke just as she was pulling the lasagna out of the oven.

"Oh, that smells delicious."

"I hope it is. I don't have your kind of magic."

"You have plenty of magic of your own, my dear," Birdie said with a fond smile.

"It needs to rest for half an hour now, then it will be ready."

"Oh good. I'm suddenly starving," Birdie said with some surprise. "I just need to wash up then I'll be ready to eat. Would you mind taking Dash out?"

"Not at all."

After helping Birdie to the bathroom, she waited until she

could resettle her grandmother on the lift recliner before finding the dog's leash.

When she walked outside, she found a vast, clear sky dotted with stars that gleamed and winked. She and Dash made a circuit around the building, where he sniffed at every single inflatable decoration as if he had never seen them before. When she returned to the apartment, she felt invigorated by the cold and the exercise.

The rest of her Christmas Eve with Birdie was quiet but enjoyable. They ate lasagna with cheesy bread sticks, then watched her grandmother's favorite Christmas movie, *It's A Wonderful Life*. This time Birdie stayed awake for the whole movie, listening intently to the classic tale.

"Do you know, I think I enjoy it more now that I can't see the action," Birdie said halfway through. "It's like listening to an old-time radio drama from the days of my childhood, especially because I can picture that handsome Jimmy Stewart."

Despite her enjoyment of the film and all her best intentions, Birdie almost nodded off before the movie was over, jerking as the bell rang and Clarence the angel received his wings.

"Let's get you to bed," Amanda said gently. "You would be much more comfortable in your own bed than here in the recliner."

She certainly knew Dash would be more comfortable. The dog was anxious to be snuggled up next to his person on the bed. Amanda would have insisted on the dog sleeping out here in the living room if she thought it was worth wasting her breath. Her grandmother loved that dog and no doubt would find just as much comfort and warmth in cuddling him.

"Would you mind taking Dash out one last time. You don't have to walk him. Right before bed, we usually just head outside, he does his thing, then he's ready to settle down for the night."

"Of course I don't mind."

She threw on her coat and walked with the dog outside again. Birdie was right, Dash didn't dawdle, whether from the cold or his own eagerness to be with Birdie. He seemed in a hurry to go back inside to the cozy apartment.

When she returned, Birdie had changed into her nightgown and had already climbed into bed. The dog jumped up beside her, stretching out at the foot of the bed.

After making sure Birdie had everything she needed, Amanda adjusted the blankets one more time.

Birdie touched her arm. "I'm afraid this was a very boring Christmas Eve for you."

"Are you kidding? There's nowhere else on earth I would rather be than right here with you." She kissed Birdie's forehead, deeply grateful she had at least one more Christmas with her grandmother. After giving a pat to Dash, she headed for the door. "I'll leave the door open slightly. Griffin and I will try not to wake you when he arrives and I take off. Merry Christmas, Grandma."

She wasn't sure Birdie even heard her. She had pulled on her CPAP mask and already had her eyes closed.

Outside in the living room, Amanda settled onto the sofa, hoping she could stay awake until Griffin arrived. She read only a few pages of her book before there was another soft rap on the door. She opened it for Griffin, who came in bearing two wedge-shaped containers.

"Liz insisted I bring you and Birdie some cherry pie."

She did enjoy Liz's cherry pie. If she weren't so tired—and if she could dredge up any sort of an appetite—she would find some ice cream in Birdie's freezer and have a slice right now.

After talking with Griffin for a few moments about his evening and the girls' funny skit they performed for the family, Amanda couldn't hold back a yawn. Though it was barely 8:00 p.m., she was ready to go to bed.

Exhaustion pressed in on her like a dense fog as she walked

outside. The clear skies of earlier had given way to random clouds that trickled out a light snow to brush against her cheeks and melt in her hair.

The church parking lot next door to the apartment building was full. She considered slipping inside to enjoy the evening service, but decided she would probably fall asleep on the pew. And wouldn't that be embarrassing?

Anyway, she should probably get back home to her poor, neglected cats, who would be happy to see her for more than the few quick visits she had made home in the past twenty-four hours to make sure they had water and food.

If she could stay awake, she would try to watch the Pope's televised midnight mass from St. Peter's Basilica in Rome and marvel at the gorgeous building and the tradition and ceremony, as she did every Christmas Eve.

As she pulled into her driveway, her little tree twinkled merrily in the window. She had to force herself not to look down the street toward Rafe's house or to wonder how their Christmas celebrations were going.

When she let herself inside, she found Willow and Oscar both stretched out under the tree. This time, they didn't come over to greet her, probably demonstrating their annoyance at her long absence.

Now that she was home, in her own space, the fog seemed to lift and she felt strangely energized. After hanging her coat in the hall closet and storing the pie slice in the refrigerator to enjoy as a special Christmas treat the next day, Amanda turned on piano Christmas music on her smart speaker. She added more water to the cats' bowls and made sure they had food.

When she sat on her favorite chair in the living room, Willow jumped up for a moment of affection before wandering off again.

Amanda picked up the Christmas book she had been trying to read all season and enjoyed the lights and the music and the story. This was a perfectly lovely way to spend Christmas Eve, she told herself, even if her beloved cottage did seem quiet.

She had read perhaps half a chapter when her doorbell suddenly rang, making Oscar bounce in the air like he had been zapped with an electrical shock.

Amanda glanced at her watch. Still not yet 9:00 p.m. One of her neighbors was probably out taking treats around this evening. Sometimes Delores Parker down the street liked to make peanut brittle on Christmas Eve and take it around to the neighbors.

She opened the door with a ready smile that froze with shock when she found not her elderly neighbor but Rafe and Isaac standing on her porch.

All the things she had said to him the day before jumbled through her mind in an instant as her heart seemed to squeeze with love and sorrow at the same time.

For one wild moment, she wanted to slam the door shut again and lean against it to keep them out. She had found some measure of contentment this evening. Why did he have to show up with his adorable son and ruin it for her?

Oscar had joined her at the door to investigate the newcomers. Only when his back arched did she realize they had a small cream-colored dog with them, who had blended in with the snow in the darkness.

"Hi, Amanda. Merry Christmas. Look what we have!"

She managed a smile for the boy, who wasn't at all to blame for her emotional tumult. "Oh my. Did you get a dog for Christmas?"

"Nope. This is my cousins' dog. Her name is Sophie and I think she's the best dog in the whole world, besides Dash."

"Did you dognap her?"

He giggled. "No. We're dog sitting. Jade and Samuel went to see their other grandma and grandpa. They live in Utah and they didn't want to take Sophie because she gets carsick, so me and my dad are watching her for Christmas."

"That sounds very fun."

"I'm going to keep her in my room so she can't bark at Santa Claus and scare the reindeer."

"Great idea."

Rafe, she couldn't help but notice, hadn't said a word throughout this exchange, or when Isaac reached inside his coat and pulled out a small square gift covered in red plaid wrapping paper.

"I brought you a present," Isaac said cheerfully. "You can open it if you want. I made it at *Abi* and *Ito*'s house tonight after we had dinner."

Amanda gazed at the present, feeling the heat of tears beginning. Only because she was so tired, she told herself. "Oh, how nice of you. Come in."

"Is the dog okay inside?" Rafe finally spoke, his voice gruff.

"Sure. The cats will probably make themselves scarce in my bedroom. They like to hide out under my bed when they're nervous."

Isaac giggled again as he carefully wiped his boots on her mat, then walked inside. Rafe followed him with a reluctance that was obvious in every hard line of his body.

"Sit down," she said, gesturing to her sofa.

Isaac plopped down instantly. Rafe hesitated, his expression remote, as if he wanted to scoop up his son and his brother's dog and head for the door. He finally sat, holding the dog's leash while Sophie sniffed the sofa and the rug and the cat's climbing gym.

Isaac held out the gift and Amanda took it, touched all over again at the sweet affection the boy offered so freely.

"It's lovely."

"*Abi* helped me wrap it."

"That was nice of her." She had to wonder if Louise had known the gift was intended for her.

She peeled away the wrapping and found a small cardboard box inside. After unfolding the top, she pulled out a clear plastic ornament, the kind sold in craft stores that could be decorated in any fashion.

Inside the ornament was a smattering of glittery fake snow in the bottom, along with a drawing created with markers on a transparent plastic sheet cut to size so it stood upright inside the ornament.

She held the clear ball so that she could see it better. The lights of her tree gleamed through and she saw there were three figures drawn with markers on the plastic, a woman with red hair, a taller man with dark hair and a small figure between them with curly hair and glasses. He was holding hands with both of them.

At least she thought they were hands. They might have been basketballs.

She looked from the picture to Isaac, her emotions tangled like strands of tinsel in a box. "Oh."

"That's us," he explained happily. "You and me and my dad."

Tears burned hotter and she blinked rapidly, aware of a deep ribbon of pain in her chest that she had been doing her best to ignore all day.

She couldn't ignore it now. It curled and twisted through her as she looked at those smiling figures inside the ornament then at Isaac and his father.

I'm falling in love with you.

She could have had that. The joy, the belonging, the *love*.

Instead, she had chosen fear over faith. She had let the pain and loss of her past taint something that could have been beautiful and right.

She forced a smile, though she could feel her lips tremble. She had to hope Rafe didn't notice.

"It's lovely. I like the colors very much."

Isaac hopped up and came over, pointing at the ornament.

"You have a green sweater on because you're always wearing red or green sweaters."

"I do like Christmas sweaters," she agreed.

"And my dad is wearing a Santa hat. Can you see that?"

She glanced at Rafe briefly, all she could allow herself, then back at the figure he had drawn. "I see that. Good job with the pompom."

He grinned at her and she hugged him, feeling her heart shatter into a thousand pieces.

"Would you like to hang it on the tree? I think it has to be pretty far up or the cats might knock it down. Maybe your dad can help lift you."

Rafe stood again. He lifted Isaac with both arms, even the one still in the brace, so that Isaac could find a spot for it in the top branches.

"Thank you. That was very sweet of you. I will treasure it."

He beamed, pushing up his glasses. "We're going to take Sophie for a walk and look at Christmas lights. Do you want to come with us?"

"Isaac," Rafe chided. "Amanda was probably in the middle of something."

She thought of her book and her music and her solitary evening. She had been trying to convince herself she was exactly where she wanted to be. Now, though, with Isaac gazing up at her out of those cheerful dark eyes magnified by his lenses, she couldn't imagine anything she wanted to do more than take a walk with the two of them on a quiet Christmas Eve.

She looked back at the ornament and the picture of those three figures.

You can do hard things.

She thought of how many times Birdie had said those words to her.

She wanted to be as brave as her grandmother, who was

willing to trust someone else with her heart, even at eighty years old.

As brave as Griffin, who had found love after his own terrible loss.

Her pulse sounded loud in her ears. This was a season of miracles. Surely she could ask for one more miracle—that she could find the strength to reach for the priceless gift of love she had rejected the day before because of her cowardice.

If Rafe still wanted to offer it, anyway.

"A walk sounds lovely," she said after a pause. "Let me throw on my boots and my coat."

She hurriedly donned her warmest parka, along with her lined boots and her favorite matching scarf and beanie set that had been knitted by Birdie before her eyesight failed.

Rafe stood by the door, watching her with an impassive expression while Isaac sat on her wood floor, petting Sophie.

"Okay. I'm ready."

They walked outside and she saw it was still snowing lightly, tiny swirling flakes that sparkled in the streetlights.

"We weren't planning to go far," Rafe said, his voice still gruff. "Only around the block."

"That sounds perfect. I would enjoy stretching my legs. I feel like I have been sitting all day, either in a hospital room or at my grandmother's place."

They set off down the street, with Isaac taking the lead, holding the dog's leash and moving ahead of them several paces.

"I'm sorry," Rafe said in a low voice, when Isaac was too busy laughing at the dog and lifting his face to the snowflakes to pay them any attention.

"My mom always has a craft project on Christmas Eve. I didn't know what kind of ornament Isaac was making until he finished it and showed me or I would have tried to talk him out of it."

"It's fine."

Better than fine, she wanted to say. That ornament might possibly become her most precious possession.

"After we left my folks' house, he insisted he had to give it to you tonight. He wouldn't rest until I reluctantly agreed we could drop it off when we took Sophie out."

"I love it," she assured him. "He's such a sweet boy, Rafe."

They lapsed into silence while Amanda fought an epic battle within herself. She had to say something but her words seemed caught in her throat.

Faith over fear, she reminded herself sternly.

Finally, she drew in a deep breath for strength and plunged forward. "Rafe, I...I owe you an apology."

He shifted his gaze from his son to her. "For?"

Amanda curled her fingers inside her pockets. "Yesterday was a rough day for me. I've had time to...to think about it, and Birdie's accident triggered old trauma in me, remembering my father's accident and all the horror that came from that. I was so scared I would lose Birdie. I was not in a good place."

"Understandable. It was a rough day."

She looked up at him, wishing she could better read his expression in the amber glow of the streetlight. "Yes. And I made it worse. I can't make important life decisions from that place of fear."

His scrutiny sharpened and she took another deep breath. This was so hard. Yet she knew suddenly that trying to live without the two of them would be so much harder.

She drew strength from the picture Isaac had drawn of the three of them together and finally went on, her voice low, "I don't want to miss out on something wonderful because I can't find the courage to take risks outside my comfort zone."

She halted on the sidewalk in front of a brightly decorated yard and he stopped with her, facing her fully now with an intensity in his gaze that both thrilled and terrified her.

"On *someone* wonderful."

She saw it then, a tiny glint of hope in his eyes. Of hope and joy and love. He didn't kiss her. Instead, after a moment, he reached for her hand.

That was all. He didn't say anything, he simply held her hand as they followed after Isaac and his cute little borrowed dog.

Happiness seemed to wash over her in warm waves, and Amanda had to blink back tears as they continued walking, boots crunching in snow and a young boy's giggles rising up through the perfect night like sleigh bells.

27

AS RAFE WALKED ALONG BESIDE AMANDA, HER COLD fingers curled inside his, with Isaac and Sophie racing ahead of them, he was aware of a soft, fragile sort of peace bubbling through him.

Despite the usual anticipation for the holidays and Isaac's infectious enthusiasm, Rafe had felt removed from everything for the past twenty-four hours, bundled in a thick, heavy darkness.

When he had kissed her the night before, he felt the same rush as when he was standing on the brink of a tough ski run, about to shove off with his poles. Exhilarated, energized, charged with adrenaline.

He had sensed they were poised on the edge of something amazing, the kind of joy he had never experienced before.

And then she had bluntly pushed him away, had told him she wasn't willing to take his hand and jump into the unknown with him, and it felt as if he had been shoved down the mountainside without skis or poles.

Now he didn't know quite what to think. Was it possible

they could find their way to happiness together? She had spoken with emotion vibrating in her voice the day before. She had meant every word.

Now she was walking with him on this magical Christmas Eve, her hand tucked into his with a trust he found humbling.

He wasn't sure where to go from here, though.

"Your house is beautiful," Amanda said when they were a few houses away. "I have been meaning to tell you that for weeks, since you hung the lights. Please don't tell me you climbed up by yourself, though, to put them up."

Rafe made a face. "I wish I could say that is what happened, but my dad and brother came over one afternoon while I was working at the market and I came home to find the job done."

She smiled, looking at the multicolored lights that lined each angle of his house. "How lucky that you have someone who loves you enough to help hang your Christmas lights."

"Yeah. I am definitely lucky."

Right now, with her hand in his, and his son running ahead on this silent and peaceful Christmas Eve, he felt like the luckiest man on earth.

Isaac and the dog waited for them to catch up near their mailbox. Rafe wondered if he would say anything about their entwined hands, but he apparently didn't think anything of it. He didn't seem to notice. Or if he did, he didn't think it worthy of mention.

"Dad, can Amanda come inside and see our tree?" Isaac begged. "I made a ton of ornaments for it."

The only other time she had been inside their home, when she had been kind enough to bring him several meals after he broke his arm, their tree hadn't been up yet.

That seemed like a lifetime ago. He felt as if his entire world had shifted in that time. His perspective certainly had.

"That's up to Amanda."

She didn't seem to hesitate. "I would love to see your tree."

"Yay!" Isaac couldn't have looked happier if they had come home to find a sleigh and eight reindeer parked on their lawn.

Sophie scampered up the steps and sat waiting by the door, tongue lolling, while Rafe unlocked his front door. He felt a little bereft having to release Amanda's hand.

As soon as they were inside, he let the dog off the leash and harness and she raced for her water bowl in the kitchen, as if she had just finished a hot and dusty marathon across the desert.

Amanda stood inside, looking around. "Have you done some work in this room since I was here last?"

"I cleared out some things and finished painting the trim."

She raised an eyebrow. "With a broken arm?"

He shrugged. What could he say? He did not like to sit still. "I paint with my right hand, anyway. I had some spare time in the mornings and I figured we didn't need to live in a construction zone for the holidays."

"It's lovely."

Rafe wasn't much of a designer. Fortunately, his mom and sister-in-law had helped him pick out furnishings and he had one of Crista's lovely watercolors, this one of Haven Lake in summer, hanging above the sofa.

It was cozy and comfortable, made more so when he flipped the switch to the gas fireplace that immediately crackled to life.

"Do you see our tree?" Isaac asked. He reached for her hand and tugged her over for a closer look. Rafe listened while his son pointed out every ornament he had made at school, at his grandparents' house or by himself.

Rafe wanted to tell Isaac to keep going. Talk to her all night. He didn't want Amanda to leave. He wanted her to stay for Christmas Eve, for Christmas morning and everything in between.

"Can I take your coat?" he asked.

She looked torn. "I should probably head home. Somebody

needs to go to bed or Santa won't be able to come," she said, with a pointed look at Isaac.

"Santa Claus comes *tonight*! I can't believe it's really here!" Isaac glowed in the flame from the gas fireplace Rafe had turned on.

"Would you stay?" Rafe asked Amanda, his voice low. "You're right, I need to get this kiddo settled for bed but I would like the chance to talk to you."

She hesitated, looking torn. She looked at Isaac then back at Rafe. After a moment that felt like it lasted a lifetime, she nodded.

As Isaac gave a shout of happiness, she pulled off her hat and her scarf. Rafe helped her out of her coat, surrounded by her scent of sugar cookies and strawberry candy canes.

"I'll go get my pajamas on, then maybe you can read me a story," Isaac suggested.

"Maybe," she said with a laugh.

He ran out of the room, a delighted Sophie at his heels, leaving the two of them alone. Rafe wanted to pull Amanda into his arms, to hold her and kiss her and tell her all the thoughts racing through his head.

Unfortunately, he knew from experience that Isaac could change into his pajamas faster than any of the guys at the station could pull on their turnout gear.

Sure enough, he had barely had time to ask Amanda if he could get her something to drink before Isaac barreled back into the room, his arms loaded with Christmas books.

"Can you read me a Christmas story? We always read one before I go to bed."

"I would love to," she said. "Shall we sit here by the fire and warm up after our lovely walk?"

He nodded and sat down on one side of the sofa, pointing to the middle cushion next to him. "Amanda, you can sit here. Dad, you sit on her other side so you can still see the pictures."

He wasn't about to complain. He sat down while she opened the book in front of her and began to read one of Isaac's favorites, a story about a lost puppy that found a new family for Christmas.

"I love that story," Isaac declared with a happy sigh when she had read the final words.

"It is a good one," she agreed.

"Will you read me another one?"

She glanced at Rafe.

"One more," he said. "How about we read the Christmas story *Abi* and *Ito* gave you tonight?"

"Oh yeah! I forgot about that one."

Isaac raced into the kitchen, where the box of things they had brought from Rafe's parents house that evening was still on the island.

He quickly returned, holding the storybook over his head in triumph and then thrusting it at her.

Amanda took it from him with a laugh. After Isaac was once more settled beside her, she began reading in her lyrical, lovely voice. This was a retelling of the original Christmas story, told from a young shepherd's perspective.

Rafe was almost as captivated as Isaac.

No matter what happened between him and Amanda, he would never forget the magic and wonder of this evening.

When she finished, they all sat in silence, none of them eager to break the enchanting spell good storytelling and the meaning behind it seemed to have woven around them.

From the floor, Sophie suddenly passed gas in a noisy burst, setting Isaac off into peals of laughter.

Rafe caught Amanda's gaze and saw her fighting a smile.

"On that lovely note, it's time for you to go to bed. Amanda is right. Santa won't be able to come until you're asleep."

"Okay," Isaac said with remarkable docility. "We have to put the cookies out for Santa first and the carrots for the reindeer."

"Right. Got it."

They went through the required steps of pulling out the special holiday china his mother had given them solely for this purpose. He helped Isaac find a cookie and a glass of milk, as well as a couple carrot sticks for the reindeer.

He might eat the cookie and perhaps a bit of carrot but he fully intended to pour the milk down the sink.

"Okay. Into bed now."

"Sophie can sleep with me, right? That's what you said."

"Yes. I did say that, didn't I? I think she probably needs to go out one more time. I'll bring her in later."

"You promise?"

"Cross my heart."

"Can Amanda help tuck me in, too?" his little manipulator of a son asked with his sweetest smile.

"Sure," she answered. She followed the two of them to Isaac's room and stood in the doorway while Rafe went through their bedtime routine: Brush teeth in the en suite bathroom, say prayers beside the bed, take off glasses and store them carefully on the bedside table, then climb between the sheets.

He kissed Isaac's forehead and pulled the blankets up more snugly.

"Good night, son."

Isaac threw his arms around his neck and clung tightly. "I love you, Dad."

"I love you too, kiddo. Merry Christmas."

"I love you too, Amanda," Isaac announced holding out his arms to her.

After a startled moment, she stepped forward and hugged him hard.

"Merry Christmas, Isaac. Thank you for helping to make my holidays so magical this year."

He yawned and she kissed him on the forehead. "And thank you for the ornament. I will treasure it always."

"You're welcome. Good night. Don't forget to bring Sophie in here after she goes outside, okay?"

"I won't forget," Rafe answered.

Amanda left the room first and Rafe turned off the light and closed the door. They both returned to the living room.

"I should probably head home. Thank you, for tonight. It was...unforgettable."

He had a hundred things he wanted to say to her but he couldn't seem to find the words for any of them. "Can you stay a little longer? I can drive you home after Isaac's asleep."

"You don't have to drive me. I'm perfectly fine walking. It's only five hundred feet."

"Okay, I'll walk you home, then. I have to take Sophie out again anyway and I have to use a leash since our backyard isn't fenced yet. I tore out the old one that was falling down."

"Did you do that with a broken arm, too?"

He made a face. "No. That was right after we moved into the house." He tilted his head. "Maybe you could help me sneak all of Isaac's presents out from the box in the garage where I've been hiding them and set them around the tree with me. You should take pity on the guy with only one working arm right now."

She laughed. "Your broken arm doesn't seem to stop you from anything else. You painted your house!"

"Only this room."

She firmed her lips as if trying not to laugh again. "Oh well, that's different."

"I really would love your help."

After a moment's consideration, she nodded. "I'll stay. I wouldn't want you to overdo or anything."

"Great. Wonderful. Can I get you something to drink? I have a can of some gourmet hot cocoa one of the neighbors brought over."

"That sounds good."

She followed him into the kitchen and they updated each other on the health status of their respective grandparents while he heated mugs of water, mixed up the cocoa and—since he was fancy like that—pulled a whipped cream canister out of the refrigerator and sprayed a healthy dollop on each.

"Wow. Looks delicious," she said with a smile.

"We can take them in by the fire," he suggested.

"Sounds good."

She carried her mug into the living room and perched on the sofa. In a blue Christmas sweater covered in sequin silver stars, she looked lovely and festive, and he decided they could no longer avoid the topic they had both been skirting around.

"About what you said earlier," he finally said. "That you were acting from a place of fear yesterday."

She released a breath, looking nervous suddenly. "Yes."

"I understand. Believe me, I get it. I've been doing that since Caitlin left, I think. Longer than that, even. Since she started using again."

"It would have been hard not to be afraid for her."

"I was," he agreed. "But I was mostly scared for Isaac. I hated knowing he was likely going to end up hurt because of my choices."

She frowned. "Not yours. Caitlin's."

"But I married her, knowing in some corner of my subconscious that she was still fighting her demons, despite appearances to the contrary. I thought love—my love—would fix everything. Obviously, it didn't."

"I'm sorry," she murmured.

"I've been…attracted to you for a long time. But I've been hesitant to do anything about it because I knew what you had been through. I could see the shadows in your eyes."

She gazed at him out of those same expressive eyes he had come to love.

He set down the mug he had only taken a few sips from and took her hand in his again, entwining their fingers together.

"These past few weeks have changed my perspective," he said. "Some people who sustain trauma hide away inside themselves or turn to behaviors that help dull the pain. Or both."

He squeezed her fingers. "Others use their pain to become stronger. They aren't afraid to reach out to others, to lift and help them."

Their gazes met and locked.

"They watch out for their grandmother and her friends, they befriend a motherless little boy, they bring meals to the ornery curmudgeon down the street."

"Oh," she whispered, her eyes glittery and bright.

He took the cocoa mug from her and set it on the side table, then finally did what he had wanted to for the past hour. He pulled her close and pressed his mouth to hers.

As Rafe kissed her, Amanda felt as weightless as a snowflake dancing on the breeze.

She had known heartbreak so deep she hadn't been sure she would endure it. But he was right. She had come through the other side with a hard-won strength and compassion.

She couldn't forgo the chance to be with him. She loved Rafe and she loved his son. She had to seize this priceless opportunity life had given her, this second chance.

The alternative was a heartbreak as deep and bottomless as Lake Haven.

She finally drew away and met his gaze. "I love you, Rafe. That is what I should have said last night. What I *wish* I had said. Yes, it scares me. But it also feels so perfectly right."

Rafe's eyes softened with tenderness as he leaned in to kiss her again, sealing the moment with a promise of love and devotion.

As they embraced on that beautiful Christmas Eve, with

snow falling softly out the window and the lights of his tree gleaming through the darkness, Amanda's fear melted away like snowflakes on her tongue. In Rafe's arms, she felt safe, cherished, utterly content.

The fear that had plagued her dissolved into the magic of the moment, replaced by a beautiful sense of peace and belonging.

Wrapped in his arms, as the world outside seemed to stand still, Amanda knew this was where she belonged. Here, with Rafe, sharing in the joy of the holiday season and the promise of a future filled with love and laughter and joy.

epilogue

OH, HOW SHE LOVED THE DECEMBER MARKET.

As Amanda walked through the crowds, her stepson holding her hand, her heart swelled with joy at the festive atmosphere surrounding them. The massive Christmas tree presided over the scene and the crisp winter air was alive with the sound of carolers, the scent of freshly baked goods and the twinkling lights that adorned every stall.

It had been a whirlwind few months since she and Rafe had exchanged vows in a beautiful autumn ceremony. Three months of married bliss had flown by in a blur of love and laughter as they settled into their new life together in Rafe's more spacious home on Huckleberry Street, which they had worked throughout the summer to renovate together.

Amanda had hated leaving Rose Cottage but knew his house, with its larger backyard and extra bedrooms, was a better fit for the family they were building together.

She was delighted that her friend Holly had been able to purchase Rose Cottage and lived there now with Lydia. Together, they were making it their own and Amanda couldn't be happier for her friend.

"I don't know what to ask for this year," Isaac admitted as they navigated toward the chalet where Santa and Mrs. Claus presided. At seven, he was on the cusp of no longer believing in the magic and wonder of Santa Claus. She wanted to hang on to it as long as possible.

She smiled at the memory of him sitting on Santa's lap the previous year, asking for a mother for Christmas. It had taken nine months for that wish to officially come true, but she was so deeply grateful that they all now had each other. This past year had been worlds better than she ever could have imagined.

"I'm sure you'll think of something," Rafe said, following behind them.

"I asked *Abuelo* and Birdie what I should ask for. Do you want to know what they said?" Isaac asked with a sudden mischievous grin.

Their grandparents were still together, delighted to have had a hand in bringing Rafe and Amanda together. Though they had each kept their respective apartments at the Shelter Inn, they spent nearly every waking hour in each other's company, sharing a deep and lasting love that inspired Amanda every time she was with them.

"Sure," Rafe answered. "What did they say?"

"They said I should wish for a baby brother or sister. Maybe even twins. That would be awesome, wouldn't it?"

Amanda nearly stumbled as his words hung in the air between them. She glanced at Rafe, whose mischievous smile matched his son's.

"Be careful what you wish for, kiddo," he said.

His hand reached for hers and he gave her fingers a meaningful squeeze They were planning to wait a year or so before adding to their family but whenever it happened, Amanda knew it would be wonderful. Rafe was an amazing father to Isaac, as she knew he would be to any children the two of them created together.

As they stood in line waiting their turn, Rafe pulled her back against his hard strength.

"Are you going to sit on Santa's lap?" he asked into her ear, his low words shivering down her spine.

She smiled at him as a wave of happiness washed over her. In that moment, standing with these two who had filled her life with so much love, she still wanted to pinch herself to make sure this wasn't one big, glorious dream.

"What would I even ask for, when I have everything I could ever want?"

He laughed softly and kissed the top of her head, and Amanda felt a sense of wonder and awe at the magic of the holiday season and the endless possibilities that lay ahead of them.

★ ★ ★ ★ ★

Fifteen summers ago, everything changed for Ava Howell. Now, back in Emerald Creek, she's grappling with a shattered marriage and a long-buried secret. Meanwhile, her sister, Madison, finds solace in their shared past and her love for the town vet. As Ava and Madison attempt to remedy the rifts in their lives and reconcile their futures, they must face the demons of their past together.

Read on for an excerpt from
15 Summers Later *by RaeAnne Thayne,*
available now from Canary Street Press!

1

The present is a delicate tightrope walk between liberation and the haunting memories that cling to us. The scent of freedom is both intoxicating and terrifying, and each step away from the compound feels like a small victory against the darkness that threatened to consume us.

—*Ghost Lake* by Ava Howell Brooks

Madison

"HERE, LET ME GET THAT FOR YOU. YOU SHOULDN'T BE grabbing heavy bags of food off the shelf without help. You might hurt yourself, honey."

At the well-meaning but misguided efforts of her seventy-year-old neighbor, Madison Howell tried not to grind her teeth.

Under other circumstances, she might have thought the old rancher was being misogynistic, assuming any young woman was too fragile and frail to heft a fifty-pound bag of dog food onto her cart.

Unfortunately, she knew that wasn't the case. Calvin Warner simply thought *she* couldn't do it.

How could she blame him, when the majority of her neighbors shared his sentiments, beliving she was forever damaged?

"It's fine. I've got it," she insisted, taking a firm hold of the bag.

"Now, don't be stubborn. Let me help you."

He set his cane aside—yes, he actually had a cane!—and all but shoved her out of the way.

Short of engaging in a no-holds-barred, Greco-Roman wrestling match right there in the farm supply store with a curmudgeon who had arthritis and bad knees, Madi didn't know what else to do but watch in frustration while he lifted the bag onto her large platform cart.

"Thank you," she said as graciously as she could manage. "Now I need five more bags."

"Five?" Calvin looked aghast.

"Yes. We have twenty-two dogs right now at the rescue. You don't need a new Aussie, do you? We have four from an abandoned litter."

"No. I'm afraid not. I'm a border-collie man myself and I have three of them. Twenty-two dogs. My word. That must be a lot of work."

Yes, the work required to care for the animals at the Emerald Creek Animal Rescue was endless. All twenty-two dogs, ten cats, two llamas, three potbellied pigs, four goats and two miniature horses and a donkey required food, attention, medical care, exercise and, unfortunately, waste cleanup.

Madi didn't care. She loved the work and adored every one of their animals. After years of dreaming, planning, struggling, she considered it something of a miracle that the animal shelter was fully operational now.

For the past three months, Madi had been running full tilt, juggling her job as a veterinary tech as well as the hours and hours required to organize her team of volunteers, hire a full-time office assistant and do her part caring for the animals.

She was finally ready to take a huge leap of faith. In only a few more weeks, she would be quitting her job as a veterinary technician at the local clinic so that she could work full time as the director of the animal rescue.

She tried to ignore the panic that always flickered through her when she thought of leaping into the unknown.

"The dogs are easy," she answered Calvin now. "Don't get me started on the goats and the potbellied pigs."

"I heard you were doing something over there at Gene Pruitt's old place. I had no idea you were up to your eyeballs in animals."

"Yes. We've started the first no-kill animal sanctuary in this area. Our goal is to take in any abandoned, injured or ill-treated animal in need, help rehabilitate them and place them in new homes."

He blinked in surprise, his bushy eyebrows meeting in the middle. "Is that right? Are there really that many animals in need of help in these parts?"

"Yes. Without question. We have no other no-kill shelters serving this area of Idaho. I'm grateful we have been able to fill that need."

For years, since finishing college and returning to Emerald Creek, Madi had been struggling to start the shelter. She had modest success applying for grants and seeking donations from various national and local donors, but it still seemed out of reach.

A year ago, the sanctuary had come closer than ever to reality when a crusty old local bachelor with no remaining family had left his twenty-acre farm, as well as a small house on the property, to the Emerald Creek Animal Rescue Foundation.

She was still overwhelmed at Eugene Pruitt's generosity.

Even so, it had taken an additional incredibly generous gift from an anonymous donor to truly allow them to be able to take care of the start-up operating expenses for the sanctuary without having to heavily mortgage the property.

As hard as she had worked to make her dream a reality, there were still plenty of people in town who would never see her as anything other than that poor Howell girl with the leg brace and the permanent half smile.

"Thank you for your help, Mr. Warner," she said, after the two of them managed to load up the platform cart.

He appeared slightly out of breath and his hand trembled as he reached for his cane. She shouldn't have let him help her. The strong, confident woman she wanted to be would have politely told him to move on. Thanks but no thanks. She could handle it, as she had been handling all the challenges that had come her way since her mother's death when she was twelve.

She had a fair distance to go before she truly was that strong, confident woman.

"Glad I could be here." Calvin gripped his cane. "You know, they have staff here that can give you a hand next time. They can probably help you take this out to your car. That's why they're here."

She forced a smile. "I'll keep that in mind. Thanks. And if you decide you need another Aussie, let me know. They're smart as can be and are all caught up on their shots. Dr. Gentry takes very good care of all of our animals at the sanctuary."

"He's a good man. Not quite the vet his father was, but he's getting there."

Before she could object on Luke's behalf and express that he was an excellent veterinarian in his own right, the rancher's eyes went wide and he suddenly looked horrified at his own words.

"I'm sorry. I wasn't thinking. Shouldn't have brought up old Doc Gentry with you."

Madi could feel each muscle along her spine tighten. "Why not?" she managed.

Calvin gave her a significant look. "You know. Because of… because of the book."

The book. That blasted book.

"The wife bought a copy the day it came out, after she saw all the buzz about it online. She's a good reader. Me, not so much. I like audiobooks, but we've been reading it together of an evening. It's awful, everything that happened to you."

Madi tightened her hands on the handle of the platform cart, fighting the urge to push it quickly toward the checkout stand.

The last thing she wanted to talk about was her sister's memoir, which had hit bookstores two weeks earlier and had become the runaway success of the summer, already going back for a third printing.

Madi didn't want to talk about *Ghost Lake*, to hear *other people* talk about it or to even *think* about it.

"Right. Well, thank you again for your help, Mr. Warner. I should get on with my sh-shopping."

Now she did tighten her hands on the cart, jaw tight.

She hated her stammer that sometimes came out of nowhere. She hated the way her mouth was frozen into a half smile all the time, how she only had partial use of her left hand and the way her leg sometimes completely gave out if she didn't wear the brace.

And she especially hated the way her sister had exposed their history, their past, their pain to the entire world.

"Take care," Calvin said, a gentleness in his gruff tone that made her somehow want to scream and weep at the same time.

"Thank you," she said, as graciously as she could manage, and then pushed the unwieldy cart toward the checkout stand.

She reached it as the woman seated on a high stool at the cash register slid a book with a familiar white-and-bloodred cover beneath the counter.

That blasted book was everywhere. She couldn't escape it.

"Hi there, Madi." Jewel Littlebear, whose family owned the

feed store, gave her a nervous-looking smile, her gaze shifting in the direction of the book.

Jewel had been in Ava's grade at school. The two of them had been friends once, before Madi's sister walked away from everything she once cared about here in Emerald Creek.

"Hi Jewel. How are things? How are the boys?"

Jewell had three hellion sons. She and her family lived on the same street as Madi's grandmother, in a small ranch-style home where the front yard was covered in toys and bikes and basketballs.

"They're good. All three of them are playing baseball this summer. I swear, I spend more time over at the park watching their games than I do in my own house."

She smiled, rose from her stool and carried the handheld scanner around the counter so she could capture the codes on the large bags of food without Madi having to lift them onto the counter.

"Um. That will be a hundred sixty-five dollars and fifteen cents. I'm sorry."

What exactly was she sorry about? That the price of quality dog food was so high? Or that Madi had caught her reading That Book?

Madi decided not to ask. She swiped the rescue's credit card and felt a burst of pride when it went through easily.

A moment later, the register spit out her receipt, which Jewel handed over with a smile.

"There you go," she said, handing it to Madi.

"Thanks. I'll see you later."

She hadn't even walked away from the checkout counter before Jewell pulled the book back out and picked up where she had left off.

Was she reading about their mother's car accident and the raw, visceral pain their family went through afterward?

Or their father's steady but inexorable downward spiral into obsession, depression, mental illness?

Or those final horrible days when she and Ava, fourteen and sixteen respectively, had escaped a grim situation that had become impossible, only to find themselves in even worse circumstances?

She didn't want to know.

Madi hurried out to her pickup, the classic, if dilapidated, teal 1961 Chevrolet Stepside pickup she called Frank that she had inherited from her maternal grandfather.

A few months ago, she had ordered a vinyl-lettered sign for Frank's side, with the stylized teal-and-yellow logo for the animal sanctuary. Now she only used Frank for sanctuary errands and for social media purposes. It photographed wonderfully and helped raise awareness for their mission.

She had considered driving the pickup in the town's Fourth of July parade in a month, maybe with a few of the animals in crates in the bed, but now the idea made her slightly ill. She could imagine how everyone would point and talk about her now.

There goes poor Madi Howell. Did you read about what happened to her?

I knew she was odd, with her perma-smile and that limp and her curled-up hand. I guess now we know why.

Renewed fury at her sister broiled under her skin. She did her best to push it away as she maneuvered the big cart to her pickup and opened the tailgate.

Though there were several vehicles in the parking lot, none of them was occupied. At least she didn't have to fend off more offers of help.

She loaded the bags by herself into the back of the truck, then paused a moment to breathe away her stress, trying to focus instead on the glorious early June day, with the mountains green

and verdant and still capped with contrasting white snow that
had yet to melt at the higher elevations.

She dearly loved living in Emerald Creek. This small community a half hour from Sun Valley was home. She could never
forget how warm and supportive everyone had been when she
and Ava moved back to live with their grandmother Leona after
everything that happened.

She had wonderful friends here, a job at the vet clinic that
she had loved for eight years, and now her passion project, the
animal sanctuary.

She had never seriously considered living anywhere else.

But sometimes she had to wonder what it would be like to
make her home in a place where she could be a little more…
anonymous.

Did that place even exist, now that her sister had spilled their
secret trauma to the whole blasted world?

She climbed into the cab of the pickup, fighting a headache,
then drove away from the farm supply store, heading through
town on her way toward the sanctuary.

It was a beautiful summer afternoon. A couple of older men
sat on a bench, shooting the breeze outside the Rustic Pine
Trading Post and she saw a healthy line of tourists waiting for
the always-busy Fern & Fir Restaurant to open.

As she turned onto Mountain View Road, she slowed down
when she spotted a trio of girls on bicycles ahead of her. Four,
she realized. One bike held two girls. She was aware of a quick,
sharp ache. How often had she and Ava ridden together through
the streets of their own town in eastern Oregon like that? Too
many to count, but that was in the days before their mother
died and everything changed.

She waved at the girls as she passed, recognizing Mariko
and Yuki Tanaka as well as Zoe Sullivan and Sierra Gentry.
Sierra and Zoe both volunteered at the animal rescue a few
hours a week.

She pulled the truck over ahead of them, and the girls rode up beside her. "Hey girls. What are you up to on this beautiful day?"

Sierra leaned into the open passenger window, her brown hair streaked with sunlight. "We were hanging out at my place and thought maybe we would ride to the Dixon's farm stand and grab some fresh strawberries."

"We really love strawberries," Zoe said with a giggle.

Madi strongly suspected the real draw wasn't so much the strawberries but Ash Dixon, the heartthrob fifteen-year-old whose family ran a popular farm stand and also had a stall at the Emerald Thumbs Farmers Market on Saturday mornings.

"Sounds like fun. Enjoy a crepe for me."

"I will. Bye, Mad. See you later."

She waved and put the truck in gear again, though before she drove away she thought she heard the words *book* and *Ghost Lake* from the girls, through her open window.

No. She was imagining things. That damn book seemed to be popping up everywhere...but only a narcissist would think everyone in town was talking about her, right?

2

I am a coward. It is a grim, humbling realization for someone who has always considered herself strong.

—*Ghost Lake* by Ava Howell Brooks

Ava

EVERYONE IN TOWN SEEMED TO BE STARING AT HER.
As she drove down Main Street in Emerald Creek, Idaho, Ava told herself she was being ridiculous. Why would they possibly be staring at her?

She had only lived in Emerald Creek with her grandmother for a few years, between the ages of sixteen and eighteen, and had been away for more than a decade, with only the occasional visit home. She probably didn't know all that many people who still lived here and those who *did* know her likely wouldn't recognize her anymore.

When she drove past the new-and-used bookstore, Meadowside Book Nook, she almost drove into the back of a big black dually pickup truck ahead of her.

Out of the corner of her gaze, Ava's attention had been caught by the window display at the bookstore. The entire front window featured the red and white cover of *Ghost Lake*, with that moody line drawing of a mountain lake.

Oh, this was bad. Really bad.

Madi must be so furious with her.

What did her sister think when she drove past this display every day?

Maybe she hadn't noticed it.

Ava knew that was a ridiculous hope. Of course Madi would have noticed it. And she was probably angry every single time she saw it.

Ava knew from her grandmother Leona in one of their frequent Zoom calls that Madi was furious about the book.

She didn't quite understand why. It wasn't as if Madi hadn't known it was coming. Ava had tried to give her sister plenty of warning the book was releasing in late May.

When she first began to realize herself that her book's journey toward publication was actually happening—and much faster than she'd ever imagined—Ava had been upfront with her sister.

Six months earlier, Ava had sent her an advanced reading copy of the manuscript, then she waited for a response. And waited. And waited.

When she nervously called a few weeks later, her stomach tangled with nerves, Madi had been nonchalant, even blasé. She had made excuses about how busy she was, still working at the vet clinic while trying to organize all the details to open the Emerald Creek Animal Rescue.

"Anyway, I lived it," Madi had finally said as their awkward conversation drew to a close. "I'm sorry, but once was enough. I don't really need to go over everything again."

Ava should have pushed her to read the book. She should have made sure Madi wouldn't be blindsided when the book started to receive prepublication buzz.

How could Ava have known everything would explode as it had? Everyone involved with the book had high hopes it would succeed, but even her publisher had to rush back to print more copies in order to keep up with demand.

Ava's hands were tight on the steering wheel as she drove through town and finally pulled into the driveway to her grandmother's two-story house, with its extravagant, colorful garden in full bloom.

She was relieved when she didn't see Madi's small SUV or their grandfather's ancient pickup truck her sister drove occasionally.

Ava would have to face her sister at some point. Not yet, though. She was far too exhausted to deal with Madi right now. After she had rested, maybe. She was tired enough to sleep for a week, though she wasn't sure even that would be enough to ease her bone-deep fatigue.

When she climbed out of the vehicle, her bones ached and nausea roiled through her.

She swallowed it down as she spied her grandmother working in one of the gardens near the house, wearing a floppy straw hat and a pair of overalls.

Her grandmother wore earbuds, her back to Ava, humming along as she clipped back her bleeding hearts. She probably hadn't even noticed the car pull in, Ava realized when her grandmother didn't come to greet her.

She moved in that direction and a German shepherd mix suddenly rose from the porch and gave a single bark. Ava froze, instant panic washing over her, icy and raw. After a few seconds, she forced herself to relax. That was only Oscar. He wouldn't hurt her.

She hoped.

The dog's greeting must have alerted Leona to her company. Her grandmother turned around, and Ava saw the shock in her eyes before Leona dropped her pruning scissors with a shriek and rushed toward her, arms outstretched.

"Ava! Darling! What are you doing here? Why didn't you call to tell me you were coming? Oh, my dear. It's so wonderful to see you, even though you're far too thin."

Leona reached her and wrapped those arms around her tightly, and Ava wanted to sink into the comfort of her embrace.

What would her grandmother do if Ava simply rested her head on her shoulder and wept and wept and wept?

Leona seemed to sense something was wrong. She pushed Ava away from her and studied her closely, blue eyes behind her thick glasses missing nothing. Ava faced her, aware of the deep circles under her eyes, the lines of fatigue she knew must be sharply etched on her features.

"What is it? What's wrong?"

So much. Everything.

She couldn't tell her grandmother yet. She would, but she needed time to figure out the words.

"I need somewhere to stay for a few weeks. Maybe even all summer. Would that be all right?"

Concern and alarm flashed over Leona's wrinkled features. "You know you're always welcome, my dear. And Cullen as well. Is he joining you?"

The sound of her husband's name was like a stiletto to her heart and it was all she could do to remain standing.

"No," she managed. "He won't be joining me. Cullen is working on a dig up in the mountains near here this summer. Some fossilized bones were found on national forest land and Cullen and his team think it might be an entirely new dinosaur species."

She tried to be casual with the words and not spill them all out in a rush. "He's ecstatic to be leading the team. It's a dream come true for him. You know what a dinosaur nerd he is."

"Indeed." Leona smiled, though that worry lingered in her gaze. "It's a good thing he likes them. It would be odd if he didn't, since he teaches paleontology. What a wonderful opportunity."

"Yes. I'm thrilled for him. We're both hoping this might help him make full professor, with tenure."

"How exciting!"

"Yes. But he'll be mostly out of reach for the summer and I…I didn't want to stay by myself at our apartment in Portland. After only a few days, I couldn't stand it, so I packed up everything and headed here. I hope that's okay."

She couldn't find the words to tell her grandmother that her marriage might be as dead as those fossils.

"Oscar and I would be delighted to have you stay with us. Won't we, Oscar?"

The dog's tongue lolled out as he studied her. Oscar. Why hadn't she remembered her grandmother and the dog were a package deal?

Every time she visited, she felt as if he were watching her out of eyes as sharp as Leona's, waiting for his moment to swoop in and attack.

The dogs are growing closer. I can hear them baying from the next ridgeline. Could our scent carry that far? I have no idea, nor do I think I can ask Madi to go through the river again to try disguising our path. We have crossed it dozens of times already. Each time, more of her miniscule energy seems to burn away.

They bark again and my heart pounds so loudly, remembering sharp teeth, slavering tongues, wild eyes. Surely the dogs can hear each pulse of my blood, each ragged breath.

She quickly pushed away the memory, the words.

"Thanks, Grandma Leelee."

Her grandmother's features softened at the nickname Ava had come up with for her as a toddler.

"You're welcome, darling. You can stay in your old room upstairs. I'll have to move a few storage boxes out. I've been clearing out closets of all my old crap and have put everything in your room so I only have to make one trip to Goodwill eventually."

"You don't have to move anything. I can work around some boxes."

"It's no problem. I'll put them in your sister's room for now, since she's living full time at the farmhouse on the animal rescue property these days."

Ava tensed at her sister's name, though Madi hadn't left her thoughts since she rolled into town. "How is she doing?" she asked, her voice low.

Leona brushed dirt off her overalls. "Well, you're not exactly her favorite person right now. Let's put it that way."

She swallowed hard. "I told her about the book. I sent her an advanced copy. She had plenty of warning."

"Yes. She knew it was coming. But you know Madi. She tends to focus on what's directly in front of her. She's been so busy trying to get the animal rescue off the ground, I think it was easier for her to put your book out of her head and pretend it wasn't really happening. Now that it's out, she can't escape it."

She had known the publication of her memoir detailing their months in the mountains and all the events leading up to it would be a pivotal event in her life. She hadn't realized how every single one of her relationships would be impacted, from her casual friendships to the guy who used to fill up her car with gas to her fellow faculty members at the middle school where she taught English.

She wasn't sure her marriage could ever recover.

You never told me half of the things you went through.

Cullen's voice seemed to echo through her memory, stunned and upset and...hurt as he looked down at his copy of *Ghost Lake* as if it were a viper that had suddenly invaded their bed.

I feel like I've been married to a stranger for the past three years.

He had been the one to suggest they use their separation while he was working in the remote mountains near here to figure out what sort of future they could salvage.

I love you, Ava. That hasn't changed. But I think we both need time to figure out where we go from here.

Her entire world was falling apart because of the words she had written. The same stark, painful honesty that seemed to resonate with the rest of the world now threatened to destroy the two things she held most dear, her relationship with her sister and her marriage to Cullen Brooks.

"Come on. Let's get you settled before you fall over," Leona said with a warm smile that made Ava again want to weep.

Her grandmother carried her laptop case into the house while Ava followed behind with her suitcase.

The house smelled of vanilla and strawberry pie, scents that made her stomach rumble with the reminder that she hadn't had anything but a few crackers since dinner the evening before.

This trip had been completely impulsive. Reckless, even. After spending three nights alone in their apartment in Portland, she decided she couldn't take the echoing silence another moment. That very morning she had awoken gritty-eyed from a night of tossing and turning. One moment, she had been brushing her teeth, the next, she'd grabbed her suitcase out from under the bed and started throwing in everything she thought she might need.

After talking to her neighbor about keeping an eye on things and picking up their mail, Ava headed out, stopping only twice during the entire nine-hour drive for gas.

What else could she do? She couldn't go ahead with the book tour, pretending everything was fine when her entire world felt…broken.

She should have told Cullen everything. She supposed she had hidden the truth because some part of her wanted, like Madison, to pretend none of it had happened. To pretend they were two average girls with an average childhood whose average parents each had died tragically, a few years apart.

That last part was certainly true, though only a small measure of the whole, complicated, messed-up story.

One could make the argument that the first part, about two average girls living an average childhood, was true as well… until the summer she turned fourteen and Madi turned twelve, when their mother died and everything changed.

Being here, in her mother's childhood home, only made her miss Beth all the more. Her mother had exemplified quiet strength and grace. She had been kind to everyone, the kind of person who drew others to her, eager to warm themselves in the bright light of joy that burned within her.

Ava missed her every single day.

Her phone rang as she carried her suitcase to the room that had been hers for the final two years of high school.

After sharing a room with her sister all her life, this room had been the first one Ava could claim as exclusively her own, and that was only because Madi's room downstairs had to be outfitted for all the things she needed to help her rehabilitation.

She pushed the memories away and pulled out her phone. Her literary agent, she saw when she checked the display.

Sylvia Wittman was a lovely woman who absolutely wanted the best for Ava. At this particular moment, they couldn't quite agree on what that was.

She sighed and let the call go to voicemail, as she had all the others that day.

Sylvia was no doubt calling with news about the various film and TV offers that had already come their way or to let her know some other book club wanted to feature *Ghost Lake*.

Most writers would consider it a dream come true to see their work go viral and generate so much interest on the national and international stage.

Ava supposed she wasn't most writers.

She only wanted to pull her old comforter off the bed, carry it to the closet and hide in the corner until all of this went away.

Tomorrow. She would deal with everything tomorrow, after she had the chance to sleep away this exhaustion that had seeped into her bones, her sinews.

Then she would have to figure out if there was anything she could do to fix her marriage or the rift with her sister...or if the wounds she had inflicted on the people she loved through her words could ever heal.

3

Blood stains the earth beneath us as the reality of our escape becomes painfully tangible. The pursuit of freedom comes at a terrible cost.

—*Ghost Lake* by Ava Howell Brooks

Luke

IF HE WASN'T CAREFUL, HE WAS IN DANGER OF BEING kicked in the groin by a goat.

Luke Gentry shifted positions as he tried to hold tight to the annoyed animal. "I'm not going to hurt you," he murmured. "I'm trying to help so you can walk better and without pain. I promise, you'll be happier when I'm done."

He continued talking nonsense to the goat as he trimmed her hooves carefully.

For a long time, he hadn't been sure this was the career choice for him. While he had always loved animals and never minded helping out at his father's veterinary clinic, he had resented everyone's automatic assumption that he would naturally want to follow in Dan Gentry's footsteps.

Luke once had other dreams. He had wanted to become an adventurer, to rock climb all the highest peaks in the world and ski the steepest slopes.

He hadn't really cared where, he had only known he hadn't wanted to be tied down here in Emerald Creek, Idaho.

Em-C, as the locals called it, was a pretty little town with plenty of recreational activities, but it had always felt too small to hold all his dreams. The world was so much bigger than this community of genuine ranchers and farmers as well as outdoor lovers and weekend cowboys near Sun Valley.

Over the years, his perspective had changed. He loved being the town's only veterinarian, building his home and his career here with his daughter, and couldn't imagine his life any other way—as long as this goat didn't manage to emasculate him, anyway.

He finally finished the last hoof and released Martha. "There you go. All done. See? That wasn't so bad."

The goat bleated at him and retreated to the other side of the pen. He opened the pen door to the outside and she escaped with a high-spirited leap into the Idaho sunshine.

He was heading to the office inside the Emerald Creek Animal Rescue barn when the double doors burst open and Madison Howell burst through, almost staggering under a large bag of dog food that probably weighed half as much as she did.

Luke had to fight down his instinctive urge to take it from her. He knew Madi well enough to know that probably wasn't a good idea.

She dropped the bag inside the barn and straightened, arching her back. Her features brightened when she spotted him. "Luke! Hey! I didn't expect you to drop by this evening, after you've already had a long day."

"So have you," he pointed out. He knew that all too well, since she was a veterinary technician in his clinic when she wasn't hauling dog food around here at the animal rescue. "I had a free few hours, so I swung in to check on Barnabas's injury and take care of Martha's hooves. He's doing fine and Martha should be good now and ready to rock and roll."

She gave her half smile, the one that always managed to brighten his entire day.

"Thanks. I could tell they were bothering her."

"She was a trooper, for the most part." He nodded toward the bag she set down against the wall. "Do you have a lot to unload?"

"Four more bags. That was all they had at the feed store."

"I can help you bring it in. Might as well at least save you a few trips."

Predictably, Madi looked as if she wanted to argue. Stubborn thing. She could be as obstinate as that goat, though he would never dare verbalize such a thing to her.

Finally, she bit her lip, the side that didn't lift. "Thanks," she said instead.

Her vintage pickup looked cheerful in the fading sunlight, all teal and yellow. Looking at the truck made him smile almost as much as looking at Madison did.

Luke hefted a bag over each shoulder and carried them back into the barn and set them against the wall, where she added the one she had carried.

"I'll grab the last bags."

He thought she would argue, but she only nodded. "Leave one in the truck, if you would. It's for Leona's dog. I'll run it over later tonight or in the morning."

When he returned to the barn, he discovered she was cradling a small calico kitten. He was familiar with all the sanctuary animals as he usually gave them a health exam when they first arrived. He didn't recognize the kitten.

"Where did you find this one?"

"On my way back from the feed store, I got a call from Charla Pope. She found a stray kitten mewling in her flower bed, with no sign of the mama cat anywhere. It's been there since last night. I stopped on my way home and the poor thing looks half-starved."

Madi had an uncanny knack for locating stray creatures. He suspected they were drawn to her, sensing a friend and savior.

She hadn't changed. She still tried to bring home every stray animal she could find, only now she did it officially, through the auspices of the Emerald Creek Animal Rescue.

"Want me to take a look at it?"

She gave him her unique smile, her eyes bright with gratitude. "Do you mind?"

"Not at all. I've got time. Let's take her into the exam room."

Still cradling the tiny kitten, Madi picked up her laptop from the office before following him into the small treatment room at the center.

She opened her laptop and created a treatment file for the kitten. "Want to name her?" she asked him.

He was lousy at picking animal names. "You rescued her. Go ahead."

She studied the kitten. "How about we call her Callie for now?"

"Sounds good."

She typed a few things onto the screen, with so much efficiency it was easy to miss how her left hand had a slight contracture and didn't work the same as her right did. It was nerve damage from injuries sustained fifteen years ago, but Madi didn't let it bother her.

He handled the animal with gentleness as he weighed it first and measured its size, reporting all those numbers for Madison to record.

"I don't see any sign of obvious disease or injury," he said after his initial exam. "She appears healthy, if a little malnourished."

"How old do you think she is?"

"Pure guesswork, but I would estimate her to be about five or six weeks old."

"That's what I was thinking. So no vaccinations for a few weeks and she's also old enough to be weaned."

"Yes, but I would still feed her kitten milk replacement along with some soft kitty chow."

"I've got some at the house. That sounds like a good plan."

"I'm going to guess she's part of a feral litter somewhere. Doesn't Charla's neighbor down the road have barn cats? Maybe this one wandered away. Or maybe something happened to the mother."

"You're probably right. I'll put the word out to Charla and others in her neighborhood to keep an eye out for any more strays. Thank you for taking a look."

"I'm happy to, but you didn't really need me."

She shrugged. "You're the professional."

"So are you."

For him, veterinary medicine was his vocation. For Madi, caring for animals was her calling. She adored them, with a depth of compassion that never failed to astonish him.

"On paper, I'm the vet, maybe," he went on. "But you know exactly what to do. You can handle anything, whether I'm here or not."

She made a face. "Tell that to everyone in town who doesn't think I am capable of even carrying a bag of dog food. Cal Warner insisted on loading my cart today. I'm not sure he even felt like I was capable of holding his cane, what with my fragile condition. And Ava has not helped matters at all with her stupid book."

Frustration shimmered off her in waves. "She has made everything so much worse. Why did she have to go and open up all those old wounds? We were doing fine."

He wasn't entirely certain that was true. Madi presented a

calm, happy front to the world, but Luke knew she had deep scars she hid from nearly everyone.

He felt fortunate to be one of the few people able to know the real Madison.

"Who did you catch reading it this time?"

"Calvin told me he and his wife were reading it together. And Jewel Littlebear at the feed store hid a copy below the counter when I checked out. I don't know why she bothered. I could still see it. Isn't everyone in town reading it?"

"Not quite everyone."

His phone rang and he glanced at the display. "That's Sierra. She's not reading it."

"No. But I think her friends are," Madi said darkly. "Or at least her friends' family members."

His phone rang again and she gestured to it. "You should get that. I saw her on my way here with her friends. They looked like they were having fun."

While she returned to the office and set down the kitten to explore her surroundings, he answered his daughter's call.

"Hey, Sierra. What's up?"

"Can I stay over at Zoe's house tonight?"

He frowned. "I thought we talked about heading into town and grabbing takeout sandwiches and then hiking up to Hidden Falls for a picnic."

"I know and I still really want to do that. But Zoe has to leave tomorrow to stay with her dad in Utah for six whole weeks. She'll be gone forever. This is, like, our last chance to hang out all summer. We wanted to do a slumber party with Mari and Yuki. Her mom says it's okay and she'll be home with us the whole night and so will Zoe's grandma."

Zoe's parents' divorce had not been amicable, he knew. Her mom currently lived with Zoe's grandmother across town.

"Sure. That's fine. I can give you a ride."

"No need. I have my bike. I'm going to grab a few things

at the house and put them in my backpack and head over now. Thanks, Dad. Love you. Bye."

"Love you back," he answered.

The click of the phone told him she had already hung up. He felt fortunate she had remembered to say goodbye as she was usually heading off in a dozen different directions.

He felt again that little tug at his heart. His baby girl was growing up. For the past four years, since her mother's death, they had been a pretty self-contained unit. He couldn't say it was them against the world, as he would have been lost without all the help from his mother and sister, as well as dear friends like Madi.

He and Sierra had a tight bond, though, and he always looked forward to the rare times they were able to hang out, only the two of them.

Apparently that wasn't going to happen that evening as he had hoped.

His sigh did not go unnoticed by Madi. "Sounds like you got stood up. Does Sierra have hot plans?"

"She wants to spend the night over at Zoe's place with Mariko and Yuki. Why not? That's much more fun than hanging out with her boring old man."

"I don't think she would agree. You know she adores you. Sounds like she got a better offer, though."

"Right. I can't really compete with a night of watching You-Tube videos and practicing TikTok dances."

"Sorry about that." She gave her half smile. "You can always come to the Burning Tree with me and Nic tonight. The Rusty Spurs are playing. Should be a wild time. If you want to play the boring-old-man card, you can be our designated driver."

He snorted. "I don't think you and my sister really want a chaperone, do you?"

"No. Absolutely not," she said, so quickly he had to smile. "But you can still come with us, have a drink, listen to the music. You deserve some fun in your life, Luke. Consider it self-care."

"I'll think about it, Dr. Howell," he said, though he expected *thinking about it* was all he would do. He would probably spend the night popping some popcorn and enjoying a beer and a baseball game.

Not a bad Friday night, in his opinion. Did that make him sound pathetic?

"Thanks again for your help," Madi said as they both headed out of the barn. The kitten was once more tucked into her bag.

"You're welcome."

Outside, the shadows of the late afternoon were long, with golden light that gleamed in the treetops and danced in her hair.

"Seriously," she said when they reached his truck. "You should come out tonight. The band starts playing at eight. If you don't want to drive us, you can meet us there. That way if you want to leave early, you won't feel trapped."

He shook his head, hand on the door frame of his blue pickup truck. "When did this become a done deal?"

"Admit it, Luke. You could use a night out. You work too hard. When you're not working, you're taking care of Sierra or helping out here at the animal rescue. Tell me the truth. When was the last time you did something simply because you wanted to?"

He snorted. "Who said I want to go hang out at a noisy bar with a bunch of half-drunk cowboys?"

"Plus your sister and me," she pointed out. "We'll be there, too. Don't you want to hang out with us, outside of work?"

"You're not going to let this go, are you?"

She grinned. "You'll have fun, I promise. It's better than sitting home on your own, watching some kind of lame sports ball."

"I happen to enjoy watching lame sports ball."

"I know, but how often do you get to watch live music surrounded by two hundred neighbors and strangers?"

"You're not exactly selling this."

"Your first drink is on me."

His mouth quirked. "Oh, why don't you say so? If free booze is involved, how can I say no?"

She laughed. "We'll save a spot for you at our table. See you there. Wear your dancing boots."

He didn't happen to own dancing boots. Or any other kind, except hiking boots, which probably wouldn't be too helpful on a dance floor.

"I'll see," he said, but she was already walking up the graveled pathway that led to the farmhouse where she lived with his sister.

Don't miss 15 Summers Later *by RaeAnne Thayne,*
available wherever books are sold.

www.Harlequin.com